LEGACY REDEEMED

NUTFIELD SAGA
BOOK 9

ROBIN PATCHEN

Print ISBN: 979-8663926829

Large Print ISBN: 979-8357624178

Cover by Lynnette Bonner

CHAPTER ONE

Vanessa Baker planted her hands on her hips. "I am not riding on that... that boat—"

"Float."

The single word from Caleb Peterson's mouth made her want to scream. Either way, it made no sense. The thing was on a street. It had *wheels*. There was no water. Thus, it was neither boat nor float, despite what the irritating man in front of her insisted. "That is what I said."

The quirk in Caleb's lips only frustrated her more. After all her years of studying and practicing English, some things still tripped her up, especially when they were completely without logic. Float, indeed. It was a flatbed truck decorated to look like it carried stacks of giant food. Emptied and reshaped appliance containers now appeared like boxes of cereal, rice, and cookies. Discarded barrel-shaped containers had become oversize soup cans. Paper mâché-covered wire molds depicted apples, bananas, and grapes the size of a human head. Though Vanessa had thought the whole thing silly, a local artist, Donovan Gilcreast, had gotten involved. He'd created the float's design and brought it to life.

People she'd known for years through her work for the food bank stood beside the pretend food, holding sacks of candy to toss to children along the parade route.

Blowing in the early autumn breeze were those silly paper... string things. Streamers, yes. Katarina had insisted she buy many packages to help decorate the truck. *Float.*

"You're the director of the food bank." Caleb's voice was steady and calm, as always. "This float represents all it's done for Nutfield and the surrounding communities. As the face of the food bank—"

"I am not the face of..." But of course that was another Americanism she didn't understand. *The face of*—as if her image were plastered across the building where she worked. "I do not wish to ride."

A float a few ahead of theirs started to move, inching onto Crystal Avenue for its slow trek in the annual Harvest Festival.

The sound of cheering arose as the parade began.

Because of her role as the food bank's director, she'd always attended the festival, but this was the first time for the food bank to participate in the parade. Always before, they'd been content with a booth to pass out literature and recruit volunteers. The volunteers had gone overboard with the float, and she was thankful for all their hard work. But why did that mean she had to ride on it?

The weather had cooperated. The early October air was crisp and cool. The trees surrounding the town were tinted with smatterings of red, orange, and yellow amidst their green. Another week, perhaps two, and the town would be an explosion of color.

"Vanessa." Caleb lowered his voice and leaned close. "The board would really like you to do this." He gestured to the truck beside them, to all the people on it. "Your friends want you to come."

She looked at them. Her *friends?* The word felt gritty and foreign. They were as near to friends as she'd ever had. People who volunteered at the food bank, others who helped her run it and keep it funded. Some of them were the people she owed this life to.

Her daughter, seven-year-old Katarina, sat atop the Campbell's Tomato Soup. Beside her, ten-year-old Johnny Thomas perched on the SpaghettiOs. Katarina would be fine without Vanessa. The women on board would look after her.

"I will go to the booth," Vanessa said.

A muscle in Caleb's jaw twitched. "There won't be anybody there until after the parade."

"Then I will have a moment of peace." She turned away from the man, got Kat's attention, and told her to stay with Johnny's mother, Rae.

"Won't you join us?" Rae asked.

"I would prefer not," Vanessa said.

"Suit yourself." Rae's smile was easy and comfortable. What would it be like to smile like that, as if life were good and one didn't have a care in the world? "Don't worry," Rae added. "I'll keep an eye on her."

Vanessa nodded her thanks and marched past her church, its white steeple reaching toward the bright blue sky. She had been raised without religion, survived years at the hands of godless men. That she was welcome in a church with the people of God, considering everything she'd done, everything that had been done to her, was nothing short of miraculous. She did love this town and the people in it. She just didn't want to be in the parade. Was that so bad?

She crossed the street and stepped onto the grassy town common.

Though she didn't turn to look, she could feel Caleb's eyes on her.

At least Rae had been kind. Caleb was angry. Perhaps the other board members were as well, but she hadn't been able to force herself onto that thing. It wasn't just because of the people who were on board who would want to engage her in conversation, but those who lined the road that led through downtown Nutfield.

She did not wish to be on display.

She did not wish to be the *face* of anything.

She did not wish to be *seen*.

Caleb had been correct, of course. His constant *correctness* was one of his most irritating qualities. Except for other vendors like herself who were setting up their booths, the grassy area on the far end of the downtown strip was empty of people. This area they called a common, a word that had made little sense. But she understood now that, when Nutfield had first been populated, the townspeople had set apart the grassy area for those who lived nearby—a place to graze livestock, to sell merchandise, and to gather in case of a threat. It was an area owned in common.

She tried to remember if there were any such areas in the town outside of Belgrade where she'd been born, but her memories of that place were dim. That life in Serbia had been lived by a different person than the one who stood here today.

She finished preparing the tent where she would spend her day soliciting donations and volunteers. Satisfied that all was ready, she wandered toward the parade route, keeping behind the crowd, hopefully unnoticed.

People lined the road on both sides, laughing, chatting, waving, as the Nutfield Squirrels' marching band passed, then the cheerleaders, then a horde of young people in various sports uniforms. There were dancers and gymnasts. Politicians waving from convertibles, firemen hanging from their big red truck, smiling business owners tossing candy to children. The

Chamber of Commerce had a float, as did the Rotary Club. Kade and Ginny Powers caught her eye and waved from that one.

She lifted her hand in response, feeling a smile on her face. As soon as she knew it was there, she stopped it. What was there to smile about?

Is life that bad, Vanessa?

This new voice in her head—was it her own foolishness?

Or was it, as Kelsey had suggested at Bible study the previous week, the voice of God? Vanessa had opened her heart to Him years before, but she didn't know how she felt about Him being in her head.

Talking to her.

Why her?

Rather than analyze whose voice it was, she focused on the question. Was life that bad? At the moment, it was not. But whenever she'd gotten comfortable in the past, danger, pain, and turmoil had followed.

She didn't trust this new, happy world she'd landed in. She didn't trust it to last, not for herself, anyway.

But for her daughter... *Protect Katarina, Lord. You alone can keep her safe.*

I will protect you both.

Bah. Foolishness. God had not protected her in the past. She wasn't believing that He would now, and she didn't deserve anything from Him. But Kat was innocent.

And would always be, if Vanessa had anything to say about it.

A dog brushed past her legs.

A little boy dodged through the crowd behind it. The boy was laughing as he chased the little mutt. He was three or four and reminded her of Milos, her younger brother. Always running away, that one, always with herself or Mama or Tata on his heels. Always laughing.

This boy's *tata* was too far behind and, based on the fear in his eyes, he seemed to have lost sight of the child. Behind him, a mama held a toddler in one arm while she gripped the hand of an older child, maybe six or seven. The mama also looked frightened.

The boy came near, and Vanessa waved to the man and caught his eye. She pointed toward the statue on the edge of the park where the dog has stopped to mark his territory. The little boy was almost to the animal. The man veered in that direction. The boy caught the dog, and a moment later, the man caught the boy. He turned to Vanessa with a smile and a wave of thanks as the mama and younger siblings arrived.

The perfect little family. Or so they seemed.

Vanessa had never had a man to help her keep her little Katarina safe. She'd been alone since she was ten years old. Now, she alone was responsible for the precious daughter she'd been given.

As the family returned to the parade route, she felt the lack keenly.

If only her daughter had a real family.

Finally, the float she'd been waiting for rolled into view. Vanessa rose to her tiptoes, straining to get a glimpse of Kat. And there she was, waving from the top of the tomato soup. Maybe now Vanessa would get her to eat the stuff. A broad smile lit her daughter's face, and Vanessa knew her own matched it.

She could smile at Kat. Only at Kat.

Johnny stood beside her, a good foot taller and three years her elder. Other children were on the float, too, waving to the crowd from the stack of faux soup cans and cereal boxes, all of them at least fifteen feet off the ground. Adults walked alongside or sat on the lower levels. It was the nicest float in the parade, thanks to the generous donation from Hamilton Clothiers. The company's owner, Chelsea, explained to Vanessa that it was because of the food bank that she'd met Dylan, her fiancé. Vanessa took no credit for their romance but happily accepted the monthly donations the woman sent.

Kat's queenly waves became a flurry of excitement when she spotted Vanessa.

As Vanessa lifted her hand in reply, a dog got loose of its owner and bolted in front of the truck.

The driver slammed on the brakes.

On the float, people and oversize groceries lurched forward.

A gasp rose from the onlookers.

Kat's eyes widened. Her arms flailed, seeking something to grasp onto and finding nothing but air.

Vanessa's hands flew to her mouth as, in her mind's eye, she saw her daughter tumble and hit the ground. She imagined that sweet little head bouncing off the pavement, imagined blood pooling beneath her cracked skull.

She imagined those beautiful brown eyes lifeless.

Like everything else Vanessa loved, Katarina would be taken away.

Kat tumbled from the soup can, but strong arms from below caught her, pulled her to a broad chest. Kat giggled and hugged the man who'd saved her, even though hugging a man—any man—was against the rules.

Caleb Peterson.

Vanessa dropped her hands. Her heart was pounding.

Back on her oversize soup can, Kat waved to her as if nothing had happened.

Caleb nodded in her direction.

He'd saved her daughter.

Despite how he annoyed her, pestered her, crowded her, she

would be grateful for that. Next time, despite how little she wanted to, she'd ride the stupid float. She'd be there for her little girl.

~

Vanessa handed out literature about local hunger, about the food bank, and about other services for people struggling with poverty. It was late afternoon when there was finally a slow-down in foot traffic. Vanessa left the job in the hands of her volunteers and took Kat for an early dinner at the tent McNeal's had set up. Poor Kat had stayed at the booth all day. At first, she'd talked to passersby, but after a while she'd become bored and sat in a corner to read while others her age played and had fun. Vanessa felt badly about that, but it couldn't be helped. She had to work, and she had to keep Kat safe.

They walked across the grounds, dodging crowds of locals, and found the back of the long line to order dinner, the aromas of frying hamburgers and steaming hot dogs greeting them. Kat let out all the words she'd surely been saving up since Rae had delivered her after the parade, words she hadn't had an opportunity to spew because Vanessa had been too busy to listen. One more thing to feel guilty about.

Kat talked about the other floats, the cheerleaders, whom she thought were "totally amazing!" She talked about riding on the float and glimpsing her friends from school. "I saw Zack and Tyler, and McKenzie. She looked so jealous." The glee in Kat's voice caught Vanessa's attention.

"It is unkind to wish people to feel envy."

Kat's smile slipped. "But she's always showing off. It was the first time I ever got to do something she didn't."

"You have much little McKenzie doesn't. You have amazing talent and kindness and generosity."

Kat rolled her eyes. "You know what I mean."

Yes, Vanessa knew. Most had more money than they did. Others lived in nicer houses than the small three-bedroom they called home. Others drove nicer cars than the beat-up minivan Vanessa had saved and scrimped to purchase. But money was only money. It was nothing compared to safety and security. Thank God Kat did not know a world where safety and security didn't exist.

Vanessa ran her hand down her daughter's braids. They'd been perfect that morning but, as usual, strands had escaped the hair ties. Even with the messy hair, her daughter, with her large brown eyes and silky light brown hair, was beautiful.

Too beautiful.

Vanessa had spent the seven years of her daughter's life fighting the urge to hide the girl away from the world lest someone decide she was too pretty to resist. Vanessa had met many such men.

If any of them came near her daughter, Vanessa would be forced to kill.

Again.

She gazed around at the crowd, but no such men leered nearby. They were safe here.

They finally reached the front of the line, and Vanessa ordered a cheeseburger and french fries for them to share— much to Kat's dismay because, as she claimed, "I'm starving, Mommy."

As if the girl knew what it meant to starve. Another blessing Vanessa thanked God for.

"If we finish it, we will find a treat. There is ice cream and fried dough and—"

"Okay! I'll share."

Vanessa paid for the meal, took the paper plate of food, and found an empty table. Despite the early hour for dinner, most of the tables were taken, either by other diners or by people who wanted to sit down for a few minutes after, presumably, seeing the many attractions. The park was filled with tents—vendors selling their wares, non-profits like the food bank drumming up supporters, politicians seeking votes, local clubs, and more. There were rides for children and games for adults and kids alike. There was a petting zoo. Vanessa had picked up a whiff of it earlier when the breeze had shifted, but fortunately she couldn't smell it now. It seemed the entire town of Nutfield, and perhaps many people from surrounding communities, had come to the Harvest Festival.

Kat squeezed ketchup and mustard onto an empty plate and mixed them together with a french fry, all the while never slowing the continual stream of words.

"And then I almost fell. Did you see? Mr. Caleb saved my life!"

Vanessa's stomach swooped at the memory, but she forced a smile. "I saw. It frightened me very much."

"I gave him a hug. I know I'm not supposed to, but I thought it would be okay. Was it okay, Mommy?"

No. It was never okay to get close to a man, any man. But she smiled at her daughter and said, "Just this once, since he saved your life."

"I wouldn't go that far." Caleb stepped to the table, a plate in one hand, a drink in the other. "Mind if I join you?"

She did mind. She was formulating a response to send him away when he added, "Seeing as how I saved her life and all. It's exhausting being a superhero."

Kat giggled. "It's okay, right, Mommy?"

Trapped. She looked up at the man and said, "I didn't realize superheroes needed rest."

"Not rest but"—he lifted the plate—"sustenance. It's hard to eat standing up."

She nodded to the empty chair. "Who knows if some other child will need your rescue tonight?"

Caleb settled in like he owned the space and engaged Kat in conversation. Was she having fun? Was the food good? Had she been to the bouncy house yet?

"Not yet. Mommy was too busy to take me before. Maybe tonight, right, Mommy?"

Caleb glanced her way. "I could take her, if you wouldn't mind. And there are pony rides, and—"

"I will take her," Vanessa said.

Caleb's easy smile faded. "Okay. I'll work the booth so you can do that."

She wanted to tell him she had plenty of help and didn't need his, but the truth was, she'd spent much of the afternoon alone in the booth while her volunteers had been with their own families.

"If you wish," she said.

"Yay!" Katarina had barely eaten a quarter of her portion of the burger when she stood. "Can we get fried dough now?"

Vanessa glanced down at her still full plate. "I'm not finished. Sit and—"

"Johnny!" Kat rushed across the space to her friend, who was walking beside an older girl, Anna Boyle, who was Marisa and Nate's daughter.

They approached, and Anna said, "We were just going to the bounce house. Can Kat come with us? I'll keep a good eye on her."

"I do not think so."

"Please, Mommy!"

Anna's dark skin and hair brought to mind Kat's father, Carlos. But where Carlos's features had always held cruelty, a kind spirit radiated from Anna. "I'm thirteen, and I babysit my own siblings and other people's kids all the time. I promise not to let either of them out of my sight. We'll hold hands when we're walking around. They won't get lost. Miss Rae said I could take Johnny to the pony rides and the games on the far side on the common, and Kat can come too, if you don't mind. Or, I can take her to the bounce house and deliver her right back to your booth."

Kat's eyes were wide and pleading.

Caleb, wisely, kept his mouth shut.

Vanessa gave her daughter a stern look. "You will stay with Anna?"

"Yes, ma'am."

"And if you get lost?"

"Find a mommy and ask for help. I can tell them which booth to return me to."

"And if someone tries to take you?"

From the corner of her eye, she saw Caleb flinch.

Kat, however, was accustomed to the question. "Yell, 'Help. This is not my daddy.'"

"Very good." Vanessa kissed her daughter's head, uttered a quick *protect her,* and said. "Be safe, *ceri.*" She handed Anna some money for the games. "Please deliver her back to the booth in an hour, and do not leave the common."

"Sure thing, Miz Baker."

Kat kissed Vanessa's cheek, waved good-bye to Caleb, and took off with Anna. Vanessa watched until they disappeared in the crowd.

"They'll be fine," Caleb said.

She turned to the man who still sat across from her. The man who'd more than once invited her to join him for a meal, and whom she had rejected every time. And yet, here they sat.

Caleb acted as if it were commonplace, so she decided to pretend to feel the same. They were colleagues, in a sense. He was on the board of directors at the food bank. He owned a chain of grocery stores, which supplied a good portion of the food that filled the shelves every week. His generous donations had helped them get off the ground and supplied much of her salary. His suggestions—those she'd decided to take—had aided her in running the place more efficiently. Thus, they were colleagues.

Nothing more.

"How's the burger?" he asked.

"Not as good as they make in the restaurant, but passable." She took a bite while he ate some of his overlong hot dog. They sipped their drinks.

"The church has its prayer meeting Wednesday night. The way you faithfully serve the community, I thought you might want to join us this month."

He'd asked her every month to attend the monthly prayer meeting, a gathering of believers from different Christian churches all over town. Every month, she declined. "I pray for the community faithfully. And there is nobody to watch Kat."

"They have childcare in the annex."

She'd heard. But who was in charge? Could she trust them? It had taken her years to get up the nerve to leave her daughter in Sunday School. Maybe it was the same people. Maybe it would be fine. But she wasn't willing to take a chance with Kat's life and health on a *maybe*.

He said, "Join us. Remember, where two or more—"

"Thank you for the invitation. I will decline." Again.

He shrugged—"Suit yourself"—and took a bite of his hot dog.

She nibbled the burger. After an awkward moment, she said, "I wanted to say—"

"You did a good job—" He spoke at the same time. He gestured to her. "Ladies first."

"Thank you for catching Katarina this morning. Not that I

believe your superhero claim, but you did save her from a nasty fall."

He dipped his head. "Right place, right time."

"Good catch."

The little wrinkles at the corners of his eyes deepened with his smile. The man was attractive enough with his dark hair, hazel eyes, and square jaw. Certainly not unattractive, anyway. He was probably a decade older than she. "Years of catching fly balls finally paying off."

"Fly balls... This is from baseball, no?"

He chuckled. "How long have you lived in America? Surely long enough to have learned the game of baseball."

"I have been busy."

He swallowed the bite and said, "Have you ever been to a game?"

"Bah. Who has time for silly games?"

Caleb sat back. "Silly? Baseball is serious business."

"I am not from America."

"No, you're from...?" His eyebrows lifted as he waited for her to supply the rest of the sentence. She did not talk about herself. Some in town knew the story of her past, but they'd held her secrets closely, thank God. Caleb knew nothing of where she came from or what she had endured. But the place of her birth did not need to be kept secret.

"Serbia," she said, "though I am an American citizen now."

"How could you pass a citizenship test without knowing baseball? Surely they had questions about America's favorite pastime."

She couldn't help a smile but worked to keep it from growing too wide. "They only tested on foolish things like the form of government and the Constitution."

He shook his head. "Shameful, your lack of education. I'll have to remedy that."

She sat back, lifted her chin. She didn't need this man or any man to remedy her education. She'd been given as much education from men as she would ever need.

He must have seen the shift in her expression, because his amusement faded. "Or not."

Not. Definitely not.

Tension stretched between them like a rubber band, and she welcomed it. She didn't need Caleb Peterson or any other man trying to get comfortable with her and her daughter. He seemed nice enough, but it was not worth the risk.

Her cell phone rang, and she pulled it from her jacket pocket and looked at the screen. She didn't recognize the number and ignored the call. "Probably one of those robots," she said.

"I was going to say you did a great job setting up the booth today and drawing people close. Every time I looked, there was a crowd there."

"It does not hurt to give away candy." Before she finished the sentence, her phone rang again. It was the same phone number. "Pardon me. I should just be sure." At his nod, she slid the call to connect it.

"Hello?"

A woman said in Serbian, "Is this Vojislava Bakočević?"

Her gasp came as much from the name, her given name, though nobody knew it, as from the language spoken. She hadn't heard her native tongue in... She could not remember when. Probably since she was taken from Belgrade as a child. Taken and sold to the highest bidder.

"Vojislava?" The speaker sounded barely more than a girl, by the high pitch of the words. She seemed... chipper.

"Who is this?" Vanessa asked.

"It's Nadia. Nadia Bakočević. Your sister."

Nadia?

It couldn't be. Nadia was a child. Just four years old when Vanessa had last seen her. But that had been many lifetimes past. Nadia would now be... she quickly did the math. Twenty years old. "I do not understand. Where are you?"

"In Boston! I met someone who knows you. He said I look just like you. He's the nicest guy. I hope you don't mind I am with him. I know you and he were close."

Close? There was nobody in her past she'd been close to. Only abusers and guards.

Nadia continued, her voice familiar despite the years that had changed it. Her sister might be twenty, but she sounded foolish and naive, like a young teenager. Like Kat, almost.

"He said you left him for another man and wouldn't care that we're together, and he's so nice. Please tell me you forgive me."

"I have no idea who you're talking about," Vanessa said. "There is no man from my past who was nice to me. They were all—"

"Abbas, of course."

Vanessa gripped the edge of the table and swallowed the nausea that rose. Of all the men in her past... "He is a monster. You must get away from him right now."

"He's not!" Nadia sounded offended. Offended, when the man himself was an offense against humankind.

Abbas, who was more monster than man.

But foolish Nadia... "If not for him, I'd never have found you. I've been looking for you forever. He helped me. He knows many people, even in the American government. They helped us find you. And now we're here, and you're just in New Hampshire, which Abbas tells me is nearby."

"You must trust me, sister," Vanessa said. "I will come to save you. I will—"

"Save me?" Nadia sounded confused. "I don't need to be

saved. I told Abbas I was going to call you, and he said that was a good idea, that he'd love to see you again. It's why we're here in Boston, so I can see you."

Vanessa pressed a hand against her stomach to hold herself together. Abbas. She couldn't face him again. She wouldn't.

But this was her sister.

Nadia had been Vanessa's little shadow, following her around as Vanessa cared for her siblings, cooked meals, and cleaned the house. Unlike the sister between them, Anya, who'd been quiet and studious, Nadia had never stopped talking.

Secretly, though Vanessa had loved all her younger brothers and sisters, Nadia had always been her favorite because Nadia had been able to make Mama and Tata laugh. And herself, back when she knew how to laugh.

Even at four years old, Nadia had been too trusting. Sixteen years hadn't changed that, it seemed. Now, she was with Abbas.

Her sister, willingly in the arms of a monster.

CHAPTER TWO

Caleb Peterson had watched the color leach from Vanessa's cheeks. Her eyes shifted from the almost genial look he sometimes caught on her face—only when she wasn't looking at him—to the hard-as-marbles stare she'd aimed his way more than once. The look didn't concern him. But the way her jaw dropped, the hand she lifted to cover her mouth...

His eavesdropping was not helping him discover what was wrong, however. She wasn't speaking English. If he'd known where Vanessa was from, he'd have been learning the language for the last two years.

The first time the Lord told him whom He intended for Caleb Peterson to marry, Caleb had laughed.

He hadn't even been praying about a wife—not that day, anyway, though he'd done plenty of praying, before then and since. More than anything, he wanted a woman to share his life with, a woman to share his wealth, and, yes, a woman to share his bed. He was tired of living like a monk. Was that so terrible?

But Vanessa? Sure, she was beautiful in an aloof, exotic sort of way. Beautiful like a prize rose, whose inviting fragrance and lovely bloom drew people close enough to be pricked by its thorns. But a rose was too common. Maybe Vanessa was more like a priceless emerald, the gem that came to mind when he gazed at her green eyes, all hard edges and sharp corners. Cold. You could admire an emerald, but you'd never want to cuddle up with one on a cold New Hampshire night.

Vanessa's image that first time God had revealed His crazy plan—complete with the white gown and wedding flowers—had surely been meant as a joke. Many times, Caleb had felt God's amusement, but not that day.

God hadn't been kidding.

But... Vanessa Baker?

Sure, she ticked a lot of the boxes on the list of things he'd prayed for in a wife. As far as he could tell, having attended the same church for two years now, she loved the Lord. He knew by the way she ran the local food bank that she was beyond competent and highly intelligent. From her beat-up car and the clothes that looked as if they came from a discount store—if not a thrift store—she wasn't greedy or focused on wealth. And she was a wonderful mother, if a bit overprotective.

But there was the one little thing Caleb had apparently left off the list of attributes he wanted in a wife, a thing he'd figured went without saying. He really wanted to marry a woman who sort of liked him.

Vanessa loathed him.

Had he really needed to add *Doesn't hate me* to his list? *Wasn't that kind of obvious, Father?*

But whenever he complained to the Lord about His choice, God was silent.

None of that mattered now, though, as Vanessa's tone shifted from confused to frightened.

Lord, whatever is happening, keep Vanessa safe. Help her remember she is loved and valued and precious. Help her trust her friends enough to ask for help. He was almost afraid to add the next sentence that popped into his head. *Help... help her trust me.*

Vanessa reached across the table and grabbed his forearm. It was the first time she'd ever touched him. Almost the first time she'd ever gotten within arms' length of him. She met his eyes and said, "Rowes Wharf Hotel."

Whatever that meant. But the One who knew what was going on prompted him to say, "Room number?"

Vanessa's words into the phone came quick and loud. She stood, listening, looking around. Probably for Kat.

Caleb touched her shoulder and whispered, "Kat's with Anna and Johnny. She's safe."

The tension around her eyes lessened. But not much. Her string of Serbian was punctuated by the English words, "Do not leave." Then a pause, and then, "Promise me, Nadia. You will be there."

A moment later, she ended the call and looked at him. Her eyes were wide. Her lower lip trembled.

"What can I do?"

"I must get to Boston."

"I'll drive."

She started to nod but stopped herself. "I have a car. I can—"

"You're in no condition to drive."

"I do not..." She sat, stood again, looked around as if she couldn't quite figure out where she was. "I do not know what to do. I cannot just... just go to her hotel room and knock. I will have to wait, to hope to see her. It may take time."

He had no idea what she was talking about or how much time she meant. Hours, days? It didn't matter. "I'm coming with you."

"I do not want your help."

He absorbed that blow. *Lord, guide me.*

She fairly vibrated with tension.

Around them, the festival continued. Children laughing, friends jabbering. Musicians on the stage at the corner of the common were warming up, the sound loud and discordant. People began streaming in that direction, while all he wanted was to get away from it so he could think, so he could figure out how to help.

Vanessa's skin was pasty white. She seemed too stunned to move.

"Take a deep breath," he said. "In slowly..." He inhaled long, and she did the same. As if she'd taken his counsel. That was a first.

He blew out his breath, and she did too.

They repeated it, and then he pulled out her chair. "Let's sit and think."

She did it. She actually did what he suggested. Two wins in a row.

Maybe, just maybe, there was hope.

"Tell me what's going on."

"That was my sister." Vanessa's voice shook with emotion. "She is with a very bad man."

"Should we call the police?"

Vanessa waved off his words. "They will not help."

How could she be sure? "But if she goes to them, they'll protect—"

"She will not. She is a fool. And they would not help because they would not care."

"Okay." He waited for her to fill in the copious blanks she'd left in their conversation. When she didn't, he said, "She's at the Rowes Wharf Hotel, yes?"

"You know it? Is it very secure? Would I be able to get in?"

"It's like any other hotel. You can walk right into the lobby. But if you don't have her room number—"

"I do. Thank you for that."

"God's direction," he said.

Her eyes narrowed slightly, but she didn't argue or ask questions.

"This *bad man*..." Caleb said. "He's dangerous?"

"*Da*. Very dangerous."

Vague but getting somewhere. *Lord, a little help here?*

He wanted to reach for her, to promise his help and protection. But he knew how Vanessa would react to that. Instead, he folded his hands on the table. "I want to come with you. I'll drive you, find a place for you to stay where you'll be safe, and accompany you to find your sister. If this guy is dangerous, it won't hurt to have a man by your side. I know you don't like that, but men are generally stronger—"

She hurled a string of Serbian his way. Though he didn't understand the words, the rage was clear in any language.

He lifted his hands, surrendering to whatever insults she'd just aimed at him.

Her shoulders slumped. "Forgive me. I have not... I am not..."

When she didn't finish, he asked, "What did you say?"

A quick shake of her head. Perhaps she wouldn't repeat the insults in English. "I am not ignorant. I know I cannot protect myself. Thanks to evil men, I have had much education in my own weakness."

Evil men. Were they the reason she didn't trust him? Didn't trust anybody?

Were evil men the reason for the way she'd grilled Kat before the girl left with Anna?

Were evil men the reason Vanessa kept herself aloof from everyone?

Too many questions, but now wasn't the time to ask them. Maybe, eventually, he'd have an opportunity. He started to speak, then stopped and sent up a quick prayer. After a deep breath, he said, "Vanessa, I would be honored if you'd let me serve as your helper and protector."

She pressed her back against her chair. "I am not interested in a relationship with you, Caleb Peterson."

As if she hadn't made that clear many times in the past.

"I actually cracked that code," he said. "What about friendship?"

"I am not good at friendship."

At least she was self-aware.

"*I* am," he said. "I'm good at friendship." Was it prideful to say so? He had a lot of friends, good friends, old and new. "I would be honored if you'd trust me as a friend. I'll drive you to Boston, find a safe place for you to stay." At her raised eyebrows, he added, "I have no expectations. You'll be safe from me, too." As if he would ever hurt her. As if he were a threat. "I'll go with you to see your sister and do my very best to protect you from harm. All I ask is that you trust me."

"You ask too much."

Her words told him she was going to refuse him, but the way she was looking at him, studying him...

"I must rescue my sister," she said.

Again, he remained silent.

"I will trust you to help me. At least, I will try."

CHAPTER THREE

Vanessa was a fool.

How could she do this? How could she face a monster in order to save a sister she hadn't seen in sixteen years?

A sister too stupid to know she was in danger.

Caleb and Vanessa fought through the crowd now gathering in front of the stage at the back of the common. A band was playing so loudly that she could hardly focus. She scanned the faces, searching for Kat, for danger.

Caleb was on the phone beside her. She paid no attention to him, though. She couldn't think about him right now.

Where was Kat?

When they arrived at the food bank's booth, she saw that, along with the regular volunteers, Ginny and Kade were there. As they approached, Kade looked at Caleb and said, "What's up?"

As if he had been summoned.

Beside her and still on the phone, Caleb said, "One second," and then said something about keys and parking.

"What is it?" Ginny curled her fingers around Vanessa's

arm, and Vanessa had to fight the urge to yank away. With all the memories and fears close to the surface, it was hard to temper her reaction.

Ginny must have noticed, because she dropped her hand. "Are you okay?"

She was not. She couldn't seem to find her voice.

Beside her, Caleb said, "Vanessa has a family emergency. Could you guys manage the booth for the rest of the day?"

"Sure." Ginny glanced at Kade. "If that's okay with you."

"Not a problem," Kade said. "Jack and I were already planning to help with dismantling it. We'll get everything back to the food bank tonight."

Managing the booth, getting it back to the food bank—as director, that was Vanessa's job. She hated that she couldn't do what she'd committed to, but what were her choices?

Studying Vanessa's face, Ginny said, "What else can we do?"

Frustration warred within her. She would not have called these people to help her. She would not have asked anyone for anything.

And Caleb knew that, which was probably why he hadn't asked her opinion.

"It is a long story," she said. "I cannot explain."

Ginny only nodded. "How can we pray?"

Before she could come up with an answer, Caleb said, "Protection, wisdom, and God's favor. We don't need to get into the rest of it." He turned to face her. "Is Kat coming with us?"

She barely stifled her gasp. She hadn't thought about what to do with Kat, but she couldn't take her to Boston. She wouldn't let her daughter within fifty miles of Abbas.

Before she could form words, he said, "Let's call Kelsey. You trust Kelsey and Eric, right?"

Kelsey and Eric had a little boy, maybe six, whom Kat

liked to play with, and a younger daughter as well. Their oldest son, Daniel, was off at college. He shouldn't pose any threat.

Eric, though. Could she trust him? He'd put himself in danger to keep Vanessa from making the biggest mistake of her life, a mistake she surely would not have been able to live with. Eric had done that to save his wife's life, though.

And then worked hard to protect Vanessa, to keep her out of prison.

Eric... he could be trusted with Kat. Couldn't he?

Caleb was watching her. He must have seen the war in her expression because he said, "They'll take good care of her," and lifted the phone to his face again.

Vanessa swallowed the terror that rose. Kat would be safe with Kelsey and Eric. Safer with them than in Abbas's crosshairs.

In front of her, Ginny said, "If she can't do it, we'll be happy to take your daughter."

No. She did not know Kade well enough. Maybe he was no different than Abbas. Maybe he would...

Ginny squeezed her arm. "Okay. It's okay. I'm sure Kelsey will do it."

Vanessa's gaze flicked to Kade. He'd stepped back. His lips were pressed together and seemed to be trying hard not to frown. She had insulted him. Without opening her mouth, her suspicions had shown on her face. She was usually better at hiding them.

"I am sorry," Vanessa said.

Ginny stepped in and hugged her. "We're here for you."

Vanessa didn't fight the hug, but she didn't return it either.

Ginny stepped back. "You just let us know what you need, my friend."

There was that word again. Friend. Did Ginny truly

consider her a friend? She should not. Vanessa was far too damaged to be anything of the sort.

Vanessa caught sight of Kat, along with Anna and Johnny, headed their way. Kat's smile was wide as she yanked her hand away from Anna's and bolted across the grassy area. "Mommy! I got to ride a pony. Her name is Mouse. Isn't that a funny name for a pony? He was *this big*"—Kat lifted her hand high—"and had a big white patch on his face."

Struggling to follow Kat's words, Vanessa only nodded. "I am glad, *ceri*." Automatically, she thanked Anna before the older girl and Johnny walked away.

"I want to stay for the fireworks tonight," Kat said. "Can we stay? Please?"

Fireworks? She didn't want to stay another moment. "I do not think so."

Beside her, Caleb said, "Great. We'll stay here," and hung up his phone. "Kelsey is on her way. You can ask her yourself."

Vanessa gathered her things and Kat's from inside the booth while the volunteers prattled about whom they'd spoken to and how many people had signed up for the raffle.

They were giving away a thousand-dollar gift card to Caleb's grocery store, which he'd donated. All the names and email addresses they collected would be added to their donor list. All to help fund the food bank.

She couldn't summon a care.

Kelsey, her long blond hair up in a ponytail and children in tow, reached the booth. She looked past Vanessa to Caleb, whose presence behind her was palpable. "What's up?"

Caleb said nothing.

Vanessa extracted herself from behind the booth and Kat's listening ears and met Kelsey on the opposite side of the table. She lowered her voice. If anybody could understand how Vanessa was feeling, it was Kelsey.

"I need help with Kat for a couple of days."

"Sure thing." Kelsey had a Southern accent. Vanessa had lived in Florida for a time, but it was different than how people spoke there. "You want her to stay with us?"

"If it will be no trouble."

"Of course not. What's going on?"

Vanessa looked behind her. Nobody was listening. She lowered her voice. "You remember our mutual acquaintance?"

Kelsey stepped back. Her skin paled.

"Before him, there was another. My sister is with that one."

Kelsey's hand covered her mouth, and tears filled her eyes. "Oh, Vanessa."

"I must help her."

Kelsey gripped Vanessa's arm. "Don't go alone. I'm sure Eric will—"

"I'm going with her." Caleb's voice was too close. Where had he come from?

How much had he heard?

"Good," Kelsey said. "Good. We'll keep Kat with us. We're going to the fireworks tonight and church tomorrow. If you're not back by tomorrow night, I can get her to school on Monday. No problem. We'll just need to get her things."

It was all happening too fast.

"We'll get her stuff and leave it on your front porch," Caleb said. "Will that be okay?"

"Yes. Fine." Kelsey leaned in and gave Vanessa a hug. "I'll be praying for you. We all will." She backed away. "I won't tell everyone else what's going on, but, if it's okay, I'll share that you need prayer."

Prayer. That should have been Vanessa's first thought. Now that she knew the one true God, she needed to learn to depend on Him. She needed Him as much now as ever.

CHAPTER FOUR

Vanessa hurried away from the town common, careful not to meet the gazes of passersby as she brushed foolish tears from her cheeks. She didn't know why she was crying. Because she'd left her daughter in another's care, something she'd sworn she'd never do? Or because Kat not only hadn't been upset but had acted as if this were some grand adventure. She'd given Vanessa a quick hug and run off to play with Kelsey's children.

As Vanessa reached her minivan and climbed in, she wondered how she'd raised such a confident little girl when she herself was filled with fear. It was not her own skill that had done such a thing. For this, she thanked God, who had created Kat to be something neither Vanessa nor her daughter's father could ever be—good and pure and innocent. The strength and confidence, though? Perhaps those came from the man who'd sired her. Carlos had been like that. He'd lorded those qualities over Vanessa. He had used them to spread evil in the world. But Kat was strong and good, confident and innocent. She was as close to perfect as anybody Vanessa had ever met.

She drove away from the festival, careful of the other cars

and pedestrians who were headed toward it. Thanks to the bands that would play tonight and the fireworks, the area was as crowded as it had been all day. Happy people without a care in the world. This town, this state, this country... It was a haven. The people on TV argued about this policy or that, this president or that. Vanessa only laughed at them. They had no idea what they had here. The beauty of a nation where people could work and earn and keep their earnings, where they did not have to fear their government or their neighbors.

She had grown complacent. She had begun to believe she was safe. But, beneath the wealth and comfort, there was danger. She'd lived it. She'd been part of it. Could it touch Kat while Vanessa was away?

You did not create her only to destroy her, da? I can trust You with Kat? She tried to pray that last with the kind of confidence her daughter would, but the pitch rose at the end in her mind. Could Vanessa trust God with her daughter?

She didn't understand how a God who had once allowed the unthinkable to happen to her could be good to her now. Where had He been for all those dark years?

A foolish, useless question.

Finally, she escaped the downtown traffic and made it to the little three-bedroom ranch she'd been renting since she'd returned to Nutfield. She felt safe here in this house, set off from the road and hidden behind trees, away from neighbors. She'd spent the money to install a security system. Brady Thomas had recommended the brand, and Jack Rossi had installed it for her.

The tree-covered lot in front of her house was just as she'd left it. Kat's bicycle rested against the side of the garage. The golf club she'd used to practice her swing was propped on the porch beside the front door, a bucket filled with white plastic balls beside it—practice golf balls. Kat had spent hours hitting those plastic balls into the forest and then collecting them. A friend had given her the club, and Kat had been begging for lessons. Vanessa would sign her up in the spring. She would find the money to pay for them, somewhere.

Vanessa packed a bag for herself, enough clothes to last four days. She hoped that was too long. She prayed she would be home the following day. But she could still hear her sister's cheerful voice, and Vanessa was not optimistic.

She went to her jewelry case, dug beneath the few items she'd gathered in recent years—costume jewelry, a frivolous expense she allowed herself sometimes. Because it was pretty. Because it was on sale. Because... there was no good reason, but still, there it was.

She found the little velvet pouch and tipped it until the ring fell into her hand. Perhaps she would need it, could use it to secure her sister's release.

No. She would not use it. She would not relinquish it now.

Despite her determination, she slid the item back into the velvet pouch and the pouch into her purse. It would be there if she needed it.

Across the hallway in Kat's room, she found her daughter's light blue duffel bag and filled it with clothes and toiletries and Kat's favorite stuffed animal, a threadbare basset hound with a dangling eye. She needed to repair that eye before it was lost forever. That was a job she would do when all this was over. She added a few toys and Kat's schoolbooks, just in case Vanessa was still gone on Monday.

She did not want to be gone on Monday.

She did not want to go now.

What was she doing? She sat on the edge of Kat's bed and stared at the pale blue walls, the butterfly decals. She and Kat had made it look as if butterflies were coming in through the window. It was... What was the word Kelsey had used when she'd seen it? Whimsical. Yes.

Vanessa scoffed at whimsy, at fun. She did not even like to smile. To smile was to invite the world to smack her down. She knew this was not true, intellectually. She knew there was a God who wanted her to smile. But she could not. Too many years had separated her from the joy of her childhood, from days when she could be happy.

But for Kat, she had found whimsy. For Kat, she smiled.

How could she leave her daughter? How could she leave the safety of her home to face Abbas again? The very thought of him had bumps rising on her arms. Her mind tried to return her to those terrifying days aboard his yacht. No. She could not think on that.

But she must. Because she was acting the biggest fool. Why risk exposing her life, her daughter, to Abbas to save a sister she hardly knew?

A sister who didn't even understand she was in danger?

Vanessa had loved Nadia once, of course. She could still remember when Mama had birthed her. They hadn't had the money for a hospital, but a midwife came and helped the screaming infant into the world. Nadia had been tiny, smaller even than Anya. Or perhaps Vanessa simply didn't remember Anya's birth as well. She certainly didn't remember her brothers' births, as she'd been a baby herself.

She'd been in the room when Nadia had come into the world. Tata had been waiting in the living room, and Vanessa's aunt had left to tend to a screaming child in another part of the small apartment they all shared. So the midwife had wrapped little Nadia in a blanket and handed her to Vanessa before returning to tend to Mama.

And Vanessa had fallen in love.

But Nadia was not Vanessa's responsibility anymore. She had her own daughter to think of now. She had done her part and more to care for Nadia and the other children. Their future had been secured because of Vanessa's sacrifice. She did not have to face Abbas again.

She did not.

She would not go.

To go was crazy. To stay was smart. Safe.

But... Nadia.

Vanessa allowed herself to return to that yacht, to the torture she'd endured at the hands of Abbas and his guards. She allowed herself to remember her wish to escape, to jump out the window into the abyss, to allow the water and sharks to take her, because then it would be over. No more torture. No more pain.

She would have if the opportunity had arisen.

Could she leave her sister to that fate?

CHAPTER FIVE

fter speeding through town, Caleb jogged into his house. *Please, don't let her leave without me.*

The prayer had been on his lips since the moment Vanessa had hurried away from the festival. If he could only hurry, he would get to her house before she left. She had promised to wait for him, but the words had been off-hand. *Da. Yes. I will wait.*

But would she? Or would all this time she was spending alone convince her she didn't need him? He didn't know what was going on, but the last thing he wanted was for his... for Vanessa to be alone with a dangerous man.

Caleb wouldn't let that happen. He'd be at the Boston hotel to protect her whether she wanted him there or not. Still, he'd prefer to go with her, not show up like some creepy stalker.

He was in his room tossing clothes into his small suitcase when he heard a knock at his front door. Then, the creak of the hinges.

"Mind if I come in?"

Eric Nolan, Caleb's accountability and prayer partner—and Kelsey's husband. "Come on back."

A moment later, Eric stepped into the bedroom doorway. He was shorter than Caleb by a couple of inches but well built. "Kelsey told me what's going on."

Caleb hadn't overheard any of Vanessa's conversation with Kelsey. He'd stepped out of the booth to reschedule an appointment and hadn't realized the women were there. He hadn't known what either said, but he'd seen Kelsey's shocked, terrified reaction to whatever Vanessa had told her.

It was enough to confirm that, whoever this man in Boston was, he was trouble.

"Maybe you could tell me, then," Caleb said. "Any light you could shed—"

"It's not my place."

Caleb froze to study his friend. "But you know? You understand what's going on here?"

"A little."

"Tell me."

"It's not my place."

Caleb's anxiety level had been running at about seven—much higher than normal, but in control. Now, it spiked to ten and tried to push past that. On his way to the bathroom for his shaving kit, he yelled, "Then why are you here?"

"Thought I'd pray with you."

"I don't have time for that." Caleb returned and shoved his shaving kit in the suitcase.

"There's more to this than you understand."

"There would have to be, wouldn't there?" Caleb snapped. "Since I know nothing." Eric was the only person Caleb had confided to about God's word regarding Vanessa. Eric had been praying with Caleb about her for over a year. All that time, Eric had known more about her than he'd ever let on.

"A hint," Caleb said. "Something, anything..."

"Be patient with her. She's—"

"Cold and closed off and not the slightest bit interested in me. I know."

"I was going to say vulnerable."

That, too.

Caleb zipped the suitcase closed and headed toward the door, which Eric still blocked. "I have to go. She's going to leave without me if I don't hurry."

"She won't," Eric said. "She's all those things you just said, but she's not stupid. She knows she can't do this alone. And the fact that she agreed to let you accompany her means more than you understand."

"I was there when the call came in," Caleb said. "And I insisted."

"She could have asked someone who knows her history. Me or Brady—"

"Brady knows, too? Who else? What happened that...?" The chief of police and a police detective both knew Vanessa's history. Had she been arrested? Or a victim?

He stopped a foot in front of Eric. "If you're not going to tell me anything, then get out of my way. I need to go."

"You can be ticked at me all you want, but I've known Vanessa a lot longer than I've known you. She's a friend, and I owe her my loyalty. Just like I would never betray your confidence, I would never betray hers."

That made a lot of sense, but it didn't help. "I get it. I have to—"

"One minute to pray." Eric didn't wait for Caleb to agree, just laid his hand on Caleb's shoulder and asked God to protect Vanessa and save Nadia and to give Caleb wisdom, insight, strength, and patience.

There was a lot of emphasis on patience.

Caleb's initial irritation eased, a sort of peace settled when

Eric finished, despite the fact that it had taken well over the promised one minute. "Thanks."

"Vanessa is not a problem to be fixed or a mystery to be solved."

"I know that."

Eric's eyebrows lifted. "You can't analyze or negotiate or purchase your way into her heart."

Caleb wanted to inform his friend that he wasn't an idiot, but Eric knew him too well. It had been through logic, negotiation, and money that Caleb had bought a fledgling grocery store chain, revived it, and built it to become one of the fastest growing businesses in New Hampshire. The world of business —that was where he thrived.

Vanessa's heart was unchartered territory.

"I can't tell you anything about her past," Eric said, "but I can tell you that it was for very good reasons she constructed those walls you want so badly to tear down. You need to be careful that your demolition effort doesn't harm the woman behind the barriers."

Eric studied him, waited for a response.

"Yeah. I'll be careful with her." He nodded to the hallway behind his friend. "Can I go now, boss?"

Eric smiled. "I like that. Boss. You should start calling me that all the time."

"Lock the door on your way out." He hurried to his car and was on the road in a matter of seconds, driving too fast on the curvy back roads on the outskirts of Nutfield.

Only the dark brown mailbox with its reflective numbers indicated Vanessa's house on the narrow road. He pulled down the practically hidden driveway to a small ranch-style home. Trees surrounded it on all sides, thick enough that there was no yard to speak of. No grass to mow. No pretty flowers adorning the front step. The cedar siding seemed dull in the evening light.

What was there released his pent-up breath—Vanessa's van. She'd waited for him. *Thank You.*

He ran to the door and knocked. A moment later, it opened. Vanessa said nothing, just left it open and backed up.

He stopped just inside the door. "You okay?"

"Da. Just..." She walked away and disappeared around a corner.

The living room was dark despite the overhead light that glowed against the old popcorn ceiling above. There were lamps around the room, but she hadn't bothered to turn any of them on. The walls were covered in seventies-style paneling, which had been painted white. A sofa and loveseat faced a small—maybe thirty-inch—flat-screen TV. The coffee table and end tables were adorned with decorative items and framed photographs—all of Kat or Kat and Vanessa together. The dingy brown carpeting had probably been in the house as long as it had been standing, but Vanessa had found an area rug that brightened the space around the couch.

It was cozy and comfortable, though not fancy. She'd done well with what she had to work with.

Vanessa had disappeared into another room, probably to finish packing. But she returned empty-handed. She stopped on the far side of the room and crossed her arms.

"I have changed my mind. I will not go."

"Oh." Good. He didn't want Vanessa to put herself in danger. Staying was the right decision. Except... she'd been insistent. Frantic, even. And she'd said her sister was in danger. "Mind if I ask why?"

"Nadia is not my responsibility. Kat is my responsibility. I will leave her here, where something might happen to her, to rush off to save my foolish sister? No, is not my problem."

"Kat'll be fine with Kelsey and Eric, though. You know they'll take good care of her."

Her hands perched on her hips, and her chin rose. "She is *my* daughter. I should be here with her."

"Do you not trust them?"

"I do not... I do not, not trust them. I believe they will take care of her. But if something happens to her while I'm gone—"

"What do you think will happen?"

"She could get hurt."

"Eric and Kelsey know where the hospital is."

"She could get sick."

"They can handle a little illness. They have children of their—"

"She could be taken."

This, he thought, was the true fear. He dared not step farther into her house without an invitation. This woman who came off fully in control at the food bank seemed as skittish as a deer right now. He didn't know what lay in her past that would make her fear her daughter's abduction, but he did know that not going to help her sister—who, it seemed, *had* been abducted—in order to protect her daughter from a very unlikely scenario seemed the wrong decision. As much as he wanted Vanessa to be safe, he wanted her to be at peace. And leaving her sister with this person in Boston would not bring Vanessa peace. Though he hated to do it, hated to talk her into doing something he didn't want her to do, he trusted this course was the right one.

"You're right," he said. "Bad things could happen to Kat. But Eric and Kelsey are capable and intelligent. Eric's a cop. He understands the dangers in the world. And Kelsey will protect your daughter like she protects her own."

Slowly, her chin dipped, then lifted, almost as if she were nodding. Though with Vanessa, one never knew. She could be building words to hurl at him. His fists wanted to clench, but he straightened them as he waited for her response. And was surprised when she said, "You are right. Nobody could understand the dangers more or be more careful about protecting Kat than Eric and Kelsey. They will keep her safe."

"So...?"

She looked past him. A clock ticked from somewhere in the other room while she seemed to debate her options. Finally, she met his eyes. "If I go, I must return. I cannot allow anything bad to happen to me, for my daughter's sake."

And mine, though he didn't say that. "I'll do my best to keep you safe."

"I will get my things."

One of the rare times she'd actually listened to him, and he almost wished she hadn't. How dangerous was this guy? Could Caleb keep her safe?

CHAPTER SIX

Vanessa didn't argue with Caleb about who should drive. His car was new and in good repair, and hers was falling apart. More than that, she didn't know anything about Boston except that she'd been told it was difficult to navigate, with the traffic and the confusion. She'd lived nearby for a time, but she'd never ventured into the city. She didn't even feel comfortable driving in Nutfield. She preferred not to drive in Manchester. She would not be able to manage Boston.

She settled in the leather seat of Caleb's sedan and told herself that it didn't matter that it was such a nice car. She'd had enough of luxury in her life. Men who could afford luxury were generally not to be trusted. But Caleb Peterson... His money came from the grocery stores he owned. He was not involved in any illegal activity. He was not like the men of her past.

This she told herself, though she startled at the sound of the trunk slamming, and her hands trembled as Caleb slid in beside her. "We have everything we need?"

Kat's duffel bag was on her lap, clutched to her the way Kat always clutched that silly stuffed dog. "I believe so."

"If you forgot anything, there are stores in Boston."

Not that she could afford to shop in any of them. Another thing she knew about Boston—it was expensive. Her budget was small. She hated that one of the reasons she'd said yes to Caleb taking her was knowing he would provide a place for her to stay. He would pay for the hotel, and he would respect her space. He wouldn't expect anything from her. This he had promised, and this she believed. Caleb had shown himself to be worthy of her trust in the past. It was a terrible thing to use a man for his money, but she couldn't do this without help. She didn't wish to go into debt, though she could use her one credit card if she had to. But Caleb had money. For Nadia, she would take Caleb's help. For Katarina, she would take Caleb's protection.

The sun was setting by the time they reached Kelsey and Eric's house on the outskirts of Nutfield. Vanessa carried the duffel bag to the front porch and rang the bell but, as expected, nobody answered. They were still at the festival.

Please, keep Katarina safe.

He would, wouldn't He? He wouldn't send Vanessa on this journey and not protect her child.

Vanessa kissed her fingertips, touched the bag, and hoped Kat would not be afraid without her. Hoped she would not be afraid without Kat. After she dropped the bag on the steps, she returned to Caleb's car.

He waited until she clicked on her seatbelt. Then, he turned to her. "Are you sure you want to do this?"

"I must."

He studied her a moment before he shifted into reverse and maneuvered back onto the road.

When they reached the four-lane highway that led to Manchester, he said, "Tell me who this person is, this bad man who has your sister."

She had only just relaxed into the comfortable seat, but now, she tensed. With effort, she forced her shoulders back down, her hands to relax in her lap. She didn't want Caleb to see how the man affected her. He didn't need to know her past in order to help her free her sister. She didn't want Caleb to know anything about that.

"His name is Abbas."

Caleb adjusted the heat, then waved to the console between them. "There's a seat warmer, if you're chilly."

"I'm fine."

A mile passed, maybe two, before Caleb said, "That's it? That's all you're going to tell me?"

"He is a bad man."

A moment passed, and then, "How do you know him?"

"I was... with him for some time."

Caleb nodded slowly. When she added nothing else, he said, "Were you his girlfriend?"

"Not exactly."

He squeezed the steering wheel. "Could you be a little more cryptic, please? You're painting such a vivid picture."

She nearly smiled at his tone. Caleb usually seemed self-controlled, but he looked rattled now. Annoyed.

He glanced at her. "What's so funny?"

Not funny but... amusing, perhaps. "I haven't heard you use sarcasm before. It doesn't sound like you."

"We're learning all sorts of things about each other. Like the fact that you used to date—"

"We did not *date*." Any trace of amusement fled.

"Okay. Then what did you—?"

"It is a very long story, one I wish to not get into. I will tell you that Abbas is an evil man, that he treats women... badly. That if my sister stays with him, I fear she will learn this the hard way."

Caleb pressed his lips together. A moment passed before he said, "Did you learn it the hard way?"

She said nothing. She didn't want to lie to Caleb, and she didn't want to tell him the truth.

He angled onto I-93 toward Boston. She rarely left Nutfield and never ventured beyond Manchester. Soon she would be farther from Kat than she'd ever been. Farther from home than she'd been since she'd returned to Nutfield when Kat was two years old.

"Is she with him against her will?"

"If she were, it would be easier to lure her away. Except, if she were held against her will, she would not have been able to contact me and would likely not be at this hotel in Boston. She would be in—" She cut off her words, unwilling to tell Caleb that much. Because to do so would reveal that she knew, which would reveal that she'd been there.

"Where?"

"Not free to come and go as she pleased," Vanessa said.

A muscle in Caleb's jaw twitched. His hands tightened on the steering wheel. He was angry.

She pressed herself against the door, as far from him as she could be. She should speak, apologize. She shouldn't have smiled at his frustration. *Stupid, stupid.* She needed his help. She needed to not make him an enemy.

He glanced her way. "You okay?"

"Forgive me. Forgive my..." What? What had she done wrong? If she didn't figure it out, then how could she make him happy? She needed Caleb on her side. She'd angered him, and she didn't know why.

"I'm not mad at you, Vanessa." Caleb stretched his hands, settled them back on the steering wheel, and held on loosely. He seemed to be working to look relaxed. "I don't like men who treat women badly. *That* makes me angry. I'm sorry for... for whatever that guy did to you."

She relaxed back into the seat. "It is over now. It's been over for a long time."

"You're from Serbia. This guy's from... somewhere in the Middle East. You don't know where?"

"He used to talk of Abu Dhabi and Doha. These are on the Arabian Peninsula, no?"

"Right. The UAE and Qatar. How did you two meet?"

The memory of that day caused heat to fill her cheeks. She would not explain. "Irrelevant."

His fists tightened again. "Okay. How did he meet your sister? Does this guy work in...? Are you from Belgrade?"

"Near there, da. My sister did not say how they met."

"Does he work there? In Belgrade? Or do business there?"

"I do not think so."

"They just... randomly met? Heckuva coincidence."

She hadn't thought of the unlikelihood that Abbas would have come to know Nadia. But... "I do not know how it could be otherwise, since..." Abbas had never known her real name. He couldn't have tracked down her family. Not easily, anyway. And why would he have bothered?

She thought of the trinket in her purse. It had been cast aside, a trifle, nothing important. He had much money, she doubted he'd even missed it.

"Since what?" Caleb asked.

She'd lost her train of thought and went back to the last words she'd spoken. "Since he does not know my family and, I believe, has no business dealings in Belgrade, I do not know how they met."

The miles rolled beneath their tires. They passed a few exits and were nearing the Massachusetts border when he signaled and exited the highway.

It was dark here. Too dark. And nowhere near Boston. She didn't know this place. Where was he taking her?

"Hey." He sounded concerned for her, as if he felt her fear. "I'm just stopping for gas."

Oh. She was being ridiculous, but the memories taunted.

He turned into a gas station, parked, and faced her. "For the record, I have never hurt a woman, and I never will. You don't have to be afraid of me."

"This I know"—she tapped her head—"here. Sometimes, I don't feel safe. It is not your fault."

A smile brightened his face. He seemed overly pleased at her words. "I'm glad you trust me. That's good." He got out, put the nozzle into the gas tank, and then sat back in the car. "It's chilly out there." He rubbed his hands together. "I should've put on my coat."

It had dropped into the fifties. Was Katarina warm enough? Vanessa had taken a coat for her daughter that morning, but would it be enough to stay outside and watch the fireworks tonight?

Kelsey would care for Kat. She needed to stop worrying.

"This is where I grew up," Caleb said.

She turned to him, then looked at the gas station.

He chuckled. "Not *here*. But in this town."

"This town is...?"

"Windham."

"It is a nice town?"

"Very nice. It's not as off-the-beaten-path as Nutfield, of course, being right on the interstate. It was a great place to grow up."

"You have family here still?"

"My parents and my youngest brother, when he's not at school."

"You have other siblings?"

"My sister, Essie, is twenty-eight. She's married. Then I have three brothers who are much younger than I am. Sam is twenty-five, Joe is twenty-three, and David is twenty."

The pump shut off with a dull thud. When Caleb had finished, he put the car in drive and said, "I'm starving. Let's get something to eat."

"We ate together. It was not that long ago."

"I just had that little hot dog—"

"It was a… a long foot."

He grinned. "A footlong."

"That is what I said."

He barely stifled his chuckle. "Hardly enough for a growing boy. And you didn't finish your burger. McDonald's or Dunkin' Donuts?"

"I am not hungry."

Despite her assurance that she was neither hungry nor thirsty, he ordered her a decaf coffee and then offered her a choice of the four donuts he'd purchased.

She wanted to refuse, but they smelled good. She chose a chocolate-glazed, which paired perfectly with the bitter brew.

After he angled back onto the highway, he held his bagel sandwich with one hand and ate while she nibbled the donut. He'd been right, as he often was—irritatingly so. She had been hungry, and the donut was the perfect snack.

They drove in silence—weirdly comfortable silence—for about fifteen minutes while he ate his sandwich. And then he ruined it by talking. "What's your plan?"

She ate the last bite and wiped her fingers on a napkin. "I do not wish to see Abbas, but my sister does not understand this. I think I will have to stay in the lobby and watch for Abbas to leave to find her alone."

"We." He handed her his empty wrapper, and she slid it

into the sack. "We'll wait, together. I'm not letting you go anywhere near that guy by yourself."

She wouldn't argue. Though she hated how needy she was, she had to think of Nadia. And Kat. "Thank you."

"I have a place for us to stay, but if you'd rather stay at the same hotel—"

"No. I do not." She breathed through the panic that had risen at his suggestion. "I do not wish to stay under the same... ceiling as Abbas."

His lips quirked. She'd screwed up the Americanism, no doubt. But he didn't correct her this time. "Good. That's good." He sipped his coffee and set it back in the cup holder. "Do you want to go to their hotel tonight, or do you want to wait until tomorrow?"

She didn't know which to choose. She wanted to see Nadia as soon as possible, but could she find her alone at night? "I do not know what we should do."

He glanced her way. "You could call her, see where she is."

Vanessa took out her phone and found the number Nadia had called her from that day. After a quick prayer, she dialed.

After five rings, she hung up. "She's not in her room."

"She doesn't have a cell phone?"

"I don't know." They crested a hill, and Vanessa glimpsed the Boston skyline ahead, the lit buildings against the dark sky. They were close, and she would have to decide.

"Here's my theory," Caleb said. "Abbas and Nadia have gone out together. If we were to go to the hotel tonight, we'd see them return together. I mean, it's already"—he glanced at the dashboard clock—"after eight. Maybe he would go back out after returning her to her room, but at this point, it doesn't seem likely that we'll catch her alone tonight. Does that make sense?"

"Where do you think they would have gone?" Vanessa asked.

"Dinner? A show?"

As if they were dating. Like a real couple. And maybe they were. Maybe that was the face Abbas was showing Nadia right now. But why? Certainly not because he cared for her. Abbas was incapable of any feelings except selfishness and greed and lust. For some other reason, he was playing a part for Nadia, convincing her he cared for her, even if he did not. But why?

Would he go to such trouble to find Vanessa? She couldn't imagine why. She was easily replaced. Interchangeable with any young, warm female body. Why would he look for her?

Caleb said, "I think we should wait and go over there tomorrow. We can find a seat in the lobby and watch for him to leave. Unless they're together all the time—"

"That does not seem likely."

"Then eventually he'll leave her alone."

Caleb made sense. She could wait until tomorrow. Tomorrow, she would find her sister and convince her to leave Abbas, to return to Nutfield with her.

She had only to survive the night with Caleb.

CHAPTER SEVEN

W hen Caleb took the Somerville exit, Vanessa stiffened beside him.

"My family owns a house in Cambridge," he said. "It's a nice place. You'll like it." When she said nothing, he continued to talk, trying to calm her. "My grandfather was the first in our family to attend Harvard. To attend any college, in fact. His parents were working class, but smart. Very smart, and my great-grandfather insisted Grandpa would go to college even if it meant joining the service to go on the GI Bill."

He glanced at Vanessa. If he weren't crazy, her expression and the way she leaned slightly toward him showed interest.

"Grandpa didn't want to join the service if he could help it. World War II had just finished, and the Korean Conflict was on the horizon. Grandpa didn't want to be a soldier."

"This I understand," Vanessa said. "My uncle died in battle when I was a child. I remember the war a little, but mostly the aftermath. The poverty and..."

Her voice trailed off. He stopped at a light and looked at her, wanting her to finish her sentence. He knew very little about the war in Serbia. He vaguely remembered hearing about the Serbs when he was a kid. That's what Vanessa was—a Serb. They'd been painted as the bad guys, he thought. As if the world could be separated into bad guys and good guys. As if her nationality could make her right or wrong. "And what?" He prompted. "What else do you remember?"

"Only that I understand not wanting to be a soldier," she said. "Please, tell your grandfather's story."

"Grandpa made straight A's. He was president of his class and joined a bunch of clubs in high school in an effort to secure a scholarship. Thanks to the owner of the factory where my great-grandfather worked, he received excellent recommendations and was admitted to Harvard on a full scholarship."

"That is good," Vanessa said. "This I love about America. A poor boy can work hard and become a different kind of person."

"Is Serbia not like that?"

"This I don't know." Her tone was clipped. "I haven't been there in many years."

"When did you—?"

"Please, tell your story."

Vanessa was not in the mood to share, apparently. Not that she ever was. "Harvard's a pretty prestigious school. It's here in—"

"I have heard of Harvard," she said. "This is impressive, your grandfather. Especially as his parents were not wealthy."

"Exactly. After he graduated, he went to work in Boston, and when he'd saved enough money, he bought a small house in Cambridge."

"This is where we're going?"

"Not exactly. He worked a few more years, paid off that first house, and then sold it and bought another, a larger house. He lived in it with his wife and kids—my father—and eventually sold it and bought another house."

"Also larger?"

Caleb smiled. "Yes. That's the house we're going to now."

"Does your grandfather still live there?"

"He and Grammy retired to Myrtle Beach, South Carolina, a few years ago. My sister, Essie, and her husband live in the house now. And my youngest brother, David, when he's at college."

"Essie? I have never heard this name."

"Short for Esther. Don't call her that, though. She hates it, despite the story behind it."

"What story?" Vanessa asked.

Surely she didn't mean... But she looked baffled. "Esther? In the Bible?"

"Oh." She faced forward. "I have read it. She was stolen from her family and forced to marry a man she didn't know. Why would anybody name a girl after her?"

That was one way to look at it. "She was made queen."

"Bah. Against her will. A queen in chains is not royalty."

He'd never seen the story of Esther quite that way before. "True, but from her position"—he conceded her point with a nod and added—"in chains, she was able to save Israel from a terrible fate."

Vanessa stared out the window. Under her breath, she uttered in a low voice, "Used by man, used by God."

He had no idea how to respond to that. He was praying for wisdom when she waved away her words—or maybe his—and said, "Continue. Your grandfather bought the house and raised your father there. Did he also grow to be successful?"

Caleb sipped his coffee to regain his equilibrium. This woman, with her strange accent and her strange ways of seeing life, with her combination of fear and aggression, had thrown him off-kilter. "Grandpa was a real estate developer. He raised his kids the way his parents had raised him, and Dad, too, went to Harvard. Interestingly, though the house is within walking distance of campus, Dad didn't live there when he attended but lived in the dorm and then in off-campus apartments."

"That seems a terrible waste of money."

"He said he needed space from his father. Grandpa could be demanding."

"Where I come from, there is no money for this kind of foolishness. You live with your family because otherwise you live on the street. You learn to get along."

"Ah. Well..." Again, what was the proper response?

"And you? Did you also go to Harvard? Did you live with your grandparents?"

"Yes, and mostly. I lived in the dorm the first year, but I grew tired of that quickly and moved in with my grandparents when I was a sophomore."

"And you studied what?"

"Business. Ended up getting an MBA."

"What is this... MBA?"

"Master of Business Administration." A prestigious degree from a prestigious school, but Vanessa didn't seem impressed.

"I see. And it helped you in your business?"

He shrugged. "I learned a lot."

"And this is why you are very successful, because of Harvard?"

He chuckled. "I don't know about that, and I'm not sure I want to send my kids there. But I can't complain about the education I received or the connections that attending Harvard afforded me."

He slowed to a stop in front of a three-story brownstone and pointed out her window. "That's the place. We'll go in through the back, though."

"It's a pretty building. Which is your family's?"

"I'll show you."

He'd never brought a woman here. Even when he was in

school, he'd never brought a date home to meet his grandparents or his parents on the weekends they visited. This house was their family's sanctuary. He knew his younger brothers didn't always see it that way. Essie had told him about a *gathering* David had had. She'd come home to find students draped over sofas and perched on the antique chairs in the dining room. An odd scent had hovered, she said, and then she realized it was from their vapes. Enough beer bottles and cans had been left about that she knew it had been no innocent party.

She'd sent everybody home, and she'd nearly kicked David out as well, but he'd promised never to do it again. A good thing, too. This was Grandpa's home. It felt sacrilegious to treat it like a bachelor pad.

Caleb angled his car down a side street and parked in the alley. The block was full of brownstones like this one, which shared exterior walls and the same brick front. The others, though, had been converted to apartments. This was the only true single-family brownstone home left in the neighborhood. "You ready?"

In response, she opened her door and stepped out.

He grabbed her suitcase and his, left them at the foot of the steps that led to the rear entrance, and unlocked the door. He pushed it open, then stepped out of the way. "Go ahead."

She moved past him, and he grabbed their suitcases and hurried back up the stairs and into the house.

She'd frozen one step into the kitchen.

The house was dark, so he flipped on a light and angled around her. "I thought Essie might be home by now, but it doesn't look like anybody is here." To be sure, he went through the kitchen to the foot of the stairs, dropped the suitcases, and called, "Anybody home?"

No response.

He returned to the kitchen and summoned Vanessa

forward. "They'll be home later. It's Saturday night. My brother's probably out with friends. Essie and Parker went to a dinner party tonight. Let me show you around."

She clutched her purse to her chest and followed. "The kitchen, obviously." She took in the space, which they'd remodeled about ten years prior. Black granite countertops, warm cabinets, travertine backsplash. She said nothing as he moved into the dining room, pushing open the French doors to show her the long antique table and the mismatched chairs that surrounded it. All unique. Somehow, the look worked. The fireplace on the far side was cold now, but it would see a fire when they gathered here this holiday season.

Usually, when he showed people the house, they remarked on all the architectural details—the unique wainscoting, the ornate moldings. But again, she said nothing, though her eyes had grown wider. Not with wonder, though. She seemed... afraid.

He pointed to the front door. "That leads to the street, where I first showed you the house." She nodded, and he moved on to the small living area, with its sofa and loveseat and the flat-screen mounted on the wall. "It's not very big, as you can see. These houses weren't built for large gatherings."

When he'd finished with the first floor, he grabbed their suitcases and started up the stairs. He was at the first landing when he looked down to find her still on the first floor. Her gaze was toward the front door.

She was scared. Not just scared. She seemed terrified. Why, though? "Vanessa, you're safe here."

She looked up at him, then back at the door. Slowly, she followed but was sure to keep a good five feet between them.

Rather than show her the rest of the house, he stepped into the room Essie had designated for Vanessa, a small room that faced the alley and was often used as a guest room. He set her suitcase inside the door and then stepped out of the way.

She took in the sage green walls, the full-size bed with the white bedspread, the original hardwood floors. Still, she said nothing, just turned to gaze at him.

He stepped into the room, and she took a step back. He stifled a sigh and turned to show her the doorknob on the open door. "It locks. Just push this button." He demonstrated, and the sound of a click filled the space. He grabbed the exterior knob and twisted it in his fist, but it didn't move. "To unlock, just..." He twisted the interior knob, and the lock disengaged. Then, he stepped back out of the room. "I promise, you're safe here. I would never hurt you."

"Your brother? Your wife's husband?"

Ah. He could see her worry.

"You have nothing to fear from them. If either one of them gives you a hard time, you let me know, and I'll handle it. I promise, Vanessa. You're safe here."

She pressed her lips together, nodded quickly.

He stepped away, tried not to acknowledge how strangely she was acting. She'd had a difficult day. Her memories, whatever they were, were too close.

"The bathroom is right next door. David and I will use the one on the third floor, so you'll only share this one with Essie and Parker."

"Okay." The single word didn't hide her fear.

He pointed to the bedroom at the end of the hall. "Theirs is the front room." He shifted to the rooms beyond hers. "As far as I know, those rooms are empty." He walked to the foot of the staircase that led to the third floor. "David's room is upstairs, and I'll stay up there tonight, too."

"Do you not usually?"

He usually slept on this floor, but... "I want you to feel safe. You are safe here, Vanessa. You know that, right?"

She crossed her arms, seemed to be working to hold herself together. "This whole place... You said your grandfather was in real estate?"

"Uh-huh."

"And your father, he does what?"

What difference did it make? "Dad's a hedge fund manager." At her blank expression, he said, "He works in finance. May I ask why it matters?"

"Wealthy people are..."

When she didn't finish, he resisted the urge to cross his own arms. Because she didn't just suspect him. She suspected his whole family. "Wealthy people are what?"

"They are... not to be trusted."

His short bark of laughter was not amused. "I don't know how you define wealthy, but I—"

"You are different. You're a nice man. I know this, and I know how you make your money. But most wealthy people are not nice. They make their money by illegal means. They are thieves, and—"

"Nobody in my family..." He took a breath, lowered his voice. The nerve of this woman. He'd dropped everything to serve as her protector. He'd brought her—the first woman ever—to his family's Cambridge home. He'd offered her a safe place to stay, and her reaction was to accuse him, accuse his whole family?

Father, what the heck? She loathes me, loathes my family, and hasn't even met them yet.

He should wait until his temper cooled, but words flew out of his mouth anyway. "I don't know what kind of people you've met in your life, Vanessa, but I can assure you, nobody in my family has made their money by illegal means. We are upstanding citizens." What a stupid thing to say. What a stupid thing to have to assure this... this crazy woman.

"Yes," she said. But she didn't seem mollified.

"What is your problem?"

"I do not trust wealthy people."

"You don't trust anybody, so why doesn't that surprise me?"

She blinked, stepped back. As if he'd wounded her.

Here he'd thought maybe they could watch a movie together. Get to know each other. It wasn't even nine o'clock, after all. But the fear in her eyes, the suspicion. The guarded expression.

Whatever. He grabbed his suitcase. "Do you need anything before you go to bed?"

"No. Thank—"

"Good night, then." He stormed up the stairs.

CHAPTER EIGHT

The little girl splashed through the still, cold water, gritty sand between her toes, cold spray on her cheeks. Tata was chasing her, and the girl ran, giggling.

Mama's voice carried in the background. "Careful! You'll ruin your dress." But Vojislava could hear the joy in Mama's voice and ignored the warning.

Vojislava didn't care about ruining her dress or about the cold that slapped against her chubby thighs. She only cared that Tata was laughing, and she was his precious daughter.

In the next instant, he caught her and scooped her up, sending water droplets over their heads and into her hair. He held her tight and tickled. "My little princess."

She giggled and giggled. "Stop it, Tata." But secretly, she loved it. She loved when her Tata was happy and played with her.

Behind them, Mama cradled Milos while Lukas played in the sand at her feet. Everybody was smiling.

And then the bad man walked toward them. He stomped the sand, which flew in every direction with each heavy footstep. His eyes were lidded, his lips pulled back in an evil sneer. He was big, a giant. Much bigger than Mama and Tata.

Tata, no. Please don't send me away.

But Tata saw the bad man, and his hands slipped from beneath Vojislava, and she fell and fell and fell.

Vanessa jerked awake, disoriented. She hadn't dreamed of her parents in years, nor had she thought of the lake. They hadn't had a lot of money, but, when she was a child, they would occasionally go to the shore to play. When there was money enough for gas, when they could take the time off of work. She longed for the little girl in her dream, the giggling, the laughing, the running.

That girl had died many years before.

Vanessa focused on the space around her, the real world and not the fantasy her mind had conjured.

Green walls. White bedspread. Sunlight streamed in through the lace curtains. She was in Boston. No, Cambridge, at Caleb's grandfather's house. Only now it was his sister's house. She'd assumed his grandfather owned an apartment in a building. It hadn't occurred to her that he could own the entire thing. In a city like this... She couldn't imagine the cost. The wealth it represented.

Her door was still locked. She'd slept all night, undisturbed. Of course she had. She felt foolish now for the fear that had propelled her into the room the night before and had her locking the door.

She checked the time on her cell phone and then sat up. It was after eight. How could she have slept so long? Of course, between thoughts of Nadia and fears about her sleeping quarters, it had taken some time to fall asleep. Her body must have decided she was safe here, because, once she'd fallen asleep, she'd slept as if she were tucked in her own bed at home.

She grabbed her toiletries and clean clothes and opened the

door. The hallway was wide, the stairway, with its shiny wooden railing, directly across from her room. She peeked both directions—nobody was there—and hurried to the bathroom.

Once she'd dressed for the day, she returned to her room, picked up her things, and made the bed. She was tempted to stay there until somebody came for her, but perhaps Caleb wouldn't. Perhaps he would let her stew in her room all day if she didn't summon the bravery to venture downstairs.

Fine, then. She was a grown woman. She could do this. She wouldn't be afraid.

Or, at least she'd hide her fear, which was nearly the same thing.

She prayed for courage, opened her bedroom door, and crept down the stairs. The foyer was also empty, but a voice came from the kitchen. A woman. The aromas of sausage and coffee and cinnamon spurred her on.

She stepped into the kitchen doorway, and the woman turned to her, a wide smile on her face. She had dark brown hair like her brother, but where his features were strong and angular, hers were delicate. Her cheeks were fuller, her body rounder, more comfortable. A cell phone was pressed to her ear, and when she saw Vanessa, she said, "Hey, I gotta go. See you there," and ended the call. She stepped forward, hand outstretched. "I'm Essie."

Vanessa shook her hand. "Thank you for letting me stay here."

The woman waved off the words. "It's as much Caleb's house as it is mine. I'm glad you're here. Coffee?"

At Vanessa's "please," Essie poured her a cup and nodded to the small kitchen table. The space had been updated, but it was still very small, the table only large enough for four.

"Sit," Essie said. "You hungry?"

"A little, but don't go to any trouble."

Essie set Vanessa's coffee on the table, followed by a sugar dish and a container of cream. "You like eggs?"

Vanessa had learned as a child to eat what was offered to her. Whether or not she liked something seemed irrelevant. "Eggs are fine." She added cream and sugar to her coffee, elements that used to seem like luxuries but which she'd become accustomed to. She was far from the poor little girl from her dream this morning.

In every way.

Essie returned to the counter, pulled a dish from the cabinet, and spooned something onto it. Vanessa couldn't fathom what else she was doing over there, but she was busy. Then, Essie set the plate on the table in front of Vanessa.

There was a square of what looked like an egg casserole along with a few apple slices that had been warmed on the stove. They had some kind of sugary substance on them. This must have been the source of the cinnamon scent. Also on the plate was a small yellowish muffin with black dots. Lemon poppy seed, she thought.

"This looks delicious. It is a breakfast fit for royalty."

Essie seemed pleased as she slid into the chair opposite Vanessa. "I rarely get to cook during the week, so I always make a big breakfast on Sundays before church."

"Your husband is... where?"

"Parker already ate. The gate out front is broken, and Caleb said he'd help Parker fix it." Essie laughed, a lighthearted sound. "What that means is that Caleb will fix it and Parker will crack stupid jokes and occasionally supply a tool. He's not exactly handy."

But Caleb was? Vanessa hadn't known that about the man, only that he was generous with his money and always full of advice Vanessa didn't want to take—even though it was usually sound. She forked a bite of the casserole. The flavors of eggs, cheese, and sausage mingled, not to mention spices she couldn't identify. It tasted delicious, and she couldn't help the little *mmm* that escaped.

"Glad you like it," Essie said.

"It is delicious." Vanessa tried the apples. Warm, sweet, and cinnamon-flavored. It was like apple pie without the crust. "How do you make? They are very good."

"Easy. Sliced apples in a saucepan with butter, brown sugar, and cinnamon."

"That is all?"

"Sometimes, the simple things are the best."

"Yes. This is true."

Essie tilted her head to the side. "I'm trying to place your accent, but I can't figure it out. Sometimes, it sounds almost French. And then..."

"I am Serbian," Vanessa said.

"Your English is excellent."

"Thank you. It is a hard language, English. Many times, it does not make any sense at all. And to speak is one thing, but to spell? I do not understand the rules. My daughter is seven, and she tells me how to spell things when I get confused. The other day, I tried to spell bologna. I thought, since it rhymes with pony, it would be b-a-l-o-n-y. But then she spells it and"—Vanessa waved as if the crazy letters were flying around her head—"I thought she was playing a trick on me."

Essie's laugh was high-pitched and girlish, which didn't go with the woman sitting across from her. It made her face seem younger, more beautiful. "I never thought of that—pony, bologna. That's funny."

Vanessa worked to stifle an answering smile. "You do not have children?"

Essie's expression shifted, became almost guarded. "Someday, maybe. I've been busy."

"What do you do?"

"I'm an OB/GYN at Brigham and Women's Hospital."

She remembered those letters. "You bring babies into the world?"

The smile was back. "It's the most amazing experience, and I get to do it every single day."

"You enjoy your job," Vanessa said, because it was obvious. "This is good, to like the way you spend your days. This I love about America—the choices. People can do what they wish if only they try hard enough."

"Not true in Serbia?"

She shrugged. "I have not lived there in many years." She returned to her meal. Who knew when she would eat again?

After a moment, Essie said, "Your daughter, what's her name?"

Vanessa set her fork down. Again, she fought the urge to smile. She sipped her coffee to hide it. "Katarina."

"I bet she's beautiful."

"Da. Yes. I think she is the most beautiful girl in the world."

"That's sweet," Essie said.

Vanessa opened her phone and showed Essie the home screen photo of Kat sitting on the shore of Clearwater Lake.

Essie gazed at the photo. "She looks like you."

"More like me than like her father. For this I thank God."

Essie's eyebrows rose. What was wrong with her, bringing Carlos into this conversation? Thanks to Nadia's phone call, the past was too close, like a stalker right around the corner, preparing to pounce.

"Her father is gone now," Vanessa said quickly. "He doesn't matter."

Essie nodded slowly. "Caleb said you have a family emergency."

"My sister... It is a long story."

Essie reached across the table and patted Vanessa's hand. "Well, you're welcome here as long as you need to stay, even if Caleb has to go back to Nutfield."

Was she serious? She would let Vanessa stay without Caleb? How generous and unexpected. But why should that surprise her? Was not Caleb the same way? She was trying to come up with a suitable response when a door opened in another room. A moment later, a man stepped into the kitchen. He was the same height as Essie, maybe five-eight, and kissed her on the cheek before turning to Vanessa, hand outstretched. "I'm Parker."

His hand was freezing when she shook it. "Vanessa. Nice to meet you."

Caleb stepped into the doorway and leaned on the door-jamb, arms crossed. His cheeks were flushed. He wore jeans and a sweater the color of pine needles that brought out the green in his hazel eyes. He sent her a cordial look.

Was he angry with her for her foolishness the night before? She would apologize later, though she wouldn't try to explain. There was no way he'd understand. "Good morning."

"Sleep okay?"

"Very well."

"Nothing, uh"—his eyebrows rose—"bother you all night?"

Definitely still angry. "I slept in peace, thank you."

"Mmm. Imagine that."

Essie watched the exchange, eyebrows hiked toward her dark brown hair. When they said nothing else, she said, "You two going to church with us? We're leaving in"—she glanced at the clock on the range—"twenty minutes."

Before Vanessa could answer, Caleb said, "We've got some stuff to do. We'll see you guys later."

"I'm going to change my clothes." Parker turned to Caleb. "Thanks for your help."

"Anytime."

Essie started to clean the kitchen. Vanessa wasn't finished with her breakfast, but she stood. "How can I help?"

Essie waved her off. "I've got it. It'll only take a sec."

While she worked, Caleb watched from his spot in the doorway. When Essie was finished, she walked out, sending a "see you later" over her shoulder.

Only then did Caleb enter. He sat at the table in the seat beside Vanessa. "You look well rested."

"I am sorry for my behavior last night."

His smile was slight, his lips closed. "I understand. New place. You didn't know what to expect."

"You can't understand, and I don't wish to explain."

He took that in with a slow nod. "Fair enough."

"You have eaten?"

"When I got up." He waited while she finished her breakfast. When she pushed the plate away, he rinsed it and slid it in the dishwasher. "You need anything else?"

"No. Thank you."

"Should we head over to the hotel?"

"Da. I should bring my things?"

He tilted his head to the side. "If we get Nadia to come with us, will you want to come back here?"

When she had Nadia, she didn't want to stop anywhere. She'd want to get out of town and away from Abbas as fast as possible. "I would prefer not."

"Then grab your stuff. Better to have it than not, right?"

"This is a good decision."

He smiled then, a real smile that made his eyes crinkle at the corners. "I enjoy the way you talk."

She went back over the last thing she'd uttered. "Did I say something wrong?"

"Nope. It was perfect." He swept his hand toward the door. "After you."

She gathered her things, sorry to be saying good-bye to the pretty room Katarina would have loved. Maybe, someday, her daughter would see this place.

Bah. Silly thought. Why would Vanessa ever be there with Kat? It was strange enough to be there herself. This whole situation was too strange. That Caleb would drop everything to help her.

That Nadia was here, in the city.

Direct us, Lord. Make Nadia trust me and come home with me. Show me how to help her. I have no resources, but You have everything. I will try to trust You.

Help me not to read into Caleb's kindness. Help him not to ruin our friendship by trying to make it something it's not. Something it cannot be.

There was much to lose on this trip, but it would all be worth the risk if only Vanessa could save her sister.

CHAPTER NINE

Caleb pulled into a parking garage a block from the hotel and took a ticket from the kiosk.

Beside him, Vanessa gasped.

"What's wrong?"

"The price is… That cannot be right."

He glanced at the sign. It was ridiculous what they charged to park per hour, but it wasn't as if there were a lot of choices. "It's not a problem."

He found a spot on the second level and parked. "You ready?"

"Da." But the word sounded tentative, and the color had left her cheeks. She was nervous. To see her sister for the first time in many years, or to see Abbas? Probably both.

He took in her appearance. Long dark blond hair, green eyes, knockout body that she'd hidden today beneath jeans and an oversize sweater. She wasn't exactly forgettable. "Do you think Abbas will recognize you?"

She dipped her head in a quick nod. "It has not been long enough."

They made their way to the stairwell, which stunk of motor oil and exhaust.

Outside, the weather was crisp, the sky bright blue. The area had already filled with tourists and locals. The streets were quieter than they would be on a weekday or even later that Sunday, but still the din of the city rumbled. Car engines, conversations. A ferry's horn sounded in the harbor. It was the perfect day to be in Boston.

The tight set of Vanessa's lips belied the atmosphere. Aside from her wide green eyes, her face was devoid of color.

"Here, let's…" He guided her to a kiosk selling souvenirs and grabbed a Red Sox cap. "You like it?"

"I do not need a hat," she said.

"I thought you could stick your hair inside, maybe pull it down over your face. Like a disguise."

Her eyebrows rose, and her jaw dropped, though she blanked her expression quickly. "You are always full of good ideas."

"When you say it, it sounds like an insult."

That nearly brought a smile, which faded when she saw the price tag. "I do not have the money."

"You like this one?"

"Are there any cheaper ones?"

He ignored the question and handed his credit card to the kid who ran the kiosk. While the credit card was processing, he faced Vanessa. "Put it on, see if you can hide your hair."

She found a mirror affixed to the wooden kiosk and did as he'd asked. He'd expected her to look less attractive in the hat. He was an idiot. With her eyes partially hidden, her lips looked… more kissable.

He'd better eradicate that thought. If she had any idea where his mind had just gone, she'd run for the hills. Or shove him into traffic. Probably the latter.

When the Lord had first told him Vanessa would someday be his bride, he'd been amused at the joke, then irritated. Caleb hadn't even liked her, much less found her attractive. Sure, she was beautiful, but to be attracted to someone meant you wanted to be near her, and being near Vanessa had always been frustrating and vaguely unsatisfying. Most women, especially single women, were overly attentive to him. Most people treated him with respect, but she'd only ever tolerated him. Barely. He'd often tried to help her, and, just as often, she'd shot him down as if both he and his ideas were unwelcome. Now, two years later, Vanessa was more receptive to his ideas. She was learning to trust him. If she could let down her walls just a little, maybe he could get to know her, and she him. Maybe God's plan wasn't crazy after all.

Vanessa had to learn to trust Caleb. Caleb had to learn to trust God.

"Is okay?" she asked.

Her hair was hanging through the hole in the back of the cap, but she'd stuffed the excess into the back of her sweater. She still looked like Vanessa, though. Nobody who got a good look at her would be fooled. "You'll have to keep your head down."

The Rowes Wharf Hotel was in front of them. Each floor of the red brick building was a little narrower than the one below, so that, from the narrow end, it had a triangular shape. "There it is."

She barely gave it a look and then only nodded.

They walked into the lobby. If he'd expected her to be impressed by the grandeur of the atrium, he'd have been disappointed. But then, his family's brownstone hadn't impressed her, either. It had only frightened her.

She looked equally frightened now.

He led her to the coffee shop and settled her in a chair that faced the doors and the front desk, where she could keep an eye out for Nadia and Abbas. "Coffee?"

"I am not thirsty."

He leaned down to whisper, "We need to look like we're here for a reason, right?"

"Da. Coffee."

He was desperate to learn what was going on in her head but knew better than to ask. "Why don't you call the room, see if they're there."

While she made the call, he ordered two coffees and waited for them by the counter, watching the lobby beyond. Of course, he didn't know what Abbas or Nadia looked like, but he could keep his eyes out for a Middle Eastern man with a young woman.

Their drinks were handed over, and he doctored them both. He'd seen Vanessa fix her coffee enough at food bank board meetings to know how she liked it.

He set the cup in front of her and slid into the seat across. "Any luck."

"Abbas answered." The words, delivered matter-of-factly, didn't hide the fear behind her fragile mask.

He needed to know what this Abbas person had done to her.

"Did you talk to him?"

"I hung up." She regarded the coffee, then sipped it. "It is perfect. Of course."

Those last two words were uttered like a complaint, and he resisted the urge to apologize for fixing her coffee properly.

He'd never figure out this woman.

Right now, though, her fearful expression wasn't hard to read.

"Why don't you tell me more about this Abbas fellow?"

"I do not know what else to say."

"What's his full name?"

She shrugged.

"You don't know?"

She sipped her coffee and stared at the lobby, head lowered to hide her face.

"How can you not know his full name?" Caleb asked.

"It was not important at the time."

"What was important?"

She didn't even glance his way when she said, "Surviving."

"How long were you—?"

"I do not wish to talk about it."

"Did he hurt you?"

"I do not wish to talk about it."

"Vanessa."

She glared at him. "I owe you much. This I know. The hat, the coffee, the parking, the place to stay. I will pay you back if you wish me to."

What did that have to do with anything? "I don't expect—"

"But I cannot talk about Abbas."

Not *will* not, but *can* not. Why, though? The need to know was eating at him like too much caffeine on an empty stomach, but he let the subject drop.

"Have you ever been to Boston?"

She didn't take her gaze away from the lobby. "For a time, I lived not too far away, but I never came into the city."

"Why not?"

She shrugged. "Kat was a baby. There was no money, and I did not wish to be around so many people. The city makes me nervous. All the people, the noise, the..."

When she didn't explain, he asked, "Did you grow up in a small town? Is that why—?"

"My first memory of a city was when we went to look for my uncle after a bombing. During the war. People were crying and screaming and digging through rubble. My aunt was..." She shook her head. "She could not be comforted. She was... beneath herself."

"Beside herself?"

"That is what I said."

His smile, which usually followed her English gaffs, didn't come. "This was her husband you were looking for?" At Vanessa's nod, Caleb asked, "Did she find him?"

A woman laughed at a table nearby. Vanessa's words belied the lighthearted sound. "His body was recovered a few weeks later."

"How old were you?"

"I do not know. Very young. My sisters were not yet born. I was at least two but not yet through my fourth year." Her gaze never left the lobby, though he longed to look at her face. Maybe she didn't want him to see how the words affected her. Maybe she was able to share this because she didn't have to meet his eyes.

"I don't understand why you were there," he said. "You were a toddler. How could you help?"

"My aunt was keeping me when she heard of the bombing, and my parents were at work. She left my brothers with a neighbor. I don't know why she didn't also leave me. Maybe the neighbor didn't like me."

"That can't be it."

Vanessa said nothing.

"Cities remind you of that?"

"Da. The chaos, the noise. It is too much."

"Is that why you didn't want to ride in the parade yesterday?"

She sipped her coffee, ignored the question.

"How did you end up in Nutfield?"

"A long story."

"We have nothing else to do."

He waited for her to speak, but it seemed he'd asked another question she didn't want to answer. He could tell her how he'd ended up living in Nutfield. He'd met Vanessa, and the Lord had told him he was going to marry her. In an act of faith and obedience, he'd moved from his home in Manchester, where his company was located, and bought a house in the small town. He'd wanted to get to know the woman God thought might someday not loathe him. Might even like him enough to go on a date with him. And then might get past the loathing and the liking to maybe even falling in love with him. But the move to Nutfield had accomplished very little in that regard.

Except now, he was here with her. She trusted him enough to let him join her on this adventure. Even if she'd only done it because she needed someone to protect her from Abbas, and someone to pay, at least she'd chosen him. Any of her other friends in Nutfield would have gladly helped if she'd asked. But she hadn't. She'd asked him.

Well, not asked so much as not refused when he'd insisted.

Still, it was astounding.

Thank you, Lord. Do Your thing here. I have no idea—

Vanessa's sharp gasp had his gaze moving to the lobby.

It was no challenge to spot Nadia. The woman looked like a younger version of Vanessa. Same long blond hair, same knockout body, and this one wasn't hidden beneath baggy clothes. Nadia wore skinny jeans and a fitted top that was so short that an inch of her midriff showed. She stood beside one of the dark sofas, a light brown leather jacket draped over her arm, a carry-on bag at her side.

About ten feet away stood a swarthy man with dark brown

curly hair and a trimmed beard. He was talking into a phone. He, too, stood beside a small suitcase.

This was the perfect opportunity, but Vanessa hadn't moved.

Her eyes were wide, her face pale as death. She was looking not at her sister but at the man.

"Are you going to go talk to her?" Caleb said. "I'll go with you. I won't let anything happen to you."

She didn't respond.

"Do you want me to approach her?" Caleb asked.

Vanessa closed her eyes and doubled over, arms hugging her stomach as if she might be sick.

"What do you want me to do?" He kept his gaze on the couple in the lobby. Nadia continued to stand and wait. Abbas continued to talk on the phone.

Vanessa continued to say nothing.

Caleb was torn. Stay, comfort her, help her through this moment? Or approach Nadia.

Vanessa would survive, and, based on the suitcases, it looked as if Nadia and Abbas were leaving. Caleb stood. "I'll try to get her over here."

When Vanessa didn't respond, Caleb wandered toward the woman. She barely looked old enough to be out of her parents' house. Vanessa had told him she was twenty. He'd have guessed sixteen.

That was probably part of her... appeal, so to speak.

The man, Abbas, looked at least forty. Maybe closer to fifty. He was paying no attention to Nadia.

Caleb would approach her, make small talk as if nothing were amiss, and then tell her Vanessa was in the coffee shop. He'd ask her to discreetly get away from Abbas for a moment to see her sister.

He'd send the sisters to the ladies' room and then stand guard. He'd call security if he needed to. He wouldn't let Abbas get past him.

If she couldn't get away or didn't want to risk it, he'd encourage her to call Vanessa again, let her sister know where she was going. *Lord, give me words.*

Either way, he had to do this without tipping Abbas off. Because Vanessa didn't seem capable of standing up to him, and Caleb was certainly not going to put a target on her back.

He stopped a few feet from Nadia. "Good morning."

She turned to him, and a broad smile crossed her lips. A smile like he'd never seen on her older sister. Joyful, carefree. He couldn't reconcile that smile with the woman who was fighting the urge to vomit on the opposite side of the spacious lobby. "Hello."

"Checking out?"

"We take short trip," Nadia said. "I will see stores." Her voice was loud. It held no subtlety, no fear. If he mentioned Vanessa, would she find a way to discreetly excuse herself? Or would she squeal and giggle?

She seemed like a squeal-and-giggle girl. Could she be any more different from Vanessa?

"Where are you headed?" Did he sound sufficiently casual?

"To the Manhattan."

"Ah. Shopping in New York. Sounds fun." He checked his phone as if he were waiting for something. As if it made sense that he was standing with this woman for no good reason. "And then where?"

"Just gone one night. Back here tomorrow."

Tomorrow. He and Vanessa could wait, come back. It would be better to get Nadia with Vanessa now, but he couldn't do it with Abbas so close, not if Nadia couldn't be trusted not to alert him. He felt movement at his side and turned to see that Abbas had approached and was glaring at him from less than two feet away.

"How you doing?" Caleb asked.

"Can we help you?" Abbas spoke with a highbrow British accent. As polite as the words sounded, he looked more threatening than congenial.

"Just killing time." Caleb glanced at Nadia. "Have fun." He turned and walked away, not toward the coffee shop but in the direction of the doors on the far end of the lobby, lifting his phone to his ear as he went as if he'd received a call.

He sat on one of the sofas and crossed his ankle over his knee. Nothing to worry about here. Relaxed as could be.

Abbas urged Nadia toward the lobby doors, shooting a glare at Caleb over his shoulder.

Caleb kept his gaze away from Vanessa. He watched as Abbas and Nadia stepped into the crisp October day, watched as they climbed into the back of a sedan. Only when the car drove away did he hurry back to the coffee shop.

The color had not returned to Vanessa's cheeks. Her arms were crossed, and she was rocking in her chair, looking toward the lobby as if she both hoped and feared Abbas and Nadia would return. "She's gone. I didn't have the courage, and now it's too late."

"She'll be back tomorrow."

Vanessa's gaze snapped to his. "What do you mean?"

"She said they're going to *the* Manhattan for one night. They'll be back tomorrow. She seemed excited. Happy."

Vanessa covered her face with her hands. "Thank you. Thank you."

He wasn't sure if she was talking to him or praying. He gave her a minute to compose herself. And worked to keep inside the words that were dying to get out. Because her reaction... Vanessa was no coward. She was one of the toughest women he'd ever met. And she was desperate to save her sister. And yet she'd been cowed by Abbas's very presence.

His own stomach roiled. And he knew he shouldn't, knew it would do no good, but still, the question flew out of his mouth as if he had no control over it.

"What did that man do to you?"

CHAPTER TEN

Vanessa had known the question was coming. But she couldn't answer. Only once had she told the whole story—to the counselor at the home where she and Kat had lived the first two years of Kat's life, where Vanessa had sought shelter after Kat was born. The kind women there had taken her in without judgment, given her a room, fed her, clothed her, and taught her about God. They'd educated her and prepared her for a life of independence. Over the two years she'd lived there, they'd taught her how to make a budget, how to pay her bills, how to survive.

From the counselor and in group therapy sessions, Vanessa had learned that she was precious and priceless, despite the fact that her father had traded her for a handful of dinars. Despite the fact that she'd been sold many times after that and, once, lost in a poker game like a plastic chip one might toss to a dealer as a tip, appreciation for a good hand.

She was not a tip or a chip or a commodity. She was not chattel.

I am precious and priceless. I am a child of the living God.

Still, she couldn't talk about it. She wouldn't dredge it up like the mud at the bottom of a lake. It would only make the clear murky. It would not help. She opened her mouth to say just that when Caleb lifted his hand.

"Pretend I didn't ask." His gaze skimmed over her face and landed on her eyes. "If you ever feel like you need to get it off your chest or... or just want me to know, I'll be ready to listen. No pressure, though."

"Off my chest?" She looked down to see if she'd spilled anything, but her sweater was free of crumbs and coffee stains.

His serious expression was replaced by amusement.

"I do not understand."

"It's just an expression. It means to unburden yourself."

Her confusion must have shown because he tried again.

"To share something that is bothering you or makes you feel uncomfortable or guilty or... just whatever."

"I do not feel guilty."

The amusement faded. "I have no idea what happened with you and that guy, but I hold him responsible."

It was good he did, but... "Why?"

He lifted his shoulders and dropped them. "Just a feeling, I guess. An instinct. But..." A muscle pulsed in his jaw. Suddenly, he pushed back in his chair and stood. "You done with your coffee?"

"Da."

He snatched her cup and his own and tossed them in the trash can. "You can take off the hat. Abbas and Nadia won't be back until tomorrow."

She had forgotten the hat. Now that he mentioned it, the hairs she'd tried to hide were scratching between her sweater and her back. She pulled the hat off, the hair out of the hole in the back of it, and shook it out. That was better. But the hat... She placed it back on her head. She had never worn a baseball cap. She liked it.

He smiled at her, an almost genuine smile. "We find ourselves with an entire day to kill in Boston. What do you want to do?"

"To kill this day?"

He chuckled. "Shopping, museums, food?"

She didn't know what he was asking. "Do you not wish to return to Nutfield? Your sister said I could stay without you."

"That's because my sister has no idea what's going on. I'm not leaving you alone."

"You have things to do, though, no?"

"There's nothing I'd like to do more than spend the day with you." He fell into the seat across from hers. "The science museum is fun. Or the Museum of Art or the Gardiner? Do you like art museums?"

"I have never been to one."

His eyebrows hiked. "Are you serious? Never?"

She hadn't done many of the things normal people did. Even if she'd stayed in her parents' house, she doubted she'd have ever gone to an art museum. At least not as a child. Were there any in Belgrade? She didn't know.

She hardly knew anything about her home country. Only that there'd been a war, and her family had been poor. Together —Tata and Mama, Vanessa and her little brothers and sisters and her aunt had all lived in an apartment, shared beds. She remembered violence on the street but laughter in the house. She remembered the lake and being caught up in her father's arms. She remembered caring for her younger siblings. She remembered Nadia. Sweet, trusting Nadia, who had been innocent before. Who had today been dressed with no shame, no sense of self-respect. Nadia, who was a captive and didn't realize it.

Caleb studied her. Did her expression tell too much? What

had they been discussing? Ah, an art museum. "Displaying art... it is only foolishness," she said. "Not important."

"That's where you're wrong. Art... beauty. These things are very important. They're vital, in fact. Come on."

❧

By the time they returned to the car, wound through traffic, and parked again, it was after eleven o'clock. "Perfect," Caleb said. "It's just opening."

They'd passed a grand, white building with a sign proclaiming it was the Boston Museum of Art before they'd turned onto this side street and found a parking spot, but he didn't walk toward that grand building. Instead, he headed in the opposite direction. Though they were still in the city, they'd left the tallest buildings and much of the noise behind. Here, the roads weren't clear, nor were they crowded. This was manageable. Vanessa had felt trapped and confined near the harbor, though that was probably due more to Abbas being close than anything else.

A crowd of college students walked by, one tossing a football in the air and catching it himself. They seemed to be headed toward a park, but Caleb led her down an even narrower road. They passed what looked like newer construction amidst the old buildings that lined the road.

Caleb nodded toward the entrance. "Here we are."

She read the sign. The Isabella Stewart Gardner Museum. "This is art also? I thought I saw another art museum..."

"This one's smaller, but I like it better."

He paid the fee and they entered.

And she was transported.

She had seen great wealth, had seen great art. But there was something special about this place, about beauty for the sake of beauty. These pieces—everything from paintings to pottery to door knockers—had been chosen for their beauty alone.

It was frivolous and yet...

Perhaps Caleb was right. Perhaps art and beauty were important.

Bah. Caleb was always right. It was his most annoying quality.

He walked beside her, letting her set the pace. When she dared glance at him, he was watching her. Why, she didn't know and chose not to consider at this moment, for this place... This place was magical.

She didn't understand any of it. She'd never studied art. When she'd lived in the group home, they'd had art therapy, but she hadn't taken it seriously. What did it matter if she painted or created? She'd been required to try, so she had always chosen a coloring book and crayons. Simple and without need for thought.

Katarina was a good artist. Even the teacher at her school said she had talent, and Vanessa had encouraged her love of drawing and painting, even though she didn't understand the point of it. For Kat, the point seemed to be the ability to create something out of nothing.

But the people who'd created these works of art, they had tapped into something deep, something Vanessa couldn't name. They had somehow brought to life emotions so vivid, Vanessa could hardly stand to look at them.

She and Caleb had completed their tour of the first floor and were on the second when she entered the Raphael Room. The walls were covered with red damask. A table in the center was surrounded by richly upholstered chairs. There were too many details to take in. Rich fabrics, gold trim, antique furniture, paintings like none she'd seen before. "It is like walking into Italy," she said.

"You've been there?"

"Da."

He studied her, but she ignored him, turning her attention to the placard beside a painting titled "Lamentation over the Dead Christ." It was painted by one named Raphael. Ah, the inspiration for the entire room. Like everything, the painting was beautiful. Like other paintings she'd seen, she had a question.

"The circles over their heads?" She glanced at Caleb, who was looking at her, not the painting, as he often had on this tour. It was unsettling. She pointed to the circles. "What are these?"

"They're supposed to be halos."

She considered the word, whispered it. "I do not know these halos."

Caleb's lips pressed together as if he wasn't sure, either. "It's supposed to be like an aura of holiness."

Frustration prickled, but she kept her tone cool. "I do not know that word, either. Aura?"

"Okay. Uh, it's as if you could see Christ on them. As if they wore their holiness or..." He stared at the painting, lips twisted. "I don't know how to explain it."

She turned back to the painting and studied the circles. She'd never seen anything like that—a circle hovering over a person's head. But she understood that *aura*. She whispered that word aloud so she wouldn't forget it, thinking of friends who carried this aura of holiness. Like her friend Kelsey, who had overcome much, who had suffered in some of the ways Vanessa had suffered, but seemed to give off goodness and holiness, almost like a pretty scent. Other friends she knew in Nutfield were the same—Samantha, Rae, Marisa. These were people who had saved her, had given her a place to go, had found her a job after she'd left the group home—when they could easily have forgotten her. These were the closest to family she had.

They had no circles over their heads, but this aura of holiness she had experienced.

Caleb shifted beside her, and she glanced his way. Perhaps he had a similar aura. Maybe. Except he was watching her again, which made her wonder. His lips tipped up at the corners, but he said nothing.

She turned back to the painting. She feared thinking of men as good. Most of those she'd known in her past had been far from holy. But the husbands of her friends and the men who helped at the food bank—Jack, Kade... And there was the artist Donovan, who had spent hours creating those silly giant food items for the parade... Dylan, who worked to find lost children and restore them to their parents, who had nearly died to rescue a woman he'd only just met. All of these had been kind to her, respectful.

None as much as the man beside her.

Caleb. Perhaps he had an invisible halo over his head. Perhaps he was as good as he seemed. If that were the case, if he did wear holiness like a crown, then he had no business with someone like her.

She closed her eyes. It was not her fault. Nothing that had happened had been her fault. She knew this. She had been reminded enough. Except, perhaps, at the very end when she'd become as bad as Carlos, as evil. When she'd fired that gun and killed him. When she'd nearly killed Kelsey.

She had murdered. She had almost murdered twice.

But she had sought forgiveness and received it. She was free of it.

Or so they'd told her.

A group of chattering people stepped into the room and yanked her out of her dark thoughts. She moved on, studied the next piece, and the next. When she came to the fireplace, she admired the rich trim of it—not Italian art but art nonetheless. And then she glanced up.

And froze.

This painting, "Lucretia" by Botticelli, according to the sign, was different. In the first part on the left, a woman was held at the point of a knife. On the far right, the same woman collapsed in the arms of others—her family, perhaps? But in the center... It was the center picture that had her staring.

The woman lay on the ground, dead, surrounded by a crowd of people.

What did it mean? The man with the knife hadn't murdered her, not if the panel on the right were accurate. She had survived. But then... died?

She had a knife in her chest in the center picture. Nobody would survive that. And the knife wasn't there in the panel on the far right.

She murmured, "I do not understand."

"Do you know the story?"

Obviously not, and obviously he did. Because he knew everything. She turned to him. "Explain, please."

"The woman was beautiful, and she attracted the attention of the king's son." He nodded to the first panel. "The man raped her at knifepoint."

Vanessa worked to keep her expression free of reaction.

Caleb turned to the panel on the right. "Filled with shame, she went to her family. They were angry, though at her or at the man, I don't remember."

"Why would they be angry at her? What could she have done?"

"Nothing, obviously. But people can be stupid sometimes."

"Da. This I know."

"In the middle picture..."

Vanessa focused on the woman with the knife in her chest. "Her family killed her?"

"According to legend, she committed suicide."

Suicide. Because of the shame. Vanessa remembered how she'd tried and tried to break the window of the room where she'd been held, desperate to hurl herself into the ocean. She did this to escape the agony she'd endured too long. But to escape shame?

"This I do not understand."

"Me, either," he said. "That's what they call a long-term solution to a short-term problem."

"Da. The knife would have been more useful had it plunged into her attacker's heart."

"I agree. But that's not the end of the story. Legend has it that the public display of her corpse incited rebels, who overthrew the regime and birthed the Roman Republic."

The end of the story was no better than the beginning. "Once again, a woman's mistreatment leads to good for others."

"What do you—?"

"Esther. A slave with a royal title is no less a slave, but her suffering led to salvation for the Jews. No?"

"Yeah, but—"

"And this woman's suffering and death led to freedom for others. Why must women always pay with their lives or their freedom for the advancement of men's causes?"

"In Esther's case, it was God's cause."

"That is not better."

He squinted and stared at the image.

The loud group neared Caleb and Vanessa, their chatter filling the space.

Vanessa moved on, through the room and into the next. But she couldn't get the image of that woman out of her head.

The shame was so bad, she'd plunged a knife into her own heart.

This, Vanessa could not understand. She had been focused on survival, not shame. Shame had become such a part of her, even now she felt it coat her skin like salt after an ocean swim.

More since seeing that painting. Others wore halos. She wore shame.

They had perused three more rooms, quicker now, as Vanessa was ready to be out of these pretty walls, when Caleb spoke beside her. "There's another way to look at it."

She didn't have to ask what he was talking about. She paused in the center of yet another room and waited.

"That woman's life was so valuable, an entire kingdom was overthrown."

"She was royalty or wealthy or—?"

"She was human." Caleb stepped between Vanessa and the artwork she'd stopped in front of and rested his hand on her upper arm, squeezing lightly. "Don't you see, Vanessa? Her prominence or lack thereof is irrelevant. God allowed that entire kingdom to be punished because one of His daughters was harmed. That's how important she was."

To be that important. To matter that much to anybody.

Caleb touched her chin.

It was an invasion of her space, and yet... yet she didn't jerk away as she should have. As she would have if anyone else had touched her. She simply looked up at him.

"Every life is valuable," he said. "Think of your daughter."

"Kat is innocent. She has done nothing wrong."

"Kat is human, just like her mother. Her value is immeasurable." He waved at the painting behind her. "These pictures are originals. They're valued at hundreds of thousands, in some cases, millions of dollars. But their value doesn't come close to yours."

Tears stung her eyes. Foolish tears. Rarely did she cry, and never in public. Never in front of a man.

Her emotions were too close to the surface. It was this place, all this artwork. This beauty. And Caleb, who spoke sincerely and seemed to peer right into her heart.

She didn't like it. She didn't like the way he knew her, the way he seemed to read her mind.

Never, not since she was ten, had she been touched by a man that her stomach didn't roil. Even casual touch, the brush of an elbow, the tap of a finger, made her want to flinch, to step back.

But Caleb...

She wanted to draw closer. She felt safe with him. She felt valued and protected.

Kind words and a gentle touch—would she be this easily tricked again?

She stepped away from him. What a fool.

CHAPTER ELEVEN

All Caleb had wanted was to show Vanessa the city, to help her relax. She'd been keyed up after seeing Abbas and Nadia, he'd thought an art museum might soothe her nerves.

Instead, he'd dredged up unpleasant memories. What lay behind the angst in her eyes, he didn't know, not exactly. But it had to be related to Abbas.

Was Abbas Kat's father? Had he cast Vanessa away when she'd become pregnant? Except... her reaction to him wasn't anger but fear. Why?

He needed to know more about Vanessa's past. He needed to know more about Abbas. A last name wouldn't hurt. At least then he could Google the man, figure out who he was, maybe find an arrest record or something.

Caleb had no idea how to proceed. He did know he needed more information, and Vanessa wasn't about to give it to him.

He waited outside the ladies' room at the museum, keys dangling from his fingers, trying to decide what to do next. And then inspiration struck.

He sent a text, received a reply, and hoped Vanessa

wouldn't mind. She needed something lighthearted, something that wouldn't dredge up any memories at all. He was pretty sure he could provide that.

Finally, she emerged from the restroom. She'd left the baseball cap in the car, and he was glad it was no longer there to hide her features. Her face had color again. In fact, it looked as if she'd splashed water on it. The woman rarely wore makeup, and she hadn't today. Not that she needed it. Her eyes were big and bright, her lashes long and thick. Her lips red and full and...

He snapped his gaze back to her eyes, thankful she didn't seem to have noticed. He should have spent more time in prayer that morning. If she picked up on his interest, she'd thicken the walls he was trying to break through.

"Ready?" he asked.

"Do we return to your sister's now?"

"And waste a perfectly lovely day in the city? Not a chance."

At her nod, he led her out of the museum and back to the car. A few minutes later, he turned into a lot on Boylston Street and searched for a spot. "This is a bit of a walk to where we're going, but we'll be glad later. Quick access to Mass Ave."

"Where are we going?"

"Brunch."

Her eyes scrunched. "I have heard this word. It means breakfast and lunch, no?"

"Right." He found a spot and turned in.

"But it is not brunch time." She glanced at the dashboard clock. "It is more like lunch and dinner."

"Linner," he said, "or dunch."

Her lips quirked. "Those are not really words, yes?"

He shouldn't tease, not when she made such an effort to speak English properly. "Just kidding. Even though they call it brunch, this place serves it until three."

"That does not make sense. To serve breakfast and lunch after lunch—"

"It's like most of the English language, right?"

"Da. Nonsensical."

He chuckled and opened his car door. Before he could walk around to open hers, she'd let herself out.

He wondered if she'd ever allow him to open a car door for her. Someday, maybe. When she trusted him. When she learned what it meant to be cherished.

Together, they walked from the lot to the restaurant and stepped inside. It was designed like an English pub, all dark wood and brass fixtures. The bar took up a good deal of the space, and people—mostly men—surrounded it. They were loud, drinking already, watching screens overhead. Not exactly the atmosphere he'd hoped to find. He spoke to the hostess and, a moment later, they were seated on the patio outside.

"Will you be warm enough?" he asked.

Vanessa settled beside him and looked at the street, the people walking by. "I think. Perhaps with a cup of tea."

It was funny how prickly she could be about some things, how flexible about others. He wore a jacket and would give it to her if she looked cold. The temperature had risen into the upper sixties, perfect for this time of year. If anything, later they'd probably both be too warm.

She perused the menu and settled on pancakes. He ordered steak and eggs—a perfect combination for a Sunday afternoon. When her hot tea and his Mountain Dew were delivered, they sipped quietly, watching the city walk by.

"This is nice," she said.

"Not too much chaos?"

"I think... I think maybe before it was worry for seeing Nadia and Abbas that had me nervous. I think this is okay."

He loved that she wasn't afraid to admit that little fear to him. He sipped his drink, thankful for the cold sweet liquid on his tongue. He hadn't realized how thirsty he was. "I'm sorry I wasn't able to get Nadia away from Abbas this morning."

Vanessa's slow nod was the only indication she'd heard him.

"I was afraid that she'd give you away, and you were in no condition to face Abbas. Your sister doesn't seem unhappy or even nervous about him."

Vanessa watched the people on the sidewalk. "She is a fool."

"Maybe he's changed."

Her gaze snapped to Caleb. "Men like him do not change."

That was quite a pronouncement, but Caleb wasn't going to argue. He didn't know what she meant by *like him*, but he did know God could change a willing heart.

The caveat—that little word *willing*.

"We'll try again tomorrow."

"We must get Nadia alone."

After the way Abbas had pounced when he'd noticed Caleb standing there, he wondered if that would be harder than they'd first hoped. Surely the man left the hotel sometimes without her. Would they have checked out of their room, though? Would Vanessa be able to locate her sister now?

Too many questions. He'd have to rely on the Lord to lead.

Caleb directed the conversation away from Abbas and Nadia, away from the art museum and all the memories it seemed to stir in Vanessa, and instead talked about his college days, about Cambridge and Boston and the trouble he'd gotten into. He'd managed to cling tightly to his faith during college, but it hadn't been easy. In a city filled with atheists and agnostics, Caleb had found a church and attended faithfully. He'd found enough like-minded friends that he never felt lonely. And he'd worked harder to understand the Bible and what he believed and why than he would have had he attended a Christian school. He emerged from Harvard with a greater faith than he'd had before.

But he skimmed over that part of his college experience, instead sharing the fun stories. Pickup football games, rowing on the Charles, and pranks pulled on fellow students.

"Pranks?" Vanessa said. "These are jokes, yes?"

"Sort of. Just... dumb things college guys do when they have too much time on their hands. Like, a girl we hung out with who lamented that there hadn't been enough snow that winter. So, we went around campus, collected trash bags full of shredded paper from... you know what a shredder is?"

"We have one at the food bank."

"Right. We collected trash bags of it and dumped it in her room. We even got some paste and made a snowman." He chuckled at the memory. "We figured she'd be mad, but she thought it was hilarious. It prompted an epic floor-wide shredded-paper-snowball fight."

Vanessa laughed. Actually laughed! He'd never heard the sound and realized in that moment that he'd gladly spend the rest of his life working to hear it again.

He scrambled for another story. A funnier story.

She schooled her expression. It was strange the way she rarely allowed herself to smile or laugh. How, even when it seemed she wanted to, she would stifle the expression. Why, though? He thought of Nadia's smile that morning. They were similar, but Vanessa's smile was far more beautiful, as her beauty was enhanced by the wisdom in her eyes, the kindness.

Her expression grew blank again. "A prank is only foolishness."

"Sometimes, you need a little foolishness in life."

"Hmm... I don't know if that is true."

"Laughter is good for you. And there've been studies that

prove that people who smile often are happier than people who don't. Admit it—you love to see your daughter laugh and smile."

That quirked her lips up. "You are right, of course."

"Of course," he said, adding a healthy dose of sarcasm.

Oh, man. Her walls were crumbling, and he really liked the woman he was finding behind them.

Perhaps God knew what He was doing.

AFTER CALEB PAID THE CHECK, he glanced at his watch. On the sidewalk, the passersby were gaining in numbers. Laughing, joking, teasing.

He stood. "Shall we?"

"We go back to your house now?"

"It's still a beautiful day, is it not?"

They left the little patio area and stepped to the sidewalk. "I think everybody in the city is here now," she said.

"Not quite." They had to move nearer the building as a throng walked past.

"There is an event? Where are they going?"

"Same place we are." He considered touching her back to guide her into the crowd but thought better of it at the last second. Instead, he nodded ahead. "Shall we?"

"You will not tell me where we're going?"

They joined the crowd behind a family of four. The father carried a toddler girl on his shoulders. She was waving to everyone who made eye contact.

"Maybe you can guess," he said.

Vanessa glared up at him, then looked around at all the people. He saw when awareness dawned on her. "They all wear things like this." She touched the hat she'd put back on after the art museum.

She wasn't wrong. All around people wore Red Sox hats, sweatshirts, T-shirts. One little boy carried a giant red-and-blue foam finger. A number of people had baseball mitts.

"We go to a Red Sox game?"

"Ding, ding, ding," he said. "We have a winner."

Another smile, though this one slight. "A baseball game. Another foolish *envedor*."

Envedor. He rolled the word around on his tongue a minute. "Endeavor?"

"That is what I said."

He chuckled. "It's not foolish, it's fun. Didn't you ever do anything just because it was fun?"

She watched the little girl on her daddy's shoulders. Her expression became unfocused for a moment, and then she shook her head. "Not since I was a child."

"What about Kat? Do you ever take her to do anything just for the fun of it?"

"She does fun things." Did Vanessa sound defensive? "She plays games with friends. She loves to draw and spends hours with pencils and crayons and paints."

"But the two of you, together?"

"Bah. There is no time for fun. I am a single mother with a full-time job. I work, I take care of my daughter. I drive, I clean, I shop, I cook, I sleep. This is my life."

Caleb understood what it was like to be busy, but he'd never been a single parent. He couldn't imagine the pressure Vanessa must feel.

"Don't misunderstand," she said. "I don't complain. I love my life and my daughter and would not change anything. There is nothing I would rather do than live this life. It is just that there is not time for fun. Or perhaps..." Again, she studied the little girl in front of them. "Perhaps for me, the fun is in taking care of her. The fun is in managing the food bank. That is my joy. Maybe not foolishness, but still..." Her words trailed off.

"I'm not judging you, Vanessa." She glanced his way, and he smiled. "You're doing a great job with Kat. She's a fantastic kid—not only well behaved, but happy and confident. I'm not a parent, but I think I understand how difficult it is in this world to raise girls who value themselves. I commend you for what you're doing."

The words, meant to praise, brought emotion to Vanessa's eyes she was quick to hide beneath that hat. He cursed the bill that kept him from seeing her face. Surely she wasn't upset by what he'd said. Maybe just pleased.

Women cried for the oddest reasons sometimes.

When she'd gotten her emotions under control, she said, "I thank you. That is very kind to say."

"Maybe you should try to add in some foolish fun every once in a while. Your daughter needs to know that life can be more than work, work, work. Maybe it would do you both good."

Vanessa scowled at him and said nothing else until they reached the field.

Way to ruin the mood.

Caleb found the young man, a recent hire to his grocery chain, whom his HR manager had sent with the tickets. Caleb thanked the kid, handed him a hundred-dollar bill—good pay for dropping everything on a Sunday afternoon to do a favor for the boss—and guided Vanessa toward the gate.

"Who was that man?"

"One of my employees. The company has season tickets, but I didn't think to bring them."

Inside the old building, they made their way to the proper section. Before he guided her toward the field, he said, "Hot dog? Popcorn?"

"You are not serious. We just finished... *linner.*"

Linner... A joke! She'd told a joke. He laughed, and her lips almost tipped into a smile.

"Indeed, *dunch* was delicious. Maybe we'll get something later."

"Your stomach is a bottomless hole, no?"

"Pit. A bottomless pit."

"That is what I said."

He chuckled and guided her up the ramp. She froze at the top and stared at the field.

There was something magical about a baseball field, about that first view from the ramp. Even though she wasn't a baseball fan, she seemed to feel the magic.

"It's strangely beautiful," she said.

"Another work of art."

"Bah. Not like before, only..." Her words trailed.

He led her, again barely keeping himself from guiding her with a hand to her back, down the aisle to their seats in the third row on the first base line.

"These are good seats, yes?"

"I like them. The best seats are behind the catcher, but those are hard to come by. I'm happy with these."

The game began, and Vanessa watched closely, her interest surprising him. She didn't know anything about baseball—as she'd told him the day before at the festival—and seemed eager to learn.

She was a wonder, this woman. He'd noticed it at the museum, the way she'd read every placard, studied every piece of art as if there'd be a test. He'd seen her repeat words she was unfamiliar with, committing them and their meanings to memory. Now, he watched those wise eyes take in this game she'd deemed foolishness.

Halfway through the second half of the first inning, the crack of bat had his attention snapping to the field—where it should have been all along—to see a ball sail over the players' heads.

The crowd collectively gasped, then groaned.

Vanessa said, "I do not understand."

"Foul ball," he said.

"Foul ball," she echoed. "Explain, please."

He did, pointing to the foul pole, then to the yellow line on the opposite side of the field.

"A foul ball is a bad thing."

"Not terrible, but if it had gone to the other side of that pole, it would have been a home run."

"Ah. And a home run is good, yes?"

Wow. She really knew nothing about baseball. He started at the beginning and explained the game to her, watching her as she took in the information, repeated words and definitions, and watched the game on the field unfold.

He'd always imagined what it would be like to teach his son or daughter the game of baseball. Now, when he did, he'd always remember this moment, teaching Vanessa.

Your bride.

The whispered words reminded him of God's promise, which, despite everything, seemed as distant as the stars. But God had made those, too. He knew what He was doing.

Guide me, Lord. I need Your help.

Because, though he'd been praying for an opening with Vanessa for years—and praying for Vanessa and Kat in general— his heart hadn't been involved. He'd trusted God, he'd believed someday he might feel for her, but before yesterday, if God had relented and given him another wife, Caleb would have been relieved.

Now, though...

As at the art museum, he watched her. When she didn't realize his focus was on her, she let down her guard. Emotions crossed her features. Right now, interest, curiosity, even amusement when her gaze shifted from the game to the little boy in front of her, who was holding his mitt in the air as if a ball would drop from the sky.

Caleb was coming to care for Vanessa more than he had ever thought possible. He squeezed his hands into fists to keep from reaching out and touching her.

He was falling for her. Which was good, as long as God knew what He was doing. Because, if Vanessa never returned his feelings, then Caleb was going to end up with a broken heart and a future void of the wife and family he longed for.

CHAPTER TWELVE

The Red Sox won the game with what Caleb called a walk-off home run. Vanessa considered the term as they climbed toward the exit. And then it made sense. The Red Sox player hit a home run, and the game was over. After the player ran the bases, the team walked off. Except they didn't walk. They ran and jumped into each other's arms and patted each other's behinds. Very odd, these baseball players. And amusing.

At the thought, she forced her smile away. What was there to smile about?

Despite the events of that morning, the old line didn't have the effect it usually did. There was plenty to smile about this day. Caleb and the art museum and the brunch and the baseball game. The little boy in front of them who was eager to catch a foul ball. The way Caleb had explained the game to her, never growing frustrated with her questions, never seeming to tire of talking to her.

And looking at her. She'd caught him staring more than once. And never did she see the lust in his eyes she was accustomed to seeing on men who watched her. His gaze had held...

Something different. Something she didn't have a word for, not in English or Serbian. Maybe a combination of wonder and tenderness and affection.

Something that had made her forget, for a little while, her anxiety about Nadia.

Caleb, she did not understand. But not understanding did not frighten her as it usually did. Maybe, someday, she would figure out what made Caleb different.

They reached the top of the ramp and joined the crowds pushing toward the stadium exit. The people were shouting and cheering and bumping and cursing. This Boston crowd with its loud and foul language made her jumpy. She'd grown accustomed to the mild-mannered volunteers and coworkers at the food bank. Even the clients, some of whom surely used such coarse language in their regular lives, were mostly respectful when they came to collect their food. She didn't tolerate bad language, which the seasoned clients had learned. The crowd now pushing to the exit was different. The cursing was in jest, the mood jubilant, but the language felt dark.

Caleb was on one side of her, a man about her age on the other. He looked down at her... and there was the lust she was accustomed to seeing.

Something brushed her back. A hand.

She jerked at the touch. The stranger smiled.

She moved toward Caleb, bumped his arm.

He looked at her, and his eyebrows lifted, a silent question. *You okay?*

No. She was not okay. People pressed from behind. Men everywhere, pushing against her. Touching her.

Caleb took her hand, and, unlike the rest, his touch comforted her as he guided her through the crowd toward the interior wall. Caleb's was a touch of safety, so foreign to all the touches she'd known from men in the past. When they were protected from the crowd by a closed vendor's stand, he turned to face her. "What happened?"

She thought back to the moment. Nothing had happened. The man beside her had probably not touched her at all, certainly not on purpose. Now that she was out of the press of bodies, she saw they were not all men. Of course not. There were women, children, families. She was safe here.

She had panicked.

"I am okay," she said.

He nodded slowly, then leaned against the concrete wall. "We're in no hurry."

"We can—"

"Let's just wait. It'll clear out in five minutes."

Grateful not to have to dive back into the crowd, she leaned beside him, only then realizing he still held her hand. She should pull hers away, but she didn't want to. She liked the feel of him. She liked the comfort of the connection.

When was the last time anybody but Kat had held her hand?

When was the last time a man had touched her, not for his own pleasure or gain, but to protect her? To make her feel safe?

Again, her dream returned to her as it had earlier when she'd seen that little girl on her daddy's shoulders. The little girl running through the shallow water at the edge of the lake. Her tata catching her, holding her close.

Indeed, it had been many lifetimes since she'd felt that protected.

She didn't pull her hand from Caleb's as they stood there, nor as they walked out of the stadium, back down the street, less crowded now than it had been earlier, and to the car. Only when he opened her car door did she relinquish his hand.

A tiny smile graced his lips as he waited for her to settle into the passenger seat. It broadened just before he pushed the door closed. He was pleased—with himself, with her? This, she didn't know. It was not a... winning smile? Was that the word? No, perhaps... yes, triumphant. It was not that kind of a smile, the kind that would worry her. It was a gentle smile, as if he felt content.

The traffic slowed them, but soon enough they crossed the river and were back at his sister's house in Cambridge. It was nearing nine-thirty by the time Caleb grabbed their suitcases from the trunk and led her into the kitchen. The room was dark and empty, but the faint sound of a TV carried in.

Caleb whispered, "Shhh." He set down the suitcases, took her hand, and then tiptoed through the kitchen and down the hallway. Was something wrong? An intruder, perhaps? Her heart thumped against her chest as she followed, and she was thankful for the presence of his hand over hers. Only one small lamp glowed in the living room, most of the light coming from the TV mounted on the wall. A man sat with his back to them, only a bit of hair showing over the top of the sofa.

Skulking low, Caleb approached the man.

Though Vanessa had at first been fearful, now she realized Caleb's plan.

He got within a foot of the stranger on the couch, landed his big hand on the head, and yelled, "Boo!"

"Aaaagh!" The stranger shot off the couch, stumbled over the coffee table, and nearly fell into the TV as he spun.

Caleb's laugh filled the room.

Vanessa clamped her hand over her mouth to keep her own laughter in.

The man looked furious, but his gaze turned to Vanessa, and the anger slipped away as he faced Caleb. "You're supposed to be the adult, man."

Caleb mopped tears from his cheeks. "Even us old guys like

to have fun every now and then." He glanced at Vanessa, who was failing to contain her giggles. "Totally worth it."

The stranger scowled and stepped around the sofa. "David Peterson. Youngest and clearly most mature of the Peterson boys."

"You wish," Caleb said. "This is my friend, Vanessa Baker."

Vanessa shook David's hand. She saw the resemblance, but where Caleb's hair was dark brown, David's was lighter, his eyes brown, not hazel. His jawline wasn't quite as defined as his older brother's, and he was slighter as well. Like his brother, he was handsome, and like his brother, amusement danced in his eyes now.

"Wow, you brought a woman to the Cambridge house."

Caleb's amusement faded. "Vanessa is my friend."

"But you never—"

"Keep your thoughts to yourself." Caleb's words held a warning tone that prickled up Vanessa's spine.

What hadn't Caleb told her? What was he keeping from her?

Nothing. There was nothing to fear with Caleb. This she knew. She would not let fear overtake her again.

David's eyebrows rose, and his attention returned to Vanessa. "Well, friend of Caleb's, welcome. Where've you two been?"

"Caleb took me to my first baseball game." Vanessa didn't know where the words had come from. Easily, she could have just said they'd gone to a game, but she made it sound as if they'd been on a date. As if Caleb had done something special.

She would need to temper her tongue.

"Great game," David said to Caleb. Then, as if her words had just penetrated, he turned back to Vanessa. "Your first *Red Sox* game?"

"First baseball game ever." Vanessa glanced at Caleb and

caught him watching her. She tried and failed to temper the smile this time. "It was quite fun. A little boy in front of us lifted up his mitten every time the ball was hit."

Caleb said, "Mitt."

"That is what I said."

David's chuckle filled the room. "Wow. Just..." He scratched his head and glanced at the TV, which glowed with highlights of the game they'd just seen. Vanessa was tempted to sit and watch to see how it had looked on TV.

David said, "You guys wanna watch something? Maybe a movie, or—"

"I don't." Caleb looked at her. "Unless you want to."

"It is too late for a movie. And I am..." Hungry—that's what she'd almost said. But would it be rude, after everything, to ask for food now? He would feel the need to feed her, and he had done enough.

"Tired, I'm guessing," Caleb said. "But you never would let me buy you a hot dog. Want a snack before bed?"

As if he'd read her mind. Which should have made her nervous but didn't. Without waiting for an answer, because of course Caleb already knew how she felt—the man knew everything—he turned to David. "We're gonna get a snack and then head up. By the way, Vanessa's staying in the green room, and I'll be on three with you."

David groaned. "Ugh, if I'd known, I'd have stayed at my buddy's another night. You snore like a lawnmower."

"That's Sam," Caleb said. "I don't snore."

"Oh, yeah." David studied his brother a minute, and then said, "You talk in your sleep. I remember the time when you were having that dream about—"

"Vanessa doesn't need to hear all my dirty secrets tonight." Caleb settled his hand on the small of her back and guided her back to the kitchen.

This hand... She used to think of it as a possessive claim of ownership. Now, it felt comforting. She didn't understand her own reactions.

David's footsteps followed them.

Caleb flipped on the overhead in the kitchen and opened the refrigerator. "What are you in the mood for?"

Before she could answer, David said, "I could use a burger, if you're cooking."

Caleb glared at his younger brother over the open refrigerator door. "For her, yes. For you, not a chance."

David only chuckled. "We could order a pizza."

"Didn't you eat?" Caleb asked.

David shrugged. "I could eat again."

The refrigerator door slammed. "Or you could go away and leave us alone."

"Why? You two are just friends, right? You won't mind a third wheel. Besides"—he eyed Vanessa—"your friend is—"

"Too pretty for you," Caleb said.

David pressed both hands against his heart. "Oh! Your words cut like knives. Never shall I recover."

Vanessa giggled, then slapped her fingers over her mouth.

Caleb turned his glare on her. "Don't laugh. You'll only encourage him."

"I don't mind if you encourage me." David waggled his eyebrows.

His words, though laden with suggestion, didn't bother her at all. He was only teasing. That she recognized it surprised her. "I am too old for you, young David."

"You ever seen *The Graduate*."

Caleb growled, a low hum she barely heard. "Do me a favor and take our bags up. Then stay in the living room."

"*The Graduate*?" Vanessa said. "This is a TV show?" Her gaze flicked from Caleb to David.

David said, "Great movie."

At the same time, Caleb said, "She's not that old."

They both looked at her. "I do not know what you are talking about."

"Consider yourself lucky." Caleb stepped closer to his brother. Since his back was to Vanessa, she didn't see his face nor hear what he said, but David peered around Vanessa and said, "I'll be watching TV if you want to join me."

"Nice to meet you."

David winked, grabbed their suitcases, and walked out.

Caleb turned to her. "He's harmless, I promise."

"I am sure he could do harm to young hearts, but I am not afraid."

Caleb's tight expression loosened. "I didn't want..."

She knew what he was thinking of—her terrible behavior the night before, her irrational fear. "I feel safe here now."

"Good, good." He returned to the refrigerator and started pulling out plastic bags and setting them on the small island. "Look in that cabinet"—he pointed to one closest to the kitchen table—"and see if you can find some crackers."

She found a box of Ritz and pulled it out.

Caleb set a plate on the counter and arranged cheese, sausage, and thin slices of some kind of ham on the plate. He added olives and baby carrots. He pointed to the space leftover. "Crackers there."

She opened the end of the long tube and slid a few onto the plate.

"You can do better than that."

She slid some more on, and he set the plate on the kitchen table. "Water, soda?"

"Water is fine."

He fixed two glasses and sat beside her. "Voila. Dinner."

She popped an olive in her mouth and savored it with a low "mmm."

He did the same, then added cheese and the skinny ham to a cracker and took a bite.

She lifted a slice of the ham and studied it. It was familiar. She'd had it before, a long time ago. She vaguely remembered. "It is called...?"

"Prosciutto."

"Da. Yes. I remember."

"That's right. You said you've been to Italy."

She shrugged and ate the meat with a thin slice of cheddar.

"Vacation, or—?"

"I do not wish to talk about it."

He sat back. "Sorry. Another landmine."

Landmine. She had heard this word, but... "It is an explosive, no? In the ground?"

"Yes." His frustration faded. "Just a metaphor." He watched her, perhaps to see if she knew that word. She nodded to indicate she did. "Basically, I asked a question that triggered a negative response."

"Not quite as explosive as a mine, though, no?"

"Just hyperbole."

Bah. He was doing it on purpose, using words she didn't know. "This is what... hy-per-bo-le?" She tested the word on her tongue. A fun word to say, though she didn't know what it meant.

"Like exaggeration."

"So... landmine is a difficult subject, and to call a difficult subject a landmine is hyperbole, which is an exaggeration. Da?"

"Da." At her raised eyebrows, he said, "I should learn your language, too."

In Serbian, she said, "You couldn't learn my language in a million years. It is far too complex for your tiny little brain."

He glared, and she laughed.

"What did you say?"

"You do not know? But you know everything."

He pointed a carrot at her. "Your claim, not mine."

She shrugged and bit into a slice of sausage.

They finished their snack and chatted about the game, the day, as the clock ticked past ten o'clock. She refrained from mentioning Nadia, tried not to think about her sister right now. To think of her would not help, after all.

She yawned at the thought of how late it was. She had called Kat twice that day, the last time after she'd run to the ladies' room during the game. Her daughter was fine, Nadia was in New York for the night, and there was nothing Vanessa could do but rest and enjoy herself.

She'd done quite enough of the latter for one day. When the plate was empty, she took a last sip of her water and pushed back in her chair. "We will clean up."

He brushed the crumbs from the plate into the trash can and slid the dish into the dishwasher, then added their glasses and started it.

While he did that, she closed the Ziploc bags of meat and cheese and returned them to the fridge, then put the crackers away. Two minutes, and it was clean.

She found, though it had been her idea, she was sorry to go to bed, sorry to put an end to this day. Partly because she'd enjoyed it—too much—and partly because, tomorrow, she must rescue Nadia, and risk facing Abbas.

Caleb flipped off the light and led her through the hallway to the stairs. At the opening to the living room, he called, "Good night, goober."

David answered, "G'night, Vanessa. G'night, meathead."

She giggled at the name. "Meathead. This is funny."

He gestured to the stairs as he said, "You find my brother hilarious."

"You both, together." She started up the stairs and realized that, soon, they'd be at her door. As they climbed, her foolish anxiety pumped. Though she knew she was safe, though she had no reason to fear Caleb, she couldn't help the tremble in her hands. At the landing at the halfway point, she turned to him, and he almost bumped into her. Unaware she'd planned to stop, he was close enough that, if she tipped forward at all, her forehead would meet his chin. She would step back, but there was no room on the small space.

"You okay?" His voice was husky.

"I wanted to say thank-you. For going with me to the hotel this morning, and then for distracting me all day. It was a good day."

His lips rose, and his eyes crinkled. "The best day I've had in a long time."

"Da." She should turn, resume the climb to her room, but she didn't want to leave his presence.

And then she realized what she was thinking. She turned and hurried up the last of the stairs. Both of their suitcases were at the top of the steps. She gripped the handle of hers and crossed to her door but didn't open it. She didn't want him to think there was an invitation, that there was more than just a thank-you to be offered.

He followed and stood opposite her, staring down at her. His gaze met hers, then lowered toward her lips. Then rose again almost instantly as if he realized what he'd done.

He wanted to kiss her.

The truth of it sunk down to her stomach, but it didn't grow into a pit. No, it grew into... desire? She *wanted* him to kiss her.

What was wrong with her? She told herself to send him away, to make him leave. But she could not. Did not want to.

He studied her as if he could see into her heart. As he always could, which should have frightened her.

He rested his hands on her shoulders and pressed a kiss to her forehead. "Sleep well."

She leaned against her door as he continued to the third floor. In her room, she sighed. Sighed as she imagined a school girl would over her first crush. It was foolish and silly, and she had nothing but disdain for foolish and silly women. But, when she went to the restroom to brush her teeth, she caught herself smiling.

Vanessa had the dream again that night. The little girl running through the water, laughing. The mother with the small children on the shore. The man giving chase, lifting her up, tickling her. Only by the time the man caught her, she wasn't Vojislava anymore. She was Vanessa, a grown woman. And the man wasn't the father who'd betrayed her.

It was Caleb—who never had.

CHAPTER THIRTEEN

The Vanessa who joined Caleb for breakfast the next morning was not the same Vanessa he'd nearly kissed the night before.

Her walls, which he'd labored to tear down, had not only gone back up overnight but had been fortified. With concrete and barbed wire. Lots of barbed wire.

She sat across from him in the sunny kitchen, back straight, gaze on the toast he'd fixed for her. Or on her coffee. Or on the window.

Anywhere but on him.

He'd already asked how she slept—"Fine." If she was hungry—"A little." Now was certainly not the time to ask anything important. She'd shut him down in a heartbeat. He could chatter to break the tension, but he didn't want to do that, either. If she wanted to shut him out, so be it. She was stuck with him today, regardless of how she felt about it.

He stood and cleaned the mess he'd made fixing eggs and bacon—which she'd eschewed. He pointed to her plate of almost untouched toast. "Did you not like it?"

"I've had enough."

He felt the same way. Her behavior, after everything...

Patience.

Patience? He'd tried patience. He'd been patient for two years. *What do You want from me?*

Patience.

He wanted to growl but took a deep breath instead. His patience felt as brittle as her attitude.

Stupid Caleb. He thought they'd begun a friendship the day before. That they'd forged new ground together. Today, it was as though yesterday hadn't happened. She was back to the same distrustful... shrew... she'd been Saturday night.

Patience.

Whatever. "What time do you want to leave?"

She rose and pushed in her chair, then gripped its back and met his eyes for the first time that morning. The effort seemed painful. "I can be ready in five minutes."

"I'm taking my laptop into the hotel. I think we should look like we're doing something besides staring at the lobby. Do you want a book?"

"How can I read a book and watch for my sister?"

She could pretend to read the book, but he didn't say that. He'd grab one for her and offer it when they got there. Maybe by then she wouldn't be so closed off.

Had he done something wrong? He couldn't imagine what. They'd had a fun day—a day of laughter and smiles and connection. Was it the peck on her forehead?

He didn't understand women. Even Essie had never behaved like this. No, it wasn't women in general, it was this woman who made no sense to him.

She carried her coffee cup to the sink and dumped the remainder in. She'd hardly touched it. She slipped the cup and her plate into the dishwasher.

"We take our things again?"

"Yup." God willing, they'd head back to Nutfield today with Nadia in tow.

And then his opportunity to get to know Vanessa—and for her to get to know him—would end. Would it be another two years before he got another?

Thanks to Monday morning traffic, it took forever to go the few miles from Cambridge to the harbor. More than thirty minutes after they'd left the house, they found a table at the Rowes Wharf's coffee shop. He ordered them both coffee and then sat across from her. She was wearing the cap again, barely a disguise.

"We need a plan."

Staring at the lobby, Vanessa said, "We wait until Abbas leaves alone."

"I've been thinking about it. They'll be getting back from New York. And you said that Nadia told you they were only here to see you."

"Da."

"It's not as if he has business to attend to. Why would he leave her alone? Unless... Do you think he wants to see you, too? Or would he prefer to avoid you, like you want to avoid him?"

"I cannot understand what Abbas wants." Her words carried more emotion than anything else she'd said that day. "I will not try to get into his mind."

"Obviously, I can't guess, either. But I think we should assume that he wants to see you. Otherwise, why would he have gone to the trouble of helping her find you? Unless it was kindness—"

"Bah. Not kindness. He does not have a kind... thing in his body."

"Bone. A kind *bone* in his body."

"That is what I said."

Her stock answer, uttered with pure loathing, didn't make

him smile as it usually did. She lifted her coffee cup with trembling hands.

He should have gotten her decaf. She was already too keyed up.

She should have eaten more than a single piece of toast. He'd buy food soon and leave it between them, but he wouldn't suggest she eat it. She was angry, inexplicably angry. She'd probably starve before she took his suggestion. Especially since he had another one for her.

"If he didn't help her find you out of kindness, then he must have done it because he wanted to find you. Maybe he wants to apologize." He watched for a reaction, but she gave no indication she considered the words, or even heard them, as she watched the lobby. "Maybe he wants to meet his daughter."

That got her attention. If looks could kill, he'd have disappeared in a puff of smoke.

Was he right? Her expression was as open as a maximum security prison.

"What other reason might he want to see you?" He posed the question as if they were brainstorming together. As if she'd answer, which, of course, she wouldn't.

But her gaze flicked to her purse, which she'd set on the third chair at their table.

"Something in there?"

"I told you, I do not wish to know what he wants or why he cares to look for me." She adjusted her chair to better see the lobby—and avoid looking at him. "I only want to save my sister."

"But that's the point. If he wants to find you, then will he leave your sister by herself?"

Her shoulders lifted, dropped. "I have prayed God will allow it. I am trying to trust. God knows I cannot face Abbas again. That I will not. I asked for help and have to believe He'll send it."

"He has already." Caleb immediately wished the words back.

Vanessa glanced his way but didn't hold his eye contact. "This I know. I could not do this without you, and I thank you."

The words were grateful, even if the tone was grudging.

"My pleasure." Which it had been the day before. "Here's what I think. Abbas and Nadia are going to return after a busy day of shopping and traveling. Maybe he'll take her to their room and then go out, but maybe not. Maybe, if he wants to see you again, he'll stay. Did you tell your sister you were coming?"

"Da. That I would rescue her. She is too stupid to know she needs to be rescued but said she wanted to see me. But they went to New York, and she did not tell me. I do not understand this."

He didn't, either. If they'd come to see Vanessa, why leave? And why hadn't Nadia called again?

"Do you think he knows you'd rather avoid him?"

Her chin dipped, a quick nod.

"If he wants to see you and he knows you don't want to see him, he won't leave her alone and risk missing you. Right?"

She faced Caleb then. "I do not know what to do about this."

"I suggest that, when we see them, I try to head him off, keep him down here to talk to me. Hopefully, Nadia will grow bored and go to the room, and you can follow her there. If I can detain him long enough, maybe you can get Nadia away."

Her expression never shifted, but neither did she look away. He could see in her eyes that she was considering it. "But if she doesn't go to the room?"

"Then I'll tell him I've come as your emissary."

"Do not do that," she snapped. "Use normal words."

He bit back the retort. Emissary wasn't that uncommon a word, after all. "Your representative. I'll tell him you weren't willing to come but that you sent me, and I'll ask him if I can speak to Nadia for a moment. Maybe I can get her to come with me."

"He might allow you to speak with her, but he will be present, and he will not allow you to take her."

"In a hotel lobby with security all around, he won't be able to stop her from leaving him if she wants to. This is America, after all. We don't allow slaves."

Her nearly silent *pfft* was the only response she gave.

"You have a better idea?"

"She will not go with you. No. We wait until she is alone. Eventually, he will leave her alone."

"Maybe. But if I'm—"

"If you don't wish to wait with me, then go." She waved toward the door. "Go home. I will get Nadia and find a way to bring her back to Nutfield myself."

"I'm not leaving you."

"I do not need your help."

Pfft. That earned him an icy stare. "Nevertheless..." He ground out the word, then forced a casual tone. "Like it or not, I'm not leaving you here with a man you called dangerous."

She shifted her focus back to the lobby.

The silence between them crackled with tension.

He studied her profile as he'd done often the day before. Standing beside her as she'd been mesmerized by the artwork, sitting beside her as she watched the baseball game. When she didn't know, she had let her guard down, almost seemed to be enjoying herself at times. Whether she realized she was being watched or not, anytime a smile would inch across her face, she would temper it—almost as if she put effort into it. As if smiling were a weakness.

Maybe because her smiles were rare, but when, in an

unguarded moment, she allowed one, her face lit up. He'd never seen a more beautiful smile.

If only he could learn to make her smile. If only she'd let him.

Still, his suggestion floated over them like the scent of coffee on the air. "What do you—?"

"Fine. It is a fine idea." She didn't turn his way. "You will try to detain him. I will find my sister and coax her away."

"When he's on his way, I'll text you so you can get out. What room are they in?"

She rattled the number for a room on the fourth floor, and he committed it to memory.

"Even if you have to leave Nadia there, you'll get out of the room, right?"

A pause. Then, she tipped her head down. "I cannot see him."

"Meet me back down here, okay? If you go another way, call me. I don't want him catching up to you alone." He waited, but she said nothing. "Okay? Vanessa?'

"Da. Yes." She still wouldn't look at him. "I will do as you say."

He rolled her answer around on his tongue. "I'm not trying to tell you what to do. If you have a different idea—"

"What will you say to him?"

"Um..."

"When you try to detain him, what will you say?"

He'd hoped she wouldn't ask. Because he had a vague plan. Regardless of whether Nadia went to the room or stayed, Caleb would tell Abbas he was acting as Vanessa's emissary in hopes of getting the man to spill the beans about why he wanted to find her.

And maybe hint at what he'd done to her, at why Vanessa was afraid of him.

Clearly, Vanessa didn't want Caleb to know her history with Abbas. Maybe he shouldn't pry. But he needed to know what he was dealing with. He thought about Eric's warning—that Vanessa had built her walls for good reason. Abbas was part of that reason. Maybe if Caleb understood, it would help him take those walls down without harming the woman behind them.

Caleb hedged. "I'm not sure exactly what I'll say to him." Which was true. He had yet to figure out how he'd broach the topic of Vanessa's past with the man. "I'm going to trust God to lead me." Also true. Surely God wouldn't disagree that Caleb needed to know Vanessa's past. Surely.

Was he being dishonest? No, he didn't think so. She would worry too much if he told her his plan. She was already worried enough.

Vanessa studied him.

"What kind of business is he in?" Caleb asked.

"Imports. This is why he travels. He brings goods from the Middle East—rugs, pottery, clothing—to western countries."

"That's good, then. I can talk about my business as if I want to sell his goods."

"You own grocery stores. His are luxury goods. They would not sell in your stores."

"He won't know that. And I understand the language of commerce. I think it'll work."

It would be an opening, anyway.

"Bah. It will not work. His business is only a..." She waved as if the word needed to be brushed off her tongue. "A thing for fun."

"A hobby." When she didn't respond at all, he added, "It'll be fine. I'll wing it."

That made her head tip to the side, and he considered what he'd said.

"Uh, I'll play it by ear." Based on her glare, that wasn't better. "I'll adjust my plan according to his reactions."

"Ah. I see. This is to wing?"

"It's just an expression."

"English is maddening."

Said the most maddening human being he'd ever met.

"Do we have a plan, then?" he asked. "I think this will work, but—"

"It's fine. You're right. You're always right."

Again, the words felt like an insult.

"What's your problem today?"

She said nothing.

"Look, if this is about that little kiss to your forehead—"

"I do not wish to talk about that."

"Of course not. God forbid you should talk to me. Never mind that I'm here with you. That I dropped everything to—"

"Yes, yes. I know. You keep telling me how much I should be grateful."

"That's not what I'm saying. I'm just... If I offended you, then you need to tell me. If I hurt your feelings or... or—"

"You did nothing wrong. Only that..."

The anger in her expression dissipated, replaced by a slight smile. Almost like the woman he'd spent the previous day with. Then, she shuttered the look and turned to face the lobby again.

"Vanessa."

She ignored him.

"Would you look at me, please?"

Still, she ignored him.

"I never took you for a coward."

At least that got her turning his direction. "You do not understand."

"Explain it, then."

"I am not interested in a romantic relationship with you, Caleb Peterson. I can tolerate being your friend."

"Tolerate it, can you?"

"I don't mean... I'm not trying to insult you. Only to say that I don't wish for more. And I don't wish for you to wish for more."

Too late for that. Despite everything, his feelings for her hadn't dimmed. Her fear, the way she was pushing him away, only made him want to know her better.

That was his personality, though. Give him an obstacle, and he'd find a way to climb it. Tell him no, and he'd get to yes. Maybe that was why God had chosen him for Vanessa—because He knew Caleb wouldn't give up on her. But did he want to win this woman's heart? When he did, what would he find? Flesh? Or stone?

Or glass.

The words were a whisper. Glass?

What did that mean?

Glass. Made of sand, a material so common, it was used as a metaphor for plenty. *Descendants as numerous as the sand on the seashore,* the Bible said. But glass was made from melted sand. Extreme heat made it clear and beautiful. And breakable.

Lord, I don't want a woman with a hard and breakable heart. I want a woman with a flesh-and-blood heart. A woman who loves me back.

But God didn't respond to that.

What Caleb wanted was irrelevant.

CHAPTER FOURTEEN

The coffee shop in the hotel lobby was subdued, the low overhead music occasionally interrupted by customers giving their orders, the grinding of coffee beans, the distant ding of the elevators. Most of the people who stepped into the luxurious lobby wore suits and serious expressions. The air that had seemed filled with expectation the day before, thanks to the vacationers and the children, was now all business.

It was a workday for most people. It should have been for Vanessa, too. Normally, she'd be at the food bank by now, checking inventory, managing volunteers, and calling her more at-risk clients to see how their weekends had gone.

Her job was of no import compared to Caleb's. He employed hundreds, possibly thousands, of people. Yet he was here with her.

She'd been unkind to him when he'd been nothing but kind to her. That was the problem, though, his kindness. She'd given him the wrong impression the day before. Today, she must remedy that impression. Today, she must be sure he understood that they could be nothing more than acquaintances.

This was her fault. She shouldn't have agreed to let him

bring her to Boston. Eric would have done it, and Kelsey wouldn't have minded letting Vanessa spend the day with her husband. Kelsey and Eric understood what Vanessa was dealing with, and Eric was married and devoted to Kelsey. There would have been no question of romance. There would have been no kiss on the forehead.

No art museum. No baseball game. No conversation beyond the friendly and safe. No dreams of a man who might care for her.

But that was the problem, was it not? The way she'd dreamed of Caleb. The way she'd laughed with him and smiled with him and trusted him. The way she'd longed to see him at breakfast, even though she'd spent all of yesterday with him.

Never had she been with a man by choice. Never had she thought she could trust a man with her heart—or her body.

She was tempted to believe Caleb was as good as he claimed to be. Which made her the worst kind of fool.

He tapped on his computer across the table from her. Since they had made their plan, he had quit trying to draw her into conversation and had turned his mind to work. He had handed her a book he'd brought from the house and said, "Pretend." She didn't know why it mattered, but she opened the book as if she were reading, rarely taking her gaze from the lobby.

The remnants of their late breakfast sat between them. He'd ordered two breakfast sandwiches and set them on the table with a muttered, "Help yourself if you want."

Though she'd thought to refuse the food, to do so would have been pride. Her stomach had churned with coffee and worry, and she'd learned years before that to refuse what she needed—even when it was offered by an enemy—was foolishness.

And Caleb was not an enemy. This she knew, though she couldn't order her thoughts to figure out exactly what he was.

Friend. More than a friend. She'd seen in his eyes the night before that he wanted more than friendship from her. He didn't understand what he was asking. He didn't know that the part of her that might have loved a man had shattered years before. There was nothing left in her to love him. And if he knew the story of her past, there would be nothing in him to love her.

She set down the book and glanced at her phone to check the time. It was just after one o'clock. They'd been sitting there more than four hours, which felt like twice that. Would Nadia never return? Would she and Abbas stay in New York all day and return tonight?

There were doors on the far side of the lobby. Her sister wouldn't come in that way, surely. They would be delivered by a car at the front, but still, Vanessa let her gaze wander that direction occasionally, just in case. She turned that way now and caught sight of Caleb watching her. He gave her a tight smile. "You okay?"

"I do not like this long wait."

"Hmm. I guess I'm not the only one who suffers from a bad case of impatience."

"You do not seem bothered by the wait."

He tapped the laptop. "I have a distraction."

"Da." Except when she'd glanced at him, he hadn't been focused on his distraction but on her. Why? He was such an intelligent man, how did he not see Vanessa for who she really was? How did he not see all the stains?

His head dipped to the side. "What are you thinking?"

She turned back to her vigil. Caleb was too perceptive, and though she questioned why he didn't understand what kind of person she was, she was glad of it. She didn't want him to know the truth.

She was lifting the book again when the lobby doors

swished open. She watched, expecting to see a business person walk in.

It was Nadia and, a foot behind her, Abbas. They both pulled their small suitcases. Nadia also carried a large shopping bag.

Vanessa stood. "They are here."

Caleb snatched the book out of her hand, closed his laptop. "Get out of sight. I'll see if I can head him off."

Caleb slid the things into his case.

Vanessa stared at her sister, who looked happy and carefree, which didn't make sense.

Caleb whispered in her ear, "Go, Vanessa. Remember our plan. When I text, you leave, even if you have to leave her. Take the stairs so you don't bump into him. Promise?"

"Da." Heart pounding, she started toward the elevators, doing her best to not let Abbas see her. Maybe she could head Nadia off before she went upstairs.

Except Nadia might give her away. No, better to meet her at the room. Vanessa pushed the button and rode to the proper floor. This hotel was all luxury and wealth, and she pressed her hand to her stomach to settle the nausea that churned as she traveled the hallways. She'd been to plenty of places like this, though not as a guest but as the provided entertainment. Only with Carlos had she had a measure of freedom, and even that had proved a lie.

She found Nadia and Abbas's room and, just beyond it, a small space with ice and vending machines. Here, she hid. Despite the baseball cap, Abbas would know her if he saw her up close. Would her sister?

She didn't know. She only knew she wouldn't let Abbas see her. She couldn't. She wouldn't risk her life, wouldn't risk a run-in with Abbas. When Caleb texted, she would run. For Katarina, she would run. She had to.

But he hadn't texted, which meant he was talking with Abbas now. Would Nadia come?

Please, God. Please send my sister. Let her listen to reason. Give me wisdom to know what to say to separate her from Abbas. Her prayers continued as she listened and finally heard the distant ding of the elevator.

She peeked, and there Nadia was, walking toward her.

Vanessa waited to be sure Abbas didn't follow. She stepped into the hallway just as her sister opened the hotel room's door.

"Nadia."

She turned and, at the sight of Vanessa, squealed like the child Vanessa remembered. Nadia dropped the shopping bag and left the suitcase blocking the door and ran to Vanessa. "You're really here." The sound of her own language was nearly as beautiful as the girl in front of her. "I can't believe you came!" Nadia wrapped Vanessa in her arms, and Vanessa held her close. She couldn't force words out. This was Nadia, her baby sister.

Her family.

She hadn't seen her in sixteen years. Now, her arms held the one she'd loved dearly.

Tears filled her eyes and dripped down her cheeks. She couldn't cry. She had to think.

She backed away from the embrace and held her sister's shoulders. "We have to go. Quickly. Get your bags and—"

"Go? No. You'll stay here! Abbas wants to see you. He said he could get you the room next door." Nadia took Vanessa's hand and dragged her toward the door. Vanessa let her only because that was where Nadia's things were. "I know it'll be weird, since I'm with Abbas now, but he really wants to see you again."

"You must come with me. He is a dangerous man."

Nadia pushed into the hotel room, a lighthearted laugh

trailing her. "Don't be silly. He's charming and sweet, and he loves—"

"Do not be a fool!"

Nadia was halfway into the room when she turned to face Vanessa. "I understand it will feel awkward for you, since you left him. I can't imagine why you would have, though." She spun in a circle. "Look at this place."

Kitchen, table, sofa. A door on the right must have led to the bedroom. In front of her, a wall of windows that looked out over the harbor. Likely, the walls were soundproof here. Nobody would hear the screams.

"Please, Nadia, I don't have time to explain. Grab what you need and come with me."

Nadia went to the door that led to the hallway, opened it, and put the lock bar there to prop it open. "Abbas is on—"

"I will not see Abbas." Vanessa forced herself to calm down. She wasn't going to convince her sister that Abbas was a monster, not in the time she had. "I have a little girl. Her name is Katarina, and she reminds me of you. I want you to meet her."

Nadia's eyes, already filled with such joy, brightened further. "You have a daughter? I would love to meet her. Where is she?"

"Come with me, and I'll introduce you."

"I'm not leaving Abbas."

God, please help me. She forced herself to go slowly, to think. To listen to the voice of God. "I understand how you feel. You care for Abbas."

"He's the sweetest man I've ever met."

Vanessa managed to keep her retort to herself—proof of God's intervention. "I understand he is very important to you."

"I *love* him," Nadia said. "And I really want you two to get along." She took Vanessa's hands and squeezed. Nadia looked much like Vanessa had at that age. Long blond hair, large bright green eyes. Except her eyes were filled with life, not death as the ones that had stared back at Vanessa from the mirror every morning for years. Yes, Vanessa had come to life again. Maybe she'd never be what she could have been, what Nadia still was, but she was no longer the walking corpse she'd been for a decade.

"I understand that you care for him," Vanessa lied. "But I'm not ready to see Abbas, and I must go home today. Maybe, if you tell me about your relationship, how he treats you, maybe I will want to see him."

"That's such a good idea! He's probably changed since you were with him. Once you hear—"

"Will you come with me then? We can spend time together, you can meet your niece and tell me about our family, and then I will return you to Abbas. Then, I will see him."

Nadia stepped back. "I don't want to leave."

"Only for a couple of days, and it's not very far from here. I promise."

"But—"

"Are you afraid he'll hurt you if you leave?"

"Of course not! He would never hurt me."

Vanessa couldn't imagine this Abbas, one who was gentle and kind. She didn't believe he was real, only that he'd fooled Nadia. Eventually, he would show Nadia his cruelty. Eventually, if Vanessa didn't save her, Nadia would know Vanessa had been right about him. But then it would be too late.

"Two days, maybe three," Vanessa said. "It is not long. Please, come with me."

Her phone dinged. She slid it from her pocket and glanced at it. Caleb's text read, *Run. He's on his way.*

She couldn't leave without Nadia. She'd said she would. She'd promised. But Nadia... Still sweet and gentle. "We must go now."

"I'll just talk to him when—"

"No. You come with me now, or I am leaving without you. We will never see each other again." She tempered her frustration and took her sister's hands again. "I am begging you. Please."

Nadia studied Vanessa's eyes. Finally, she nodded. "Okay. I'll call him later. He'll understand."

"Da." He would understand far better than Nadia did.

Nadia stepped into the bedroom. "Let me just grab—"

"We must go. You have a suitcase packed."

"Only a minute. I need to grab a couple of things."

Vanessa was halfway to the bedroom to implore Nadia to come when the hallway door swung open.

Abbas stood in the opening.

Terror flowed through her brain. She gasped, tried to force the air out on a scream, but it was caught in her throat.

She was trapped.

Abbas crossed the space in a second, shoved her against the wall, and covered her mouth with his hand. With the other, he squeezed her neck, pressed against her windpipe. "If you alert Nadia, I'll kill you. And then I'll treat her as I did you until she is spent and useless. And then I'll kill her. You understand?"

His voice, the refined English accent, the confidence and casual tone to speak such hatred. In a heartbeat, she was the slave she'd been for so long, in his grip, as she'd sworn she would never be again.

"Do you understand?"

She tried to nod.

He removed his hand from her mouth and barely let up the pressure on her neck. He flipped the hat off her head and sent it flying across the room, then closed the space between their faces to mere centimeters. "Where is it?"

"I do not know—"

The hand on her neck tightened, silenced her. "If Nadia walks out and sees this, you'll leave me no choice but to kill you both. Where is it?"

"I sold it. I sold it to—"

The fist came so fast that she didn't have time to brace for it. Her head exploded in pain.

In the other room, Nadia yelled, "I just need to use the restroom. Make yourself comfortable."

"Answer her," Abbas said.

She considered warning her sister. She could speak Serbian to do it, but Nadia wouldn't believe her, and Abbas would only punish her. In English, she called, "Take your time." *Please, God. Protect Nadia.*

Abbas studied her face. "I hope for your sake you're lying," he said. "Or I have no reason to keep either of you alive."

"I can get it. I can—"

He squeezed her neck, not the windpipe, but the blood supply. "I can't decide if I should believe you. Perhaps you did sell it. You are stupid enough to pawn a priceless piece of art. But perhaps you decided instead to keep it, a way to remember our time together. Either way, you will get it for me, or you'll wish you'd never been born."

His voice was fading. The room was darkening at the edges. She could feel her legs growing weaker but had no power to hold herself up. He would kill her now. Kill her and kill Nadia, and all would be lost.

CHAPTER FIFTEEN

C aleb checked his watch again. He stood in the center of the lobby, gaze flitting from the elevator to the stairs and back. Where was Vanessa?

She'd promised to leave when she received his text. It had been delivered, but minutes had passed.

He hadn't detained the man nearly as long as he'd hoped to.

He replayed the conversation in his head.

"Sir," he'd said as he stepped in front of Abbas, barely glancing at Nadia.

Abbas had turned to him, recognition in his expression.

Caleb stepped forward. "I think we have a mutual friend."

Abbas's gaze skimmed the lobby, the coffee shop, the doors.

Nadia realized Abbas had stopped, and she came back. "Oh, it's you again."

Caleb held out his hand to her. "Caleb Peterson."

"Nadia Bakočević."

It didn't surprise him that her last name wasn't Baker like her sister's. Obviously Baker wasn't a Serbian name.

"Pleasure to meet you, Nadia." Caleb turned to the man, hand again outstretched.

Abbas said, "Nadia, go to the room and await me there."

"Happy to. My shoes are killing me." After a smile directed at Caleb, she turned to the elevators.

Only then did Abbas shake his hand. "Abbas bin Fahd al Sahim."

It took all of Caleb's self-control not to react to the name. *Al Sahim?*

"You said a mutual friend?" Abbas prompted.

"Vanessa asked me to speak with you regarding her sister."

"Vanessa," Abbas said. "That is not the name she was called when we were together."

Because it seemed the proper response, Caleb said, "What did you call her?"

Abbas's lips didn't part but quirked at the corner. His eyes remained cold. "Is she here?"

"She couldn't make the trip. I do a lot of business in Boston, so she asked me to come by."

"You were doing business here yesterday when you accosted my friend?"

Caleb forced a chuckle, as if Abbas were trying to be funny. "I hardly accosted her. We just talked. Vanessa had worried about her well-being."

"As you saw, she is fine."

"I told Vanessa that last night. She was pleased to hear it."

Again, Abbas's gaze skimmed the lobby.

"She's not here," Caleb said.

"Yet, you are." Abbas studied Caleb head to foot, and Caleb did the same to him. He was shorter than Caleb by inches with a dark, swarthy look. The black bushy eyebrows and trimmed beard matched Caleb's idea of a Middle Eastern man. The deep-set eyes flashed with anger and suspicion. "What do you want?"

"I want to know what happened between you and Vanessa."

Slowly, the man's lips separated to reveal straight white teeth. The evil in his eyes had Caleb's adrenaline pumping.

Caleb said nothing, just waited.

Abbas, too, said nothing.

A couple walked past. A crowd of business people exited the elevator and headed toward the coffee shop.

When it was clear Abbas wasn't going to answer, Caleb asked, "You two dated?"

Abbas chuckled. "When we met, she was desperately poor. I suspect it was my money she was attracted to, and my ability to get her out of Serbia. Foolishly, I believed she cared for me. We spent years together, most of that time on my yacht, but often I indulged her, as I do her sister. We would visit places like this." He gestured to the grand lobby. "I would take her shopping, buy her whatever she wished. I thought she was happy with me. But then"—he shrugged—"she found another. Though he can't have been wealthier than I, he lived in America, and she had often begged me to bring her here. I refused, however, since my business was in Europe. She discarded me and moved on."

Caleb didn't believe a word that came out of the man's mouth. The Vanessa he knew wasn't the woman Abbas described.

"You're in love with her," Abbas guessed. "Based on that alone, I know you're wealthy. Am I wrong?"

"We're only friends." Caleb wished it weren't true, wished there were more. If Vanessa were interested in wealth, she'd have been more receptive to him. Clearly, she wasn't the gold digger Abbas made her out to be.

Abbas's eyes held amusement and a hint of condescension, as if Caleb were naive and he the wise one. It irritated Caleb, but Abbas did know more about Vanessa than he did, or at least about her history.

"I would caution you to hold your valuables close," the man

said. "Not only do her loyalties shift with the wind, but she has sticky fingers."

"You're saying she stole from you?" He couldn't keep the incredulity from his voice.

"Water under the bridge." Abbas checked his watch. "I must go now. Nadia will be looking for me."

"Before you go... Vanessa said you deal in Middle Eastern imports. I own a chain of stores and—"

"I do not wish to do business with you, Caleb Peterson." He turned toward the elevator while Caleb scrambled to find some way to detain him further.

Then Abbas turned back. "You asked me what I called her when we were together." He closed the small distance between them and whispered in Caleb's ear. "I called her whore."

The word hit him as the man had surely hoped it would. Abbas barely concealed his sneer before he swiveled, marched to the elevator, and mashed the button. The second the doors closed behind him, Caleb texted Vanessa.

Whore.

The elevator dinged now, snapping him back to the moment. Two people stepped off. Not Vanessa. She'd promised to take the stairs, but she hadn't come out. Should he go that way? Maybe Abbas had seen her and followed her.

The elevator was there, though. He'd check the room first.

He stepped on and pressed the button to go to Abbas's floor. *Lord, keep her safe until I find her. Please...*

Abbas's suitcase was in the hallway outside the hotel room—not a good sign. Caleb could hear nothing on the other side of the door. He banged his fist against the wood. "Open up!"

A moment later, it swung open, and Abbas stood in the

entrance. "I guessed you'd lied about Vanessa," Abbas said. "Fortunately, I was able to intercept her before she left." Abbas backed away and turned to Vanessa, who was on her hands and knees on the floor.

Abbas spoke to Caleb over his shoulder as he reached Vanessa. "Your knock startled her, and she tripped." He grasped Vanessa's arm, but she shrunk back, terror in her eyes.

"Let me help you," Abbas said.

She yanked away and spat something in Serbian.

"Back off." Fury coursed through Caleb's veins.

Abbas stepped away from Vanessa, hands raised.

Caleb took Vanessa's arm and helped her up. Her eyes seemed to struggle to focus. "What did he—?"

"I'm ready." Nadia stepped in from another room carrying a patterned duffel bag. "Vojislava!" The bag dropped and she rushed to Vanessa's side as more words flew from her mouth. Serbian words.

Abbas barked, "English, Nadia. Your sister is fine. She tripped."

Nadia turned to Abbas, shock registering in her features.

Abbas said, "Forgive me. I find myself confused with the crowd in my hotel room."

"Sorry, my love," Nadia said. "Vanessa wants me to go with her to—"

"We go now." Vanessa shook off Caleb's hand and stepped out of the room, unsteady on her feet.

Nadia's joyful expression shifted as she studied Abbas. "What happened to her?"

"I told you, she tripped. I think perhaps she bumped her head." Abbas approached Nadia and took her in his arms.

Caleb didn't want to witness whatever was about to happen. He wanted to rush into the hallway to make sure Vanessa was all right. But he stayed where he stood against the wall and waited. It seemed Nadia had decided to go with them, and he wasn't about to let Abbas talk her out of it.

Abbas said, "You are leaving me?"

She giggled. "Vojislava wants me to meet her daughter."

Interest flashed in his eyes.

Caleb resisted the urge to tell Nadia to shut up.

"But she promised to bring me back in two days," Nadia said. "She said she'd talk to you then, but maybe since you two already—"

"We haven't had nearly enough time to catch up. I will look forward to your return."

"You won't miss me too much, will you?"

He nuzzled her ear. "I will hardly rest until you're returned to my side. Be safe." He whispered something, quiet enough that Caleb couldn't make out the words.

She giggled and said, "I promise."

Nadia seemed reluctant to leave as she turned to Caleb.

He snatched the duffel bag from the floor and nodded at the suitcase she'd left just inside the door. "That too?"

"Yes, please."

He pulled open the door, and Nadia stepped out in front of him.

Vanessa wasn't there. Surely she hadn't gone to the stairs, not as unsteady as she'd been.

They walked to the elevator, his gaze flitting everywhere. Finally, around the corner in front of the elevator doors, they found Vanessa sitting on a bench. She stood when they neared.

"Are you all right?" Caleb asked.

Vanessa barely nodded but focused on her sister. "He didn't give you a bad time?"

"He told me to have fun." She turned to Caleb. "Why didn't you tell me before you were Vanessa's friend?"

The elevator arrived, and the three of them stepped on.

Caleb hit the button for the lobby and met Vanessa's eyes. He had no idea what to say to this girl.

Vanessa said, "I asked him not to. My experience with Abbas isn't the same as yours, and I worried for your safety."

"Abbas has never been anything but kind to me. I don't know how he treated you, but—"

"Not kindly," Vanessa said.

Caleb pulsed with anger and worry. He could hardly stand the sound of Nadia's cheerful voice as they walked across the lobby and out the doors. He couldn't help an occasional glance behind him to see if Abbas followed. He didn't, but he didn't have to. He was confident enough in Nadia's devotion to know she'd come back to him.

Unfortunately, Abbas was right. Nadia wouldn't be convinced her boyfriend was trouble. She'd insist on returning to him. And then what would Vanessa do?

And what would Caleb do? If he had to choose between protecting Vanessa and protecting this naive sister of hers, he'd choose Vanessa every time.

He feared he wouldn't be able to protect them both.

CHAPTER SIXTEEN

When Vanessa stepped into the cool October air, the last of the dizziness faded and her head cleared. She pulled away from Caleb, who, until then, had carried both of Nadia's bags in one arm, along with his own laptop case. He'd kept the other arm around Vanessa's back for support.

He glanced at her as they neared the street. "Are you all right?"

"Better now. Thank you." She was better. Out of that stifling luxury and back in fresh air and sunshine.

She couldn't help a look behind her. Was Abbas following?

She didn't see him, but she couldn't help but notice that Caleb's head swiveled back as well. Nadia, however, seemed delighted as she gazed at the buildings around them. "Such a pretty city," she said. "Quaint, da?"

She spoke English well, better than Vanessa would have guessed.

"Vojislava, do you spend—?"

"My name is Vanessa," she snapped.

Hurt filled her sister's eyes. "It will take some getting used to. Forgive me."

After crossing the street, they entered the parking garage and took the stairs to the second floor. Caleb stayed behind Vanessa and her sister all the way to the car. He set the bags by the trunk, then opened the rear door. Nadia slid in.

"You can sit with her, if you want." Caleb's words were spoken low so only Vanessa could hear, his expression tight and anxious. It made her stomach hurt again.

She whispered, "She is cheerful. I might slap her if I'm too close."

Caleb smiled, as she'd hoped he would. Not that she should care.

He slammed Nadia's door, his smile fading. "What did Abbas—?"

"I do not wish to talk about it."

"Considering everything, I think you should—"

"Yes, yes. I owe you much. This I know."

He opened her car door. After she climbed in, he slammed it too hard.

The traffic was bad, and, though she longed to put miles between herself and Abbas, she told herself to relax and tried to respond gently to Nadia's incessant chatter. The feeling that Abbas was on their heels wouldn't fade. In a break in Nadia's talk, Vanessa angled to face her. "Will you please let me see your phone?"

"Why?"

"Does Abbas pay for it?"

"What does that matter?" Nadia asked.

"I worry that he tracks your location. I know you trust him, and perhaps he has changed since I knew him. But because I don't know for sure, I don't wish him to know where I live. I would like to turn off your location services so he cannot find us."

The carefree tone that had filled Nadia's voice almost constantly since Vanessa had seen her now faded. "I can't believe this. You're being ridiculous. He's not going to track me, Voji—"

"Vanessa."

"He's a good man. You're the one who's changed. I'm sorry I ever came with you."

Vanessa reached into the backseat, palm up. "It's just for a couple of days. You can live without Abbas for two days, can't you?"

"I love him. But maybe you don't know what that means. All these years, you've never contacted Mama and Tata or any of—"

"You have no idea what you're talking about, what I've been through. What Tata did—" She cut off her own words and glanced at Caleb.

He kept his eyes on the road, but the muscles in his jaw tensed. She realized now that, at some point during the conversation, she and her sister had slipped into Serbian. To Caleb, she said, "Forgive me. It is very rude to not speak English."

"It's fine," Caleb said. "You two have a lot of catching up to do."

"Da." She glanced at Nadia over her shoulder, who'd crossed her arms and was looking outside. "I had wanted her to meet Katarina and to see where I live, but she does not wish it. We must take her back to the hotel."

"What?" Nadia said. "No, I want to go with you. I came all the way here just to see you!"

"Ah," Vanessa said, "and yet, you cannot do this one thing for me."

Caleb glanced sideways at Vanessa, one eyebrow lifted.

"I asked her only to shut off her cell phone's location so Abbas can't track us, but—"

"It's not necessary," Nadia said.

"Then what does it matter, hmm?" Vanessa asked.

Nadia said nothing.

Caleb glanced in the rearview mirror, probably to see the sulking girl in the backseat, and then flipped on his blinker. "No problem, Nadia. I'll have you back at the hotel in—"

"I wish to meet Katarina. I wish to go—"

"Then give me your cell phone."

With a huff, Nadia swiped it on and handed it over.

Vanessa found the setting for location services and turned it off. She turned to face her sister again. "You need to promise me you won't turn it back on. If Abbas wants you back, I will take you back. If he wants to know where you are, you tell him New Hampshire and nothing else. Can you promise this?"

"You're being ridiculous," Nadia said.

"Nevertheless, I ask for this favor. As your sister."

After a long silence, Nadia huffed and held out her hand. "I promise."

Vanessa planted the phone in it. "Thank you. I will trust you."

Nadia said nothing, and the silence in the car grew thick. Caleb broke it with, "You like music, Nadia?"

Her sister's face lit up. "Yes! I love to dance. Voji... Vanessa, do you like to dance?"

"I do," Vanessa said. "I have not had much opportunity, though."

"Abbas takes me dancing all the time. We went to this club in Manhattan last night and danced until my feet ached."

"What kind of music do you like?" Caleb asked.

She rattled off names of bands and artists Vanessa had never heard of. Not that she had much time in her life for such foolishness. Caleb did, and he found a radio station that pleased Nadia, who sang along with the lyrics, dancing in her seat, all frustration with Vanessa seemingly forgotten.

When the traffic eased, Caleb got into the right lane and hit the blinker. "I need a restroom."

Vanessa did, too. All that coffee, and she'd been afraid to leave the lobby for fear of missing Nadia. "This is good, da."

A moment later, he pulled into a McDonald's parking lot. Nadia's squeal was louder than the music. "I love McDonald's. Abbas can't stand it. He rarely lets me have it."

Vanessa climbed out of the car and waited for Nadia to do the same before she said, "He does not have the right to tell you what you can eat."

Nadia only laughed. "Oh, it's not like that. When I want to go to McDonald's, he laughs and takes me for what he calls *real* hamburgers. He thinks I like McDonald's because it is American."

That Nadia and Abbas had these kinds of conversations, Vanessa couldn't understand. She tried to imagine Abbas in the role Nadia painted for him, but the image wouldn't come.

Caleb held open the restaurant door for Vanessa and her sister. "Do you want anything," he asked Vanessa.

"I am thirsty. A Diet Coke?"

He handed Nadia a fifty and said, "Get two sodas for us and whatever you want for yourself.

A wide smile on her too happy face, she said, "Thank you!"

"We'll be right back."

He led Vanessa around the corner to the bathrooms but stopped her with a gentle grasp of her upper arm before she went inside. "Are you all right?" When she turned to him, he touched the side of her head and angled it to the side.

She didn't flinch. Rather, she leaned into the warmth, the tenderness. As much as she'd wanted to distance herself from this man, she couldn't pretend she didn't care for him. She did. And she trusted him. She let him examine her, let his fingers stay against her skin, his gaze on her injuries. "He hit you?"

Only one customer sat nearby, and he was staring at his phone, paying them no attention. Nadia must have still been ordering her food. Quietly, Vanessa said, "Da."

"And Nadia just—"

"She was in the other room. He told me if I alerted her, he would kill us both."

The color drained from Caleb's face. "Is that why you were woozy?"

"I do not know this word, woozy."

"Befuddled. Dizzy. Did he do anything else to you?"

She touched her neck, and Caleb lifted her chin. Gently, he traced the marks Abbas's fingers must have left. Then, he shifted his touch from her neck to her shoulders and closed his eyes. He seemed to force a deep breath before he opened them again. "He nearly killed you."

"He was not trying to kill. Only to scare."

Caleb took her hands. "I'm so sorry. I should never have left your side. I swore I'd protect you, and then... I thought I gave you enough time to escape."

"It was not your fault. I promised to leave when I got your text, but I had to convince her to come."

"I should have known."

"I should have done what you said."

They stared at each other. Try as she might, she was unable to erect the walls again. Perhaps Abbas had torn them down. Perhaps she didn't have the energy. Perhaps she desperately needed somebody to be her protector, to take on some of this responsibility for her.

Caleb let go of her hands and pulled her close, wrapping his arms around her. "I will never let him hurt you again."

She let herself relax against his broad chest, let herself feel safe in his strong arms. But she didn't let herself believe his words. Because she'd done something she'd sworn she would never do. She put herself in Abbas's sights. She might have rescued her sister, but she'd put herself—and her daughter—in danger in the process. Nadia's phone location off or on, it wouldn't matter. Eventually, Abbas would come.

She'd not allowed herself to think of what would happen once she rescued Nadia, but now she must.

She must deal with the truth of this situation today. She would have to leave her job, her life, her home. She would have to take Katarina—and Nadia, if she would come—somewhere safe. Somewhere Abbas could never find her. He claimed to want the item she'd stolen from him. Priceless work of art? She'd seen only a bauble, a piece of jewelry he'd kept in his drawer. Was it truly that valuable?

She should simply return it.

Except he'd gone to a lot of trouble and expense to find her and that bauble. Surely, his anger had burned against her ever since he'd realized she'd stolen it—when she'd thought he wouldn't even realize it was gone.

She'd been a fool. And now... She knew Abbas well enough to know he would not be satisfied with the return of his property and leave her be. He would exact his revenge. He would make her sorry for what she'd done.

Tears filled her eyes, and she pressed her cheek against Caleb's sweater. She didn't want to leave Nutfield and the life she'd made there. She didn't want to leave this man.

But she had no choice.

CHAPTER SEVENTEEN

The traffic was steady but moving at a good clip as they neared the New Hampshire border. Caleb figured they had another thirty minutes before they got back to Nutfield. Thirty minutes to figure out what to do next.

Nadia and Vanessa had been chatting, mostly in English, since they'd left McDonald's. They'd kept the conversation light. Vanessa asked her sister about the places she'd visited, and, while Nadia had gone on and on about Greece and Italy and Morocco, Caleb had tried to block her out.

He needed to think, and he was running out of time to make a plan.

Because the meeting with Abbas had told him a few very important things.

Abbas was a master manipulator. He was a man who could be charming to one sister and abusive to another. He was a man who could shift from his true, evil nature to the face of courtesy in a matter of seconds and keep the mask on for long periods of time.

The man who'd left those bruises on Vanessa while her sister was in the next room—that man was a sadistic monster who'd learned to hide behind his refined English accent and his money, a man who'd learned to present himself to the world as a civilized human being.

But the most disturbing thing Caleb had learned was the man's full name. Abbas bin Fahd al Sahim. Abbas, son of Fahd, House of Sahim. It was that last part that had his heart racing. If Abbas was to be believed, he was part of one of the oldest royal families in the world. It was a big family numbering, if Caleb's memory served, around fifteen thousand members. A couple of thousand held most of the power. Though they didn't currently reign over any nation, their influence in the region—and thus, in the world—was impressive. Whether Abbas was one of those elites, Caleb couldn't know for sure, but did it matter? Surely he knew those powerful people even if he wasn't one of them.

What did Caleb know so far? That Abbas was manipulative, sadistic, powerful, and connected.

And for some reason, he'd gone to great lengths to find Vanessa. But why?

He glanced at her now. She was turned to her sister in the back seat. Nadia was telling Vanessa about all they'd done on their short trip to New York, and Vanessa was listening and nodding along, though he could feel tension radiating off her.

Or maybe that was his own tension reflecting back to him.

He needed to understand more. And his window for gleaning information was closing as they neared Nutfield. At a break in the ladies' conversation, he said, "Nadia, tell us how you tracked down your sister. That can't have been easy, considering she changed her name."

"Abbas did most of the work," Nadia said. "He has friends everywhere, and he found someone in American immigrations to help us."

"Helpful that those records are public," Caleb said, feigning casual. "But still, with the name change—"

"He couldn't have done it without me." In the rearview, Caleb saw Nadia's proud smile as she spoke to her sister. "Even with his connections, he could never have found you without my help. The man had your Serbian name but wouldn't share your English name unless a family member requested it. Fortunately, I was able to provide enough information to prove we were related, and he told us you were now Vanessa Baker and had last lived near Boston. It must have been fun living close to Boston. Did you have a job? Did you have a lot of friends?"

Vanessa sighed, probably praying for patience. "I had a baby. I didn't spend time in the city."

"Too bad," Nadia said. "When you take me back to Abbas, we can explore together. I want to go to an American football game. Have you done that?"

Vanessa explained that she had not but then told Nadia about the baseball game they'd attended the day before. Nadia seemed enthralled. Meanwhile, Caleb tried to fit this new information in with what he knew.

Maybe Abbas had tried to find Vanessa sooner but had been thwarted by his connection's insistence that he wouldn't share Vanessa's new name with anybody but family. Was that normal procedure for the US Customs and Immigration Service? He couldn't imagine, unless she'd been given political asylum. And anyway, with the money Abbas had, he probably could have offered enough in bribes to get the information. Had he truly needed Nadia's help, or had he just told her that to make her feel a part of the search?

Or... Abbas said he hadn't known Vanessa by that name. Maybe he hadn't known her as Vojislava, either. Maybe he'd never known her real name. But then, how had he found her sister?

When Nadia quit peppering questions at Vanessa about the baseball game, Caleb asked, "How did you and Abbas meet?"

Nadia's smile beamed in the rearview. "It was romantic. I was at university—"

"University!" Vanessa's outburst almost sounded angry. "How? How did you pay for that?"

Nadia sat back. "Tata paid for it, and Milos helped. He had graduated and gotten a job."

"Milos went to university, too?" Vanessa asked. "What of Lukas?"

Nadia was silent, and Caleb glanced back to see why. The girl blinked a couple of times. "You don't know?"

"I know nothing," Vanessa snapped. "How could I know?"

Nadia leaned forward and placed her hand on Vanessa's shoulder. "Lukas had a breathing disorder." She said something in Serbian, then in English added, "I'm sorry, Caleb. I don't remember the English word, but he struggled sometimes to get breath."

"Asthma?" Caleb suggested, shooting a look to the woman beside him. Vanessa's eyes brimmed with unshed tears as if she knew what was coming.

"Da." Nadia's voice was gentle. "He came down with the flu. We all got it, but with the breathing disorder... He couldn't fight it."

Vanessa swiped at her eyes. "How old was he?"

"Sixteen."

After a moment, Vanessa asked, "Everyone else is okay? Mama? The baby?"

"Mama is... sad always. After losing you and then Lukas... she does not smile."

Like mother, like daughter.

"Milos is married and works in Belgrade. Anya will graduate from university this year. Tasya is home still, annoying as ever."

"I only knew her as an infant," Vanessa said. "She was never annoying to me."

"These are your siblings?" Caleb asked.

Vanessa said, "Da. I am the oldest. Lukas would be twenty-five, Milos is twenty-four. Anya is... twenty-two, yes?"

Nadia said, "Da. I am twenty, and Tasya is sixteen."

"When did you last see them?"

Nadia started to speak, but Vanessa cut her off with, "It has been many years."

Silence filled the car while Caleb put this information together. Vanessa's brother had died nine years earlier, and Vanessa hadn't known. She was maybe twenty-six, which meant she hadn't been home since she was seventeen? Or even earlier?

Why?

He tried to shake off the question, but it held on. He'd learn her history one of these days, surely. But right now, more important was the question he still waited for Nadia to answer. When she said nothing else, he asked Nadia, "You were at university when—?"

"Abbas saw me on the campus and told me I reminded him of someone he'd once known. We talked a long time and discovered that his old friend was my sister. We shared stories about our Vojislava and"—she shrugged—"we fell in love."

Vanessa's scoff was probably only audible to Caleb. She turned back to face her sister again. "You were in school. Did you not have the money to stay, or—?"

"Why do I need college when I have Abbas? He takes care of me."

"But you had the opportunity..."

Wise not to argue with Nadia right now. The girl was clearly smitten, and neither of them would be able to talk her out of her feelings.

"What did Tata think about you leaving with Abbas?"

Nadia waved the question away. "Tata is suspicious of all foreigners and told me I would regret it. Even when I promised to find you and send word, he..."

"He what?" Tension hummed in Vanessa's question.

"He said you were long gone. That if you hadn't contacted us, we should assume you were dead. But I had met someone who knew you. For the first time, I had hope I could find you." She leaned forward, reached between the seats, and squeezed her sister's arm. "I am glad I found you."

Vanessa's lips trembled. She seemed unable to speak.

He wanted to comfort her as he'd done at McDonald's. That moment with her in his arms... It had almost felt like a spiritual experience filled with God's presence, God's pleasure.

To be trusted, to be believed... What Caleb had felt could only have been a pale reflection of how the Lord felt when His children trusted Him. Caleb longed for more of it, more of her.

Not her beautiful face or her shapely body—not that he hadn't noticed those. He was a man, after all. A single man who'd fought his very human urges for years, over and over choosing purity over all its pale substitutes.

But what he'd enjoyed when Vanessa was in his arms was much more than physical. It was her trust, her confidence in him, that encouraged him now to offer her comfort.

But Nadia was here. Vacuous, silly Nadia... who seemed neither at this moment as she gripped her sister's hand.

There was more to Vanessa's story than Caleb understood. How long had it been since she'd left home? Why hadn't she ever reached out to her family? If the expression on her face proved anything, it proved that it wasn't a lack of care for them that had kept her away. But what?

He had none of those answers and knew that if he asked, Vanessa wouldn't tell him. Not now, when she must feel raw and exposed.

He needed to focus on the task at hand—keeping Vanessa, Nadia, and Katarina safe.

What did Abbas know? He knew Vanessa's real name, knew she lived in New Hampshire, and knew her cell phone number. That hadn't concerned Caleb too much. When Vanessa had first started working as the food bank's manager, she hadn't had a cell phone. Caleb had insisted she needed one and convinced the board to provide one for her. That number was published on the website, as was Vanessa's name. He remembered that she'd asked they not publish her name, but the board had insisted. She hadn't put up much of a fuss at the time. He hadn't thought her objection anything more than the typical attitude they got from the prickly woman. But now... Had she known Abbas might be looking for her?

Surely not, or else she'd have insisted her name be hidden.

Her address... Would that be searchable? Her little house was rented, so it wasn't as if her name would show up on any title records. Leases weren't public information. But she had a driver's license. Her address was out there, and with enough money and connections, Abbas could locate her easily enough. And he had Caleb's name too.

Which meant she wouldn't be safe at home.

Caleb wouldn't leave her where she might be in danger.

She needed a safe place to stay. As soon as he had a private moment, he'd secure her one.

CHAPTER EIGHTEEN

Vanessa was still trying to fit the pieces together. Nadia had been at university? Milos and Anya, too? How had Tata paid for that? When Vanessa had lived at home, there'd hardly been enough food to survive, and that was with both Tata and Mama working many hours. Now, there was enough left for education?

Had Tata been given that much when he'd sold Vanessa?

Or perhaps her family's fortunes had changed. Perhaps they always would have, and if Tata had only held out, Vanessa, too, would have stayed in her parents' home where she was safe. She'd have had more years with her closest brother before he'd passed away. She'd have gone to university and studied... What? She didn't have any idea what that Vojislava would have loved or wanted to do.

Vojislava had died many years before.

She didn't wish to think about that. What was done was done. She hadn't been valuable enough to keep around, and maybe the money Tata received had lifted the family out of poverty. Maybe knowing that should help her feel better about what she'd been through.

It did not.

They were long off the highway when Caleb turned toward the outskirts of town.

"This is not the way to my house," she said.

"I'm going to swing by and get Kat. She'll be there, right?"

"If you will take us home, I'll get Katarina."

He pressed his lips together. Glancing in his rearview mirror, and saw that Nadia was looking out the window, paying them no attention. He leaned in Vanessa's direction, voice low. "What if Abbas knows where you live?"

She gasped and kept her voice just as low. "Do you think he might?"

One curt nod was all the answer she needed. "If so, then why—?"

"Let's talk about it later."

Because Nadia didn't understand. This would be difficult, to convince her sister that Abbas was not to be trusted. Vanessa would need to tell her sister everything.

At the moment, the bigger issue was the immediate one. Where would she go?

"We'll pick up Kat now," Caleb said. "I'll take you back to your house, and while you get some things together, I'll secure a place for you to stay."

"But you have done enough already. I will..." What could she do? She could use the credit card tucked in her wallet, the one she'd gotten for emergencies but had never used. But it would only last a short time. She needed time to make a plan, to sell what she could to raise the funds to relocate. But how could she do that if Abbas already knew where she was?

If he did know, why had he not come for her already? Perhaps he'd thought it would be easier if she came to him. Perhaps all he wanted was his property back. Could she be rid of him that easily?

Nadia gazed out the rear window at the deep forests all around. Would Abbas be satisfied with the jewel Vanessa had stolen, or would he want Nadia back as well?

Whatever he said, could she trust him to keep his word?

No. That she knew already. The man lied as easily as he breathed. Her thievery was only one reason Abbas had to punish her. If he had figured out the rest...

She could not think about what he would do to her. Not just to her, but to Nadia.

To Katarina.

The images came too fast. She couldn't control them. All the practice she'd done in controlling her thoughts seemed useless now as she saw Abbas's evil sneer, the face of her sister. The face of her daughter.

Nausea churned, and she doubled over.

"Hey," Caleb said. "What's wrong? Are you sick?"

She couldn't respond. She inhaled through her nose, exhaled through her mouth, and lifted prayers that amounted to no more than, *Please, God. Please, God. Please, God.*

"Want me to pull over?" The car slowed, the blinker clicked. The tires left pavement and bumped onto the narrow shoulder and came to a stop.

Behind her, Nadia said, "What is it? Are you all right?"

Another inhale, another exhale. She didn't have time for this. She had to get to Katarina and get to safety. *Please, God. Please protect us.*

Rarely did she hear the voice of God. Rarely did He speak back to her, but now, she felt His response in a gentle whisper. *You are my daughter, a daughter of the Living God. Trust Me.*

The God who created the universe called her daughter.

Daughter.

The last one who'd called her daughter had sacrificed her.

But this One... Her true Father had let His Son die to save her.

This, she did not understand, but this she believed.

Slowly, she became aware again of Caleb beside her. His hand was on her back, rubbing in slow circles.

Nadia had leaned between the seats. Her hand was on Vanessa's arm.

Neither of them knew what thoughts had stalled Vanessa, but they were with her, silently encouraging her. She felt her sister's worry. She felt Caleb's prayers.

The future was uncertain, but God was there. She could do this. She had no choice but to do this.

She straightened. "I am okay."

Nadia squeezed her arm. "Maybe you should eat something. I think I have some pretzels from the plane." Nadia started digging through her purse.

Caleb's eyebrows lifted, a silent question.

"I'm okay," she said again. "Let's go get Kat."

FIVE MINUTES LATER, they pulled into the driveway of Kelsey and Eric's house. As they exited the car, the front door banged open. "Mommy!" Her daughter flew down the front steps and into Vanessa's arms. She looked happy and healthy and perfect. "I'm glad you're home. I had so much fun. We went to fireworks, and they were pretty, except too loud! And yesterday at church, I met a new girl, and she was in my class at school today! Isn't that cool? And we got to—"

"*Ceri*, there is plenty of time to tell me everything. Let me say hello to Miss Kelsey, please."

"Sorry, Mommy." Kat ran around the car and launched

herself at Caleb, hugging his waist. "Hi, Mr. Caleb. Mommy said I could hug you now because you saved my life."

That wasn't what she'd said, and now the nausea that had begun to settle stirred up again.

Caleb patted Kat's head. "Sounds like you had fun." Gently, he extricated himself from her embrace, glancing at Vanessa as if he understood her fear. As if he ever could. "I hope you'll tell me all about your weekend."

"I will, but Mommy says I have to wait." Only then did Kat seem to notice there was somebody else there. She turned to Nadia, who'd stepped out of the car, and said, "Hi."

"Hello, Katarina."

"You say my name like Mommy does."

"Da." Nadia smiled and ran her hands over Kat's light brown hair. "The proper way."

Kat turned to Vanessa. "She talks like you, Mommy!"

"*Ceri*, this is your Aunt Nadia, my little sister."

Kat's grin spread wider, and she hugged Nadia's waist. "I have an aunt? I didn't even know."

"I didn't know I had a niece, either."

Vanessa couldn't take her eyes off them, these two she loved dearly.

Kelsey joined them in the driveway, Kat's bag in her hands. "Looks like you had success." She lowered her voice. "Did you see the guy?"

Low, she answered, "It was not good."

At the questions in Kelsey's eyes, she said, "I will tell you another time." Then, she called, "Nadia."

Her sister rounded the car, Kat at her side.

"Nadia, this is Kelsey Nolan. Kelsey, my sister."

Nadia held out her hand. "It is a pleasure to meet you."

"You, too. I'm glad y'all found each other."

Nadia's eyes widened in wonder. "You are from a different place? Your accent is lovely."

"Georgia, in the South," Kelsey said. "Though I worry I'm losing my accent."

Caleb's chuckle was low. "Doesn't sound like it to me."

"Well, good," Kelsey said. "I love New Hampshire, but y'all talk funny."

Kat giggled. "Everybody here except me and Mr. Caleb talks funny."

He high-fived her. "You tell 'em, sister!"

"Do not encourage her." But Vanessa couldn't help the smile. Now that she had Kat back, she felt almost normal again.

She hugged Kelsey. "Thank you for keeping her."

"Anytime. And if you need anything else, anything at all"—she gave Vanessa a knowing look—"y'all just let us know. Eric and I... the whole crew... you know we'll do everything we can."

"Da. This I know. You have been good to me."

"It's what friends do." Kelsey ruffled Kat's messy hair. "Let's do it again sometime."

They loaded into the car, and Kat started chattering to Nadia in the backseat. The two were so similar, it was almost laughable. But the lighthearted mood she'd almost reached dissipated as they neared her house.

They pulled into the driveway. Kat's bicycle was still outside, her golf club still on the porch. Vanessa ignored those things as she unlocked the door.

Caleb followed Vanessa inside but stopped just beyond the front door.

Kat came in next, dragging Nadia through the house to show her around.

This house, her house, was nothing like the luxurious places she'd visited and even, for a time, lived. Fancy hotels, the yacht, the beach house in Florida. But it was also nothing like the cold wet basement where she'd been kept for years, starved, beaten, broken.

This place was all the luxury she needed. It was the home she'd made for herself and her daughter. She didn't want to leave it.

She didn't want to leave this town or her job.

Caleb reached out to her, but his arm dropped before he touched her. "Get whatever you need. I'll find someplace for us to stay until we can figure this out."

"I do not... wish to need your help."

He smiled at that.

And then his words penetrated. "For *us?* You are not going to stay with us."

"I'm not leaving you alone until this is all straightened out."

This would never be... straight. There was no way to fix it. But to say that would make it too real, and she didn't wish to have the conversation now with Caleb, who would surely try to talk her out of what she planned.

"You have responsibilities. You have wasted enough—"

"You are not..." That muscle in his jaw ticked. "You are not a waste, Vanessa. You are precious, and you are worth my time and my resources. You're a daughter of the Living God. I'm not doing this for you. I'm doing it for Him."

A daughter of the Living God.

The same thing she'd heard God tell her just minutes earlier.

That Caleb would use that same statement, it meant something. It meant... She had to trust God with this. And for some reason, He wanted her to trust Caleb.

It was one thing to place herself in Caleb's care. It had been a risk, a calculated one, but nevertheless. But to trust Caleb with Nadia?

To trust Caleb with Katarina?

How could she do this? How could she trust any man?

Except... that phrase. She could still hear the echo of what God had said to her. *You are my daughter, a daughter of the Living God. Trust Me.*

She realized that to trust God right now meant to trust Caleb.

<h1 style="text-align:center">CHAPTER NINETEEN</h1>

The guard at the entrance to the posh neighborhood made a call, and a moment later the gate swung open. Caleb drove up the short rise, and, when the car crested the hill, he got a view of the lake and the little town of Nutfield. The vista never ceased to inspire him.

In the backseat, Nadia said, "Oh, it is beautiful. And the town from here is... I do not know English word for it." She rattled off something in Serbian.

Vanessa supplied, "I think photoesque?"

"Picturesque," Caleb supplied.

"That is what I said."

Caleb chuckled as he meandered the pretty streets of the housing development.

He hadn't wanted to take Vanessa and her family to his house. He'd given Abbas his real name—a mistake, in retrospect. He wouldn't let Abbas track Vanessa through him.

He also hadn't wanted to take Vanessa to a hotel. Hotels weren't nearly secure enough. He'd considered Angel and Donovan's bed-and-breakfast, but they were booked solid, thanks to the leaf-peepers who always descended on New

Hampshire this time of year. Even Samantha Kopp and Jack Rossi, friends who owned rental properties in town, hadn't had anything available.

He'd called Kade, thinking there might be a house in his development that was available but not yet sold. Kade had suggested this solution.

Ginny and Kade would stay in a hotel, which Caleb would pay for. He'd considered having them stay at his house, but that would make them targets, if Abbas came looking.

Caleb, Vanessa, Nadia, and Kat would stay at Ginny and Kade's house. With all the security around this neighborhood, and all the security in their house, it was a great solution. They'd stay here until... Well, until Caleb figured out what to do next.

He had no idea what that would be, but God must have a plan. He must.

"Look, Mommy, a golf course," Kat said. "Can we play golf?"

"Not today, *ceri*."

"I saw your golf club at the house," Caleb said. "You like to play?"

"Mommy's going to let me take lessons in the spring."

"It's a fun game," he said. "Maybe we can go to the driving range and hit some balls while you're here."

"Can we, Mommy? Can we?"

Beside him, Vanessa said, "We will see."

He turned into Kade and Ginny's driveway, and Nadia *oohed* again.

"This is the prettiest house of all the houses," she said. "Vanessa, you know who lives here?"

"They are friends."

"You have rich friends." The awe in her voice was unmistakable.

"I have good friends." Vanessa opened her car door but

turned to face her sister. "Whether they have money or not, I do not care, only that they are kind."

"Doesn't hurt when they're rich, though."

They all climbed out of the car. Caleb punched in the code on the oversize door, stepped into the foyer, and turned off the alarm. When everybody was inside, he turned it back on. Just in case.

The ladies had frozen in the foyer. Beside them, a small table held a giant vase of silk flowers.

"It is like... like fancy hotel, no?" Nadia turned to Vanessa. "You have been here?"

"No. I knew these houses were nice, but this is..."

Her words trailed. The two-story foyer was impressive. Beyond it, Caleb could see through the living room to the wall of windows that overlooked the lake. Everything was beautifully decorated in whites and grays with a touch of teal here and there.

Kat was standing at those windows. "Look, Mommy! There are boats! Can we go on a boat?"

Vanessa said, "I do not think so, *ceri.*"

At the same time, Caleb said, "I'll see what I can arrange."

Kat apparently only heard Caleb's answer, because she squealed.

Vanessa shot him a look, and he shrugged. "No promises."

Nadia peeked into the room inside the door—an office. "They have many family members who live with them?"

"They don't live with extended family in America," Vanessa said. "I believe only Ginny and Kade live here." She turned to Caleb. "Yes?"

"I think they're hoping to fill it."

"I know Ginny wants children," Vanessa said.

Caleb hadn't been here, either, but Kade had given him a quick rundown on the rooms. "There are two bedrooms on this floor, both with en suite baths. We probably shouldn't stay in the master, but the guest room will work. There are three bedrooms upstairs. Vanessa, you decide where everyone will sleep, and I'll deliver the suitcases."

"You will stay in the room down here," she said.

Closer to the door, closer to intruders. "Good." He left his bag in the foyer and carried the rest up the grand staircase.

The rooms upstairs were similar to each other. Vanessa gave Nadia the largest.

Caleb stepped in with the younger woman and set her suitcase on the bed while she opened the blinds. Her room looked out over the lake. "It's lovely here." She turned. "When can we go out on the boat?"

"I think Kade has one," he said. "I'll ask him. But I need you to do something for me."

Her head tilted to the side, and her lips tipped up at the corners. "What can I possibly do for you, Caleb?" Her words, the look... It was almost as if she were flirting, though he doubted she realized it. Most likely, she saw him as so old that he was harmless.

And, despite her pretty face, he wasn't the slightest bit attracted to her. "Promise me you won't tell Abbas where you are."

Her flirty look disappeared. "He is a good man."

"You may be right, but your sister believes differently. Respect her wishes—and mine—and keep your whereabouts secret. Please."

"You are both wrong about Abbas. Why do you think he is bad?"

"You'll need to talk to Vanessa about that. I'm just trying to keep you all safe."

"From Abbas we do not need to be protected."

"Nevertheless, will you honor my wishes?" He let the question hang.

After a moment, she said, "What if I want to go back?"

"All you have to do is ask me."

"You will take me to Boston, to Abbas?"

He wanted to check behind him to make sure Vanessa wasn't listening. Because she'd be furious if she heard this, but Caleb wasn't going to keep Nadia against her will, and he wasn't going to let Nadia put Vanessa and Kat in danger.

He lowered his voice. "Anytime, day or night. I promise."

"Da. Then I will not tell him where we are."

"Even if he asks. Even if he demands you tell him—"

"I will not. I give my word."

"Thank you." He took the other two suitcases and delivered them to Vanessa's and Kat's rooms. When he caught Vanessa's eyes, she seemed content enough, which meant she hadn't overheard his conversation with Nadia.

He left the women to get settled upstairs. Kade had told him to help himself to whatever they could find in the kitchen, but he'd order some groceries to be delivered. No need to further impinge on his friends' hospitality by gobbling up all their food.

Caleb's house was nice—a Colonial in a newer neighborhood—but it was nothing like this. Caleb wasn't one to flaunt his wealth, and, as only one person, he hadn't needed much. Someday, he'd buy something bigger, a place like this, a place to fill with love and laughter and children.

Kade and Ginny's kitchen, like the rest of the house, was bright and airy. An oversize island had four stools pushed up to it. The round table in front of the bay window overlooking the lake was large enough for six. Kade had designed this house—and many of the properties in this development. Caleb had known his friend was talented, but this was beyond impressive.

Voices carried from upstairs, coming from the wrong direction. Caleb wandered around a wall and found a rear staircase. Good. If Abbas should find them here, the ladies would have two ways of escape.

He had no idea what the next step should be. God had a plan. He must. Caleb would hang onto the promise God had given him two years before and trust that somehow, God would get them from here to that promise.

It had taken more than forty years for Caleb's namesake to receive the promise of God. Forty years of wandering in the desert, not to mention the years of battle to take the Promised Land from those who inhabited it. But eventually, the Caleb of the Old Testament had settled in his promised land.

Caleb believed he would receive God's promise as well. No matter how long it took, he'd wait for the bride God had given him. He'd believe, despite all evidence to the contrary, that Vanessa would someday return his feelings. That they would be safe and secure. That they would have their own home to fill with children.

He leaned against the wall and listened. Was this what it would be like to have a family of his own?

Nadia's and Vanessa's voices sounded similar, though Nadia's accent was thicker. Then there was little Katarina, whose higher pitch was often filled with joy, as it was now.

"Look how high I can jump, Mommy."

"Don't jump on the bed! You'll break it."

"But it's fun!" This from Nadia, who, it seemed, had joined her niece in the mischief.

Caleb feared he'd be replacing something before their stint here was over, maybe multiple somethings. But the laughter—Vanessa's laughter, if he wasn't mistaken—would be worth every penny.

He sat at the island and pulled out his computer, trying not to eavesdrop. They clearly weren't aware he could hear. He should probably tell them. He would... later. Right now, he'd simply enjoy their pretty voices.

He searched Google for Abbas's name, hoping perhaps Abbas had lied about his connection to the Sahim royals. Unfortunately, the man's name and image appeared, along with a detailed explanation of his lineage and his net worth. Caleb's low whistle echoed off the quartz countertop.

Abbas's wealth made Caleb's family look like paupers.

With that much money... he must be well connected within the royal family.

That wasn't good. It was one thing to have an enemy. But to have an enemy who was nearly untouchable? An enemy with unlimited resources?

Caleb read all he could find on the web about Abbas bin Fahd al Sahim. As Vanessa had said, the man's company sold Middle Eastern goods throughout Europe. He had no outlets in the US. Was he here to make connections, to expand his company's reach?

Based on the way he'd shut Caleb down that morning, he wasn't interested in doing business in the US. But perhaps that refusal had been personal. Perhaps he was trying to find American retailers to carry his goods.

Or perhaps he'd only come to find Vanessa.

Why, though? Why would a wealthy Middle Eastern prince care about Vanessa, a woman he'd deemed a...

Caleb didn't want to even think the word, but there it was, against his will.

Whore.

He inhaled a clean breath, blew the ugly word out. Whoever Vanessa had been before, she was no longer. She was a Christ-follower now. She was redeemed, a new creation.

And for some reason, she was valuable enough for a multimillionaire to chase all over the world. Why? He'd said she was a thief. Was it related to that?

The voices he'd been trying to drown out reached him now, and he focused on them.

"He's handsome, your boyfriend." Nadia's voice was tinged with teasing.

"He is not my boyfriend," Vanessa snapped. "Only a friend."

"I think more than a friend. What do you think, little Kat? Does Caleb like your mommy?"

Kat giggled. "I think so, but Mommy says men are not to be trusted. Right, Mommy?"

There was a long pause. Caleb turned toward the back staircase, wondering how Vanessa would answer that.

Finally, she said, "Most men—this is true. I think Mr. Caleb is the exception. Perhaps."

Wow. Rousing endorsement.

"Because he saved my life?" Kat asked.

"What is this?" Nadia again. "How did Caleb save your life?"

Kat described the moment she almost fell off the float and how Caleb had grabbed her. "I woulda landed right on my head. Mr. Caleb saved me."

"He's like Superman, no?" Nadia said.

Kat giggled. "He's too old to be Superman. Maybe Iron Man?"

Caleb would take that, though Robert Downey, Jr., was at least a decade older than Caleb. To little Kat, they'd both be in the category of *old*.

Nadia said something in Serbian, and Vanessa replied in the same language. He had no idea what they said, but the frustration in Vanessa's voice was evident.

"Well, he is handsome," Nadia said. "This is all I am saying."

Which led to a string of Serbian words Caleb could only guess were all the reasons why Caleb would never be Vanessa's boyfriend.

All he'd done, all he was still doing, and Vanessa still didn't see him as anything more than a friend.

Patience, the Lord whispered.

Not my strong suit.

Like all of My gifts, you'll learn this one through practice.

Great. Something to look forward to.

Vanessa pushed away the half-full plate of Chinese food Caleb had ordered. The meal had been delicious, but she couldn't eat another bite.

Kat, who'd never eaten Chinese, had gobbled up her sesame chicken like a starving girl and was now watching TV in the attached living room.

Nadia was still eating. It was hard to talk and eat at the same time, and Nadia rarely stopped doing the first long enough to focus on the second.

On the far edge of the round table, Caleb was nodding along to Nadia's latest story about her travels. Abbas had taken her to many of the same places he'd taken Vanessa, though Nadia had gone as a companion. Abbas had taken her shopping and out to dinners and to the opera.

Nadia had loved the opera. Tears filled her eyes as she recounted the evening. Nadia was wiser and deeper than Vanessa had first imagined. That she'd been completely fooled by Abbas wasn't that surprising. Very few people knew the depth of Abbas's evil. He kept that side of himself hidden from the world, only brought it out in front of trusted guards and defenseless women. He'd successfully hidden it from Nadia for months, but that wouldn't continue. If Nadia went back to Abbas, now that he had found Vanessa, he would no longer hide his true nature.

Vanessa had to protect her sister. She wouldn't let Nadia endure what she had, not if she could help it. Which meant she'd have to tell her sister everything.

Finally, Nadia took a bite of her chow mien, and Caleb shifted to Vanessa. "Maybe your sister would like to hear about your work."

Nadia swallowed her bite. "Please. I would love to hear of this."

"I manage the food bank," Vanessa said. "We provide groceries to people who cannot afford them."

"I thought everybody in America had money," Nadia said. "There are poor people here?"

"There are poor people everywhere." Her sister's naivety and innocence were almost refreshing. Vanessa forced away the urge to smile. Poverty wasn't something to smile about. "There are many people who have lost their jobs, people who are under-employed."

"This means what?"

"They have jobs, but their jobs don't pay enough to live on. Perhaps they work minimum-wage jobs, or perhaps they make decent money but their expenses are too high. Some have many children. There are single mothers who get no support from their children's fathers. Some have medical bills or expensive prescriptions that eat up their salaries. Some have made poor choices that led to drug addiction, alcohol addiction, gambling addiction. There are many grandparents who are caring for their grandchildren because the parents are in prison or are strung out on drugs."

"I had no idea," Nadia said. "I thought all Americans lived the American dream."

"What I love about this country is that the people are very generous." Vanessa's gaze flicked to Caleb, who gave a half-smile. "People like Caleb and"—she gestured to the house—"Kade and Ginny and many others give not only their money but also their time and resources. Jack, a friend on the food bank's board, helps with maintenance. His wife, Harper, volunteers in the senior center."

"This senior center—this is what?" Nadia asked.

"Just a room where local senior citizens hang out. Harper spends many days there. She makes sure they eat well and are healthy. She plans games and outings, sometimes.

"And then there are others. Angel organizes our community events and provides food that draws a crowd. Her husband is the artist who designed the parade float Kat was telling you about. Rae Thomas often writes about the food bank in the newspaper. Marisa runs a once-a-week class for non-English speakers. Samantha and Kelsey are both regular volunteers at the food bank. Funds are provided by faithful donors, people like Dylan and Chelsea O'Donnell. She owns HCI Clothiers, and even though they don't live in Nutfield, they give generously, as do other local business owners—like Caleb." She nodded his direction. "By the time all of them do what they are good at, I hardly have to do anything."

"That's not true." The look in Caleb's eyes held such admiration, she wanted to turn and see if someone was behind her, someone deserving of it. Caleb, a man who had built a very successful business, was impressed by her little job? "You keep it all running smoothly. You're the one who makes sure there's food on the shelves. You're the one who makes sure the food ends up with the people who need it."

She waved away his words. "Much of our food comes from Caleb's grocery stores."

"And others," he added.

"Generous people, generous companies. I am a small part of a big thing, and it is an honor."

Caleb reached across the table and set his hand on top of hers. Where was the instinct to yank away from him?

"Before we hired you," Caleb said, "the place was a mess. You've transformed it into the best food bank in the state."

"Because of you and everyone else," Vanessa said.

Nadia giggled. "You two are funny, each arguing that the other is better. I would like to see this food bank."

Vanessa pulled her hand away, and Caleb leaned back in his seat. In his eyes, she saw the warning he didn't need to issue. Abbas knew about the food bank. They couldn't go there. "We will see." She stood and gathered dishes.

Caleb started to stand, but she waved him off. "I will do it. You stay and rest."

His smile crinkled his eyes at the corners. "If you insist."

She tempered her answering smile. What was there to smile about?

Really? That voice again, His voice. *You're here with your daughter and your sister. You're safe. There's a man who cares about you. None of that is worth smiling about?*

Da. Perhaps. But Abbas—

Isn't here. Trust Me. Trust this. Practice your smile.

As she rinsed dishes and slid them in the dishwasher, she prayed for help with that last one.

To smile was foolishness. This she'd learned at a very young age, surrounded by poverty and hopelessness and despair. Even before Tata had sent her away, she'd known life was all difficulty and pain. The chaos of the war that had torn her country apart, it had left an indelible mark on her soul. Though she didn't understand even now what they'd been fighting about, she could still smell the death in the air that day she'd gone with her aunt to search for her uncle.

She could see the ruins all around her.

She could feel the dust that filled her lungs, the remains of buildings that no longer stood.

Life was not good.

Yet... she looked out the windows at the lake. The setting sun cast a yellowish glow across the dark waters. The steeple of Vanessa's church rose above the towering trees in the little town on the far side.

This wasn't Serbia. This wasn't a cold wet basement. This wasn't a locked room on a yacht in the middle of the sea.

This was a different world. This was a world of joy and happiness, of people who loved even those who were not lovable. This was a world of happy people and safety.

Could she trust it?

"You all right?" The voice in her ear, the hand on her arm—both should have made her jump.

Her body had decided Caleb wasn't a threat.

Foolishness.

She turned to face him. "Just..."

Smile.

She did, and it felt as natural as the false eyelashes she used to be forced to wear.

Caleb's eyebrows lifted. "What is that? It's almost as if you're happy to see me."

As soon as she tried to wipe the expression off her face, it turned natural. She *was* happy he was there. "I am practicing."

"Smiling?"

"Da."

"Why?"

"Because..." He'd think she was ridiculous if she told him the truth. So be it. "Because God tells me to."

"Oh." He squinted as he studied her. "That makes sense. The joy of the Lord is your strength, right?"

The joy of the Lord? "What is this?"

"It's from the book of Nehemiah."

She leaned against the counter. "This is in the Bible?" She repeated the words in her head again, let them roll around. *The joy of the Lord is your strength. My strength?* "I don't understand. Is it that the Lord's joy gives us strength? Or that we have joy through the Lord, which gives us strength?"

Caleb's mouth pushed to one side. "Hmm. I always assumed the second—that God gives us joy. But why couldn't it be both? I mean, if He gives us joy, then He must also have it. So... yeah."

"How does joy give strength? Joy makes people weak, no? It makes people"—she dipped her head toward her sister, who was sitting beside Kat on the couch, watching TV—"like Nadia. Foolish and trusting."

"You think joy equals weakness?"

"Do you not?"

He dipped his head from side to side. "No. Not at all. I think joy makes people strong."

"People who are happy are fools. Life is hard. What is there to smile about?"

He straightened his shoulders, and his head dipped to one side. "You're in a safe place with your daughter and your sister. You have a full belly. You have a job you love, friends who adore you. Can you think of nothing to be thankful for?"

"I do not... You think I am ungrateful?"

"Uh... yeah. A little bit."

"That is not how I feel. I am very grateful to you for all you've done, to Ginny and Kade. To all the people in this town who've helped me."

"And yet…?"

Ugh. How to explain. How to make him understand. "Where I come from, life is only hard. Things got better for a time, and then the better was snatched away. Bombs fell. People died. Nobody smiled. Nobody was happy. Nobody had… optionism."

"Optimism."

"That is what I said."

She almost made him smile again. She liked to make Caleb smile. That was new. That was… disturbing.

He took her hands, and again, she didn't pull away as she should have. Instead, she let herself enjoy the feeling of warmth and safety.

"Hey, what happened?" he said. "You were almost smiling again."

She couldn't think about how it would all be snatched away. She'd let herself enjoy this moment with this man she was coming to trust, to care for. This man she would leave soon enough.

He lifted her hands and placed them against his chest. She could feel his heartbeat through his T-shirt. Strong and steady. Fast.

"I don't know what you're thinking," he said, "but I need you to know that I will protect you. I'm not going to let anything happen to you."

It wasn't his job, though. She had to take care of herself and her family. She just didn't know how. Or where they would go. Or how she would provide for them. The weight of it settled on her shoulders.

Caleb slid his arms around her back. He pulled her close, and she allowed herself to be enveloped in his embrace. To be taken care of by another person. This *better* would be snatched away soon enough, and she would be alone again.

He ran his hand down her hair, and something stirred in her body, something she'd never felt in the arms of a man. Never felt at all.

She should step away from him, but it was the last thing she wanted to do. This, she didn't understand.

"Vanessa." His whisper was barely audible and carried emotions she'd never heard from a man. Her name sounded beautiful on his tongue.

What did he mean by it? His feelings for her were beyond friendship. This was beyond friendship. This was...

The counter was behind her. She couldn't move. She was trapped.

He must have felt her stiffen because he stepped away. His arms fell to his sides.

She waited for him to apologize, but he didn't. He only watched her.

She didn't know what to say, what to do. Their embrace had been so lovely. It had made her hope for foolish things that could never be.

"That cannot happen again."

"It was only a hug," he said.

But it wasn't only a hug. "I told you, I am not interested—"

"You told me."

"You should not... If you knew who I truly am, you would not want..." She waved at the space between them as if it held the end of her sentence.

He dropped his head and kneaded his neck. When he met her eyes again, his were dulled with pain. He attempted a smile, but this one did not make his eyes crinkle. "You're a woman who loves God enough to smile when He tells you to. You're a woman who lets your daughter ride on a parade float even when you're terrified of it yourself."

"A mistake. She almost fell off it."

He ignored her interruption. "You're a woman who gives your cell phone number to clients when you think they might be in danger. You're a woman who is risking everything to protect a sister she hasn't seen in years. I know who you are, Vanessa. I like who you are."

"You do not—"

"Wherever you came from, it doesn't matter. I care about—"

"Do not!" She gasped and realized she'd been holding her breath during his little speech. Now, she felt as if she'd run a mile. She forced herself to inhale, exhale. "You do not know me. You cannot know me and care for me."

"I can. I do."

"You must stop."

"You don't care for me? Not even a little."

"I do not."

His Adam's apple bobbed. He stared at her, maybe waiting for her to change her mind. But she said nothing.

She let the lie stand.

She did care for him.

She should know better than to trust him. He was a man like all the rest.

Really? The Lord whispered. *All the rest? Have you not met other good men?*

All the men who'd helped her after Kat was born. Eric and Kelsey had taken her in. Nate had found her an attorney. Garrison had located the home for former human trafficking victims and gotten her a place there. Brady had fought for her when the DA had wanted to charge her with murder.

More good men had come into her life since then. Jack, Kade, Dylan, Garrison—all of these had proved to be good men.

And now Caleb, who was the best of the lot.

But the truth stuck in her throat.

Caleb swiveled and walked into the living room, where he fell into a chair and stared at the TV.

CHAPTER TWENTY-ONE

"Time for bed, little one." Vanessa kept to the edge of the living room, avoiding Caleb's scrutiny. Not that it worked. Though the sun had set beyond the wall of windows, nobody had flicked on any lamps. The TV and the dim light over the bar in the kitchen were the only sources of light.

"Please, can I stay up just a little later?"

Vanessa wasn't in the mood to argue. "You say good-night to Mr. Caleb and Aunt Nadia and go upstairs to your bedroom, or there will be no TV tomorrow."

Her daughter huffed but stood. Her little arms snaked around Nadia's neck. "Night-night."

"Have pretty dreams, da?"

"You, too." She turned to Caleb, who bent forward and tapped his cheek.

"Plant one right there."

Vanessa opened her mouth to protest, then clamped her lips shut as Kat kissed his cheek.

He took her hands. "May the Lord bless you and keep you tonight, little Kat."

Oh. His simple blessing, sweet and reverent, had Vanessa's thoughts in chaos.

Kat giggled. "You too, Mr. Caleb. 'Night!"

Kat barreled up the stairs. How could she still be so filled with energy? Vanessa wanted only to drop in bed. Her head pounded. Her throat hurt—though she blamed that on Abbas and the bruises she'd hidden behind a turtleneck. But Nadia needed to know about Abbas, and she needed to know now. Otherwise, Vanessa couldn't trust her sister not to tell the man where they were.

After listening to Kat read her a chapter, barely hearing her at all, Vanessa prayed over her and then said, "I will be in the next room. You can go through the hallway or through the bathroom to find me if you get scared. Okay?"

"Why would I be scared? You're here and Aunt Nadia is here and Mr. Caleb is here, too. There's nothing to be afraid of."

Vanessa envied her daughter's confidence. At least she hadn't passed her fears on to Katarina. At least she'd done that one thing right. "I love you, sweet *ceri.*"

"Love you, too, Mommy."

Vanessa closed her daughter's door and stood in the hallway, praying for a tiny bit of her daughter's confidence and courage. After descending the rear staircase, which Caleb had shown them earlier, she found Nadia and Caleb in the living room, watching TV. A doctor show, based on all the people wearing scrubs.

Nadia seemed enthralled with the program. Her sister... She still couldn't believe she was here. Last she'd seen her, Nadia had been four years old, Vanessa's little shadow. She was the giggliest little thing, always goofing around, always smiling. Though the little girl had disappeared and this grown woman had emerged—a woman who looked so much like Vanessa had at her age, it was eerie—she was happy and carefree in a way

Vanessa had never been. Even as a child, Vanessa had been the responsible one, caring for her siblings, trying to make everybody happy in their cramped home overflowing with people.

Vanessa perched on the sofa beside her. "Do you mind if we turn this off? I would like to talk to you."

"We can pause it." Nadia snatched the remote.

The room turned darker, and too quiet. Too exposed.

How she wished for something to hide behind or somewhere to run. Caleb stood. "I guess I'll go—"

"I would like for you to stay."

His eyebrows shot to his hairline. "I thought you were going to tell Nadia about—"

"I would like for you to hear. It will help you understand."

He sank into his chair and propped his forearms on his thighs.

She couldn't look at him.

Nadia touched her arm. "What is it?"

"I was ten when I left. You were four. Do you remember much from back then?"

"I remember you used to play games with me and make me laugh."

Vanessa pulled away from her sister's hand and rose. "When I went away, where did Tata tell you I went?"

Nadia tilted her head to the side. "He said you got an opportunity to study at some fancy school, and it would be selfish for us not to let you go, even though we all missed you terribly."

School. It was so far from the truth... *Oh, Tata. What lies did you tell yourself? What lies did you tell Mama?*

"There was no school."

"Of course there was." Nadia glanced at Caleb, and Vanessa couldn't help but do the same. His lips were pressed together, his eyes locked onto her with a palpable intensity.

"In France, right?" Nadia said. "You went to France?"

"I don't know what he thought would happen to me," Vanessa said. "I cannot believe that he understood what he was doing. Maybe he really did think I would be educated. Maybe he—"

"What are you saying?" Nadia asked.

Vanessa couldn't face her sister. And she couldn't face Caleb. She stared out the windows at the dark lake below. "Tata, he..." *Please, help me. I don't know how to do this.* She waited, tried to feel God's presence. He was with her. He'd been with her all along. "I was sold."

"What? No! He would never—"

"I was there, Nadia. I know what happened. Tata gave me to a man, and the man gave Tata a handful of bills. Big bills." As she said the words, the memory came back to her, a memory she'd buried years before.

That morning, Mama had dressed her in her nicest dress, a white dress they'd been given by a neighbor. It had pretty lace on the sleeves. Vojislava had only owned one pair of shoes, but Mama told her she wouldn't need those and gave her thick socks to wear. She'd laughed at her image—the pretty dress and the ugly black socks.

And then Tata had taken her. The place was fuzzy. They were outside in the gray early morning light. There was a building nearby, but they never went in, only stood in the cold air until a man showed up. Somewhere beyond the mist, there'd been a loud hammering, a pounding of metal against metal. She could hear that pounding even now.

The man gripped Vojislava's arm with a hot and sweaty hand, and the scents of cooked onions and vodka surrounded him like a fog.

Tata had crouched before her, brushed her hair out of her face, and kissed her forehead. "Forgive me."

And then, he walked away.

"It is a lie." Nadia's words were vicious, her expression filled with fury.

Vanessa closed her eyes. *Lord, if she doesn't believe that, then she won't believe anything I tell her.*

"Nadia." At Caleb's deep voice, Vanessa glanced over her shoulder.

Her sister faced him.

"Just let your sister tell her story."

Nadia sat back on the sofa and crossed her arms.

Vanessa perched on the chair opposite Caleb's. Without looking at either of them, she started at the beginning.

The man who smelled like onions and vodka delivered her to another man, this one tall and skinny. Vojislava couldn't remember his face. His scent—like pine and cigarettes—was always with him. He took her to his bed that night. When she fought him, he put her in a closet in the basement, where she sat on the concrete floor, legs pulled to her chest. There was no room to stretch out. Water seeped down the walls. Insects crawled on her skin, but there was no light to see them. She longed for someone—anyone. Beyond the silence, there was screaming and crying. The sounds of more girls. She didn't know why they were crying and wished to go to them. Maybe she could help. Maybe if she could help them, she would not think about herself.

She covered her ears and prayed for Mama to come. She prayed Tata would rescue her. But he didn't come.

Nobody came.

She didn't know how much time passed. She had no bathroom, had no choice but to soil the pretty dress Mama had put her in. Many times she soiled it before the door finally opened.

She was called filthy, shoved into a shower, and told to clean herself. When she was brought back to the man's room, she did what he said and didn't fight. Then she was given clean clothes and food and a blanket and pillow. She was returned to the basement, but this time to a larger room where other girls were held, most older than she, a few younger. Always, someone was crying. In the beginning, Vojislava was the one who couldn't stem the tears.

The girls huddled together for warmth, then fought over the meager food and water. There was nothing to do, nothing to look at, nothing to play with. There were only bugs and rats and wet walls and cold floor.

When her stomach would gnaw at her, when her eyes were so dry she couldn't form tears, she would pray to be let out of the room.

And then, the man would come.

She would be brought upstairs to a bedroom. If she was very, very good, they would give her food and water. At first, it had been hard to be very, very good. She would cry. She would try to escape. But she learned that fighting only brought pain and hunger and thirst.

She learned quickly. She was no fool.

How long she stayed there, she didn't know. She never thought to mark the days and wouldn't have known when they passed, since there were no windows in the basement. No light except what came from under the doorway. Only cold and hot told her the weather outside and marked the seasons. Girls came, girls went. Some girls died, and their bodies lay on the floor for days before they were taken away, usually with a warning.

"This is what happens when you don't obey. Do what you're told, and you'll survive. Don't, and the birds will pick at your bones."

Vojislava only knew she didn't want to be carried out as a corpse. She didn't want birds to pick at her bones.

So, she did what she was told. She learned to be very, very good.

And she got out of the room more. She ate more. She drank more. She grew taller until the dress she'd been given when she arrived no longer fit her. She was given a new dress and a new name. She was no longer Vojislava Bakočević. When she was asked, she was told to tell her captors her name was Maria.

"Like the virgin Mary, eh?" The tall man had laughed and laughed at that.

But she did what she was told, because she was very, very good.

And then, she was sold again, taken from that place, put in the trunk of a car, and driven far away. Out of Belgrade. Out of Serbia.

The next thing she knew, she was taken into a luxury hotel on the coast of the sea. The Mediterranean, she knew now, but at the time, she'd only known the water was very pretty and she was very ugly.

She was left in a hotel room with a stern woman and a lot of other girls. She was cleaned and scrubbed, the stern woman tsk-tsking over the dirt and grime under her fingernails, calling her a filthy little girl. She put something thick and gooey into Vojisla-va's hair, then picked through it, swearing at the bugs that had crawled all over the girls in that basement. Hours it took the woman to pull out all the bugs, yanking at little Vojislava's scalp and swearing all the while and threatening to shave it off if Vojislava moved.

Vojislava had learned long before never to complain. She sat still and let the woman do the work.

And then, she and the other girls were taken to another room, where they stood in front of a bunch of men who spoke strange languages and watched them with hungry eyes.

Cigarette smoke hung in a haze. The men held glasses with dark liquid. As the liquid went down, the men got louder. Some tried to touch the girls, but the stern woman would slap their hands away.

The man who bought Vojislava wasn't one of those trying to touch. He had blond hair and fair skin and blue eyes, and he told her to keep her mouth shut as he took her out of the hotel and put her in the backseat of a car.

Maybe he would take her home to Mama. Maybe this man was a good man. He hadn't made her show she was a very, very good girl. He'd given her food and drink and told her to sleep, for the drive was long.

For the first time in forever and ever, Vojislava was almost alone. She had a blanket of her own. She was on a soft seat. She slept and slept for hours and hours.

When she awoke, she was pulled out of the car, fed a meal, and sent to the bathroom in a roadside restaurant. "Brush your hair and your teeth. You want to look your best for your new friend."

A friend. She was afraid to believe there would be a friend, but a little part of her hoped. She made herself as pretty as she could.

And then the blond man drove some more until they stopped at a marina. Pretty boats bobbed everywhere.

She wanted to believe there was really a new friend, but her stomach knew something her brain didn't want to acknowledge. She didn't want to go on a boat and float farther away from her home.

A man with dark curly hair and dark skin approached the blond man. A handful of bills was passed over.

She was sold again.

Abbas smiled when he held out his hand to her. She slid

hers into it and smiled in return while he walked her onto his yacht and showed her around.

He made her show him that she was a very, very good girl.

But he made it clear that she would never be good enough.

CHAPTER TWENTY-TWO

"You are a liar."

Nadia's words, uttered low and angry, barely seeped through Caleb's consciousness.

His hands held his head up, his fingers gripped his hair. His eyes burned for want of tears.

The story was too real, too graphic, to be anything but true. That Vanessa had endured all that...

"I know you don't wish to believe," Vanessa said, "But you must—"

"I won't listen any longer."

A string of Serbian words had Caleb tuning out. Vanessa had bared her soul, and Nadia—foolish, vapid Nadia—refused to believe.

It took all his self-control not to stand up and force Nadia out on her skinny, stupid rear end. To take Vanessa in his arms and promise to protect her until his final heartbeat.

But the images she'd put in his mind were too vivid. He wavered between the desire to comfort her and the desire to hunt Abbas and the other men down.

And murder them all.

Then to find Vanessa's father and every other man—and woman—who'd hurt her, and murder them, too.

Vanessa's voice rose above her sister's, and the Serbian shifted back to English with, "You are a coward, afraid to hear the truth."

"As if I'd ever believe the word of a whore."

Caleb was on his feet in an instant. He took two long steps and stopped inches in front of Nadia, hands clenched at his sides to keep from touching her. "Get your things. You're leaving."

"No! She cannot." Vanessa grabbed his arm in a hard grip. "He will do to her—"

"At least she'll know you were telling the truth."

"Caleb, no." The tears in Vanessa's voice had him turning her way. He'd never seen her cry. Even when she'd recounted the story moments before, her voice had been flat, her face expressionless. Now, her cheeks were flushed, her eyes rimmed in red. Her bottom lip quivered.

He turned back to Nadia. "You will not use that word in my presence. Do you understand?"

"I do not wish to hear any more."

He glanced again at Vanessa, who pleaded with her eyes. He looked up, prayed for help.

He was angry, furious, by all he'd heard. He couldn't think straight. *Patience.* When he felt he could be kind, he returned his gaze to Nadia. "Sit down and let your sister finish her story. It's the least you can do."

"I owe her nothing." But Nadia plopped back onto the couch and crossed her arms.

Caleb turned to Vanessa. "You okay?"

She waved him back to his chair, and he sat with his hands clasped between his knees.

Vanessa stood over her sister. "You owe me nothing," she

said. "Only that, because of what I endured, you ate. The money Tata got when he sold me put food in your belly and clothes on your back."

"There was always food," Nadia said. "You lie even about that."

"You were a child. You didn't go hungry because I did."

"Lies."

Vanessa perched on the edge of her chair and dropped her face in her hands. This courageous woman seemed defeated.

"Tata would never sell you," Nadia said. "He cried for you, every night after you left. He and Mama cried."

Fresh tears filled Vanessa's eyes. "How did they explain that I never came home?"

She shrugged. "I do not remember."

"If I'd been at school, then I would have come home for summers, yes? I would have come home for Christmas. Where did they—?"

"I do not remember! I only know Lukas would cry for you, and they would say you were gone. Gone. But they never said where, only that you went to school in France."

"A pretty lie."

"I will call Tata right now. I will—"

"No!" Vanessa's eyes bulged at the phone in Nadia's hand.

It was such an odd reaction, Caleb went to her side. "What is it?"

"The idea that they are right there"—she nodded to the phone—"on the other end of the phone. That I could call them. I have never... I never thought to try to contact them."

"You are a liar. You are afraid—"

"Shut your mouth." Caleb didn't feel a bit sorry for the anger in his tone. He turned back to Vanessa. "What do you need? What can I do to make this easier for you?"

She waved a hand toward her sister. "She does not believe."

Lord, what now? Give Vanessa wisdom. Open Nadia's eyes and heart to her sister.

"I think her distrust makes sense." Why Caleb had said that, he couldn't explain. Especially at the spark of anger in Vanessa's eyes. If he'd been tinder, he'd have burst into flames. "She doesn't know you. She's spent..." He turned to Nadia. "How long have you known Abbas?"

"We met in February."

"Seven months." Caleb reached toward Vanessa, knowing she'd slap his hand away. But when it connected with hers, she didn't react. "She's known you for a couple of hours. She trusts Abbas. He hasn't shown her that side of himself. And she believes she's in love with him."

"I do love him. And he loves me." Nadia's voice came from behind Caleb, but he didn't take his eyes off Vanessa.

"Just give her a minute to catch up."

Vanessa looked defeated, stricken, he longed to pull her into his arms. After a moment, she nodded. "Da. You are right. As always." She looked past Caleb to her sister. "Can I tell you more about Abbas?"

Nadia shrugged. "I will not believe you."

Caleb resumed his seat and braced for the rest of the story.

"You have never seen that side of Abbas?" Vanessa asked. "Never seen the flash of anger in his eyes."

"He is always kind to me."

She nodded slowly. "Have you ever looked in the bottom drawer of his bureau?"

She shrugged. Which wasn't a no. What did that mean?

"You have seen his things, then? The..." She glanced at Caleb, swallowed. "You know what I mean?"

"You want me to leave?" he asked.

Vanessa said nothing, just watched her sister.

Nadia shrugged again. "He said they were for fun."

"He has had fun with them with you?"

"No!" Another flash of fury from Nadia had Caleb wondering what they were talking about.

Vanessa spoke in Serbian, her words gentle. Nadia answered her with anger, pointing her finger at her sister.

Vanessa lifted both hands. "You believe what you want to believe. But you know it is truth."

Nadia turned to Caleb. "You know what she talks about?"

"It's okay. I don't need—"

"Chains and handcuffs and disgusting things. Abbas and I do not do those things. We make love."

Caleb's stomach turned, and he swallowed. Swallowed again. This was more than he could handle. *Lord, what am I supposed to do with this? Why am I hearing this about the woman who will be my bride?*

Though no answer came, he knew one thing. God had been there. God had seen it all. As painful as this was for Caleb to hear, he couldn't imagine how the heart of God had grieved for His daughter. The tears Caleb couldn't shed clogged his throat.

Then why? Why did You let it happen?

There was no answer to that. There never was, or maybe the answer was always the same. When given a choice, men choose evil over and over again. The greatest depth of evil.

Vanessa sat beside her sister on the sofa. "I am glad Abbas hasn't shown you his true nature. But he was not like that with me." She met Caleb's eyes. "Will you please turn on the lamp?"

He didn't know what she was doing, but he flicked on the lamp on the end table beside Nadia.

Vanessa lifted her sister's hand and placed it against her temple.

Oh, yeah. The bump. "You feel that?"

"Da."

"Abbas did that today. In your hotel room."

"More lies." But she didn't sound as confident as she had before.

Vanessa pushed down the turtleneck and lifted her chin, pressing fingers against the bruises there.

Caleb angled the light to better highlight the bruises, the sight of which made his heart pound. They were darker now, the fingerprints evident on her pale skin.

"And he did this," Vanessa said. "And he told me that if I called out, he would kill me and use you as he had me until you were shattered, and then he would kill you."

Nadia touched her own neck.

Caleb set the lamp back down, resumed his seat, and waited for Nadia to say something.

"I do not..." She swallowed. "I do not want to believe you."

Vanessa took her sister's hand. "I don't blame you. It is an ugly truth about a man you care for."

"Two men," Nadia said. "Abbas and..."

"Tata."

The word held in the silent room. Their father had done this. Their father had sacrificed his own daughter.

How desperate must he have been?

There was no level of desperation that justified what he'd done.

Nadia stood. "I must think. I cannot process it. I cannot..."

Vanessa stood and pulled her sister into a hug. "I understand." Nadia seemed stiff in her sister's arms, but at least she didn't reject her.

Caleb crossed the room to the sisters and held out his hand to Nadia. "Give me your phone."

She backed up. "What? No."

"You want to call him, right? You want to hear from his own mouth that your sister is lying—or even to confirm her story. You feel like Abbas has the right to defend himself."

"He does."

"Maybe. But you're not calling him tonight. Not from this house. Give me your phone."

Nadia looked at Vanessa, then back at him. She gripped her phone against her chest as if she held a favorite child. "I will not."

Caleb didn't take his eyes off Nadia when he said, "Vanessa, grab your sister's things and bring them downstairs."

"She can't go back—"

"I'll take her elsewhere. I'll find her a hotel. If she wants to call Abbas, she can call him from there."

Vanessa didn't move.

Caleb wasn't kidding.

Nadia said, "I won't call him tonight."

"Give me your phone."

"Caleb," Vanessa said, "you're being unreasonable."

Rage he'd been tamping down for an hour rose, turned everything red. He closed his eyes, prayed for patience, remembered God's promise that he'd get a lot of practice with that particular fruit of the Spirit. This was too much, too much to ask. He turned on Vanessa. "You risked your life to save her. You risked everything for this..." He forced himself not to utter the adjectives that came to mind. Silly, stupid, foolish, brainless... "This sister. A few minutes ago, she told us she loves Abbas. Do you really trust her not to tell him where you are?"

Vanessa's gaze flicked between them. "I...I think so."

"He's a manipulator and a liar. Nadia doesn't know this about him yet. She's still processing." He didn't glance at her sister to see her reaction. He didn't care. "Your daughter is here, Vanessa. Are you willing to take the chance?" Without waiting for an answer, he turned back to Nadia. "Get your things. I'll take you back to Boston."

"You will not!" Vanessa said.

"I won't..." His voice was too loud. He wouldn't shout. He wouldn't lose control. Not now when he needed it so badly. He lowered his voice and started again. "I am not Abbas. I don't keep women against their will. If she wants to go—"

"But she doesn't understand," Vanessa said.

"Nadia is a grown woman. She can go where she wishes." He turned back to Nadia. "Eventually, you'll know your sister was right. You'll wish you'd stayed. But if you must, feel free to learn the hard way."

"No. Nadia, please don't leave."

Vanessa would never forgive him if he returned Nadia to Abbas. But at least she'd be safe.

"Please stay," Vanessa said.

"I can keep my phone?"

Vanessa pressed her lips together, glanced at Caleb. "I will not risk Kat's life. Caleb is right. You must give him your phone."

Nadia glared at him, glared at Vanessa. And then, she slapped the phone into Caleb's waiting hand and stormed up the stairs.

CHAPTER TWENTY-THREE

Vanessa gazed at the starry night, hoping the chill would blow away the memories. She hugged herself against the cool breeze.

Behind her, the sliding glass door opened and closed. She didn't have to turn to know who'd stepped out.

"I heard the alarm disengage," he said. "Figured I'd find you out here."

A moment later, a blanket draped over her shoulders. She pulled it close. "Thank you."

He stood beside her, hands in his pockets. Earlier, he'd seemed eager to touch her. But since she'd told her story...

She shouldn't have been surprised, certainly shouldn't have been disappointed. That's why she'd asked him to stay, after all. Because he'd needed to know how unsuitable she was for him. He'd needed to understand how very damaged she was. Damaged beyond repair.

He leaned his hip against the railing that surrounded the patio, facing her. "Thank you for trusting me with your past."

She shrugged. "Now you understand."

"Yeah." His voice hitched. She'd been so intent on

convincing Nadia that she'd almost forgotten Caleb was in the room. And then she'd seen him. His head had been down, his fingers yanking at his hair. As if her words physically injured him.

When he'd looked up, she'd seen the starkness of his eyes.

At least he believed her.

"How old were you when you went to Abbas?" he asked now, his voice low in the silent evening.

She shrugged. "Two winters passed when I was in the basement. I think twelve. Maybe not quite."

His arms came around her, and he pulled her close.

She was so surprised, she didn't even react. Didn't react when his hand trailed down her back, when his other hand pressed the back of her head against his sweatshirt.

"I'm sorry."

"You did not—"

"For all of it. Sorry you went through it. Sorry I never understood. Sorry I was ever impatient with you, or demanding. Sorry I can't fix it now. Sorry I was rude to your sister, even though..."

Even though Nadia didn't understand and could very easily have put Vanessa in danger. Nadia was a soft spot, a spot Abbas would use to destroy Vanessa if given the chance.

But the threat of Abbas felt distant here in Caleb's arms. She felt safe.

And that he would still hold her... did it mean he could still care for her? How, when he knew her past?

He backed up and looked down at her. "Do you want to tell me the rest of the story?"

Did she? She'd only ever told the whole thing once. Would he reject her when he knew the worst of her, the ugliest truths?

"You don't have to," he said. "I only thought that, since you're already raw, you might as well finish it."

"You want to hear it?"

"I want to know everything."

"Why?"

His lips nearly turned up in a smile. He brushed her hair away from her face and kissed her forehead. "I care about you, Vanessa. A great deal."

She tried to back away from his embrace. At first, he held on. And then, maybe remembering all she'd been through, his hands dropped to his sides. "I'm sorry. I'm asking too much."

"I don't understand. You should find me... ugly now."

"Why? Because you were abused, I'm supposed to blame you?"

"You don't understand."

"Then tell me the rest of it. Maybe I will."

"And then you won't care for me anymore."

His half-smile surprised her. "Don't count on that, sweetheart."

Sweetheart? This was a pet name, a name for one you cared for—a child, a spouse. Nobody had ever called her sweetheart. Did he say it as a joke? Was it sarcastic?

"You want to sit down? Or go back inside?"

"The blanket is warm. I will stay out in the pretty night, if you don't mind."

Gently, he walked her to a wicker loveseat that overlooked the lake. They sat, and he draped the blanket over both of them.

It was perfect, this night with this man beside her. If she were a different kind of woman, she might find it romantic.

But instead, she would tell her story, and Caleb would certainly retreat, though he'd be kind about it. She would not be his sweetheart. She would not be his anything but friend. And this was okay because the part of her heart that might have loved a man had been torn out many years before.

"How did you get away from Abbas?"

"This is the story I fear he has discovered, though I don't know how he could have."

Caleb put his arm around her and pulled her close. The blanket was warm, his body warmer, and she allowed herself to enjoy the embrace.

"I went with him to a high stakes poker game. I was... decoration, I suppose. I was not allowed to speak. He often traveled with guards, they were on either side of me, as if they were protecting me. Truly, they protected him and kept me from getting away. They were nearly as vicious as..." She stopped. She didn't need to tell him the details.

"There were many men in this game, but at the end, it was only Abbas and his opponent, a Latino man named Carlos. Carlos kept catching my eye. I think he found me attractive. At one point, he scowled at the guards. It seemed he saw through the farce, knew they were there to keep me in line. At one point, he suggested Abbas allow me to sit down. I had been standing like a... like those plastic people in department stores. A man-of-kin."

"Mannequin."

"That is what I said."

She knew if she looked at his face, she'd see no smile there.

"Abbas said I was fine, that I liked to stand, and I could see in Carlos's eyes that he understood that it was not true.

"Because I was behind Abbas, I could see his cards. I had watched him play many hands of poker, and I understood the game. When he was..." What was the word for it? Yes, she thought... "When he was bluffing, I showed it on my face. I don't know how Carlos knew how to understand what I was showing, but he did. He won hand after hand until Abbas had no chips left. It was foolish on my part. He was meaner when he lost. But I hated him. I thought that, when we were back on the yacht, I would tell him what I did, tell him that I'd made him fail, made him look foolish to the Latino man. I hoped he would lose his temper and kill me and throw me in the sea, and then..." Her words trailed when she felt Caleb stiffen beside her.

She whispered, "Forgive me. That is too much information."

"No." He held her tighter. "I'm just... It's fine. Go on."

"But then, Carlos did something I did not expect. When Abbas was out of chips, Carlos suggested Abbas put me in the... bowl."

"The pot?" Caleb shifted to look at her face, and she missed the warmth of his body against hers. In the dim light, she couldn't see what was in his eyes. "He added you like... like a poker chip?"

"Abbas was never one to back down from a challenge. And I knew, if Abbas won that bet, I would be the one to pay. So, I made sure Carlos won."

"And Abbas gave you up?"

"Just like that, I was no longer his property."

"You were *never* his property. People cannot be owned. People cannot be bought and sold and..." He settled her against his side again. "I'm sorry. What happened then?"

"Carlos asked me my name—something Abbas had never done. All the years I was with him, he never once called me anything but whore."

Caleb stiffened at the word.

"Sorry. I know you don't like this word."

"It's not the word that offends me, Vanessa. It's that anybody would dare hang that label on you."

She took a moment to absorb that before she continued. "He asked my name, and I told him the truth—I was Vojislava Bakočević. He said he liked my name but suggested I change it to Vanessa Baker, something more Western. I agreed, and from then on, I have been Vanessa.

"From the very beginning, Carlos was different. He was

kind to me. He never hurt me. I learned quickly, though, that he was in the same business as the people my father had sold me to. He was in Europe to purchase girls, and I did not wish to be one of the girls he sold by the hour. So..."

She didn't want to tell Caleb the rest. Better him think she was always the abused, never the abuser.

He squeezed her shoulders. "It's okay. You survived."

"Da. Survived. I made myself... difficult to live without. Important in his business. I helped him train the girls. I managed his business for him. I became no better than he was. And I convinced myself that I was an equal. He taught me how to drive, and he gave me a car, but I never went anywhere that there weren't guards behind me, watching me. I was still on a leash. It was longer, but it was still a leash. I was still property.

"Carlos was trying to find a woman he'd known years before, believing her to have become pregnant with his child. All the time I knew him, he was searching for that woman and child. That search brought us to Nutfield." She didn't tell Caleb who that woman was, who that child was. That was not Vanessa's story to tell. "At the time we learned where the woman and child were, I discovered I was pregnant. I was afraid that his first child would usurp mine, but also, I knew I had to help Carlos to keep his loyalty. So, I did. And then, I learned that it was not only the child he wanted but also the woman. And... it is a very long story. He was going to kill the woman, and I didn't care about that. I only cared that he didn't love me. Had never loved me. I shot him. I killed him."

She could still feel the cold steel in her hands, the power that coursed through her as the first bullet ripped through Carlos's body. The desire to empty the gun into him. A bullet for every man who'd ever put his hands on her. There'd never be enough bullets to make up for what Carlos and Abbas and the man who smelled of pine and cigarettes and her own father had done to her. Never.

"Kat's father is dead?"

"Da."

"It was self-defense."

"After Kat was born, after I knew I could never support myself or care for my daughter without help, I turned myself in. I thought maybe the woman Carlos had been after and her husband, maybe they would take my baby if I went to jail. They were good people, and I was desperate. And I met people here in town, and they helped me. They got me a lawyer, who argued I'd fired in defense of another. I didn't go to prison, even though I wasn't trying to save the woman. Only to avenge what had been done to me, and to protect my child. When the DA wanted to charge me with crimes related to Carlos's business, the lawyer argued something called Stockholm syndrome. When I had first killed him, I had called the police and given a tip to turn in his right-hand man. Again, I did it not to protect anybody but myself. I knew he would always be against me. When I turned myself in, they took into account that I had made that call, which had led to his arrest and, ultimately, to the dismantling of Carlos's business. Many girls were saved and returned to their families. But honestly, I did not care about that. I should have. That I didn't tells you what a terrible person I'd become. What a selfish, evil—"

"Stockholm syndrome. Do you know what it is?"

"That a victim will begin to trust her captor. I did not see myself as a captive, though."

"But you were, right? You couldn't leave Carlos."

"I didn't try. He saved me."

"From Satan incarnate."

"This is true."

"You felt like you owed Carlos. You felt gratitude for another man who hurt you, who used you."

"I am ashamed of this. Of all I did for him. Of all I didn't do to help those girls. This, I can never make up for. I can never fix. I tell myself that these sins, Jesus took to the cross. That I am forgiven. I forget, and then I remember again, over and over. But I cannot forgive myself."

"Vanessa." Caleb held her away from him to look at her face. "Sweet Vanessa, you were trying to survive. After all you'd been through—"

"How do you still look at me like that? Do you not understand what I say? I was as bad as Carlos. I helped him. I was a monster. Evil. I was…"

He pressed his fingers over her lips. "Don't. I don't see that person when I look at you. I see this one." He slid his finger over her eyebrow, down her cheek, across her lips. "I see a beautiful daughter of the Most High. I see a woman saved and redeemed, a woman who loves the Lord, loves her child, loves those who need a hand up. I see a woman saved by grace, accepted into the family of God, redeemed and forgiven."

Tears burned her eyes. "You are a fool."

"No." He wiped her tears with his fingertips. Gently, slowly, he lowered his face until she could feel his breath on her lips. "I see you, Vanessa. Vojislava Bakočević. I see you."

There was no answer. No words came. Because he was supposed to be repulsed by her now. He was supposed to move away.

But he only moved closer.

"May I kiss you?"

She had never been asked. She should push him away, try harder to make him understand how damaged she was. But all she wanted was to feel his tenderness on her lips. Her nod was slight, but he caught it.

His lips brushed hers.

Her body tingled from her head to her toes. How could one slight touch of the lips bring such a response?

He waited, maybe thinking she'd push him away. But she did not. Neither did she move forward. She stayed frozen, hoping he'd kiss her again, feeling guilty for hoping it, feeling things she should not feel.

And then, he did, his lips moving against hers in the most gentle manner. Not demanding. Not expecting.

His fingers slid into the hair at the back of her neck, and pleasure filled her every pore. Pleasure she'd never known could exist at a man's touch.

Before she was ready, he ended the kiss and wrapped her in an embrace.

His heart beat beneath her ear, strong and fast.

His sigh blew against her hair. "Thank you for trusting me."

She didn't know what to say. *Thank you for kissing me. For still wanting to kiss me, even though you know the truth.*

He touched his lips to her head and then angled back to look at her. "Promise me you won't build your walls again overnight?"

Her walls. Already, they were trying to strengthen. Already, she was afraid of Caleb. But he was not to be feared. "Da. I will try."

He smiled, and his teeth shone in the moonlight. "Good. It's not fun working to tear them down over and over."

"But if tomorrow you wake up and are sorry for..." She indicated the narrow space between them. "Promise me you will tell me. I will understand."

He swallowed. "I can easily make that promise because I know it won't happen. What I feel for you isn't that fleeting."

"How do you know?"

"You're just going to have to trust me a little more."

She laid her head against his chest again. Trust him. This, she was learning she could do.

CHAPTER TWENTY-FOUR

Caleb was adding eggs to a mixing bowl when Kat skidded into the kitchen on sock feet. "Good morning, Mr. Caleb!" She hugged his waist, and he couldn't help but look to see if Vanessa had caught it. The girl who wasn't allowed to hug men had gotten too comfortable with him. Not that he minded, but he feared her mother would. Fortunately, Vanessa wasn't downstairs yet.

Kat climbed onto a barstool. "Mommy says I don't have to go to school today because my Aunt Nadia is here. She said we're gonna do something fun."

"Did she say what?"

"No." Kat's little feet tapped against the island. "I wanna go on the lake, but Mommy said not to count on that."

Vanessa rounded the corner from the stairs. "Because we don't have a boat and it is too cold to swim."

"I know, but maybe Mr. Caleb has a boat." She turned to Caleb. "Do you?"

"I'm sorry, I don't. Kade might. I could—"

"We do not need to go on a boat today," Vanessa said. "It would be too chilly, no?"

Kat scowled at her mother, but the expression didn't hold as she turned to Caleb. "Whatcha doing?"

"Making breakfast. You hungry?"

"I don't like eggs."

Vanessa said, "Don't be rude, *ceri*. You will eat what you are given."

Caleb whisked the ingredients in his bowl. "Good thing I'm not making eggs, huh?"

"Looks like eggs."

He poured milk into the bowl. "I'm making French toast." The groceries he'd ordered the night before had been delivered earlier that morning, so he'd had plenty of choices. "This happens to be my favorite breakfast in the world."

Kat turned to her mother. "Have I ever had French toast?"

"I don't think so." She looked at Caleb, and a small smile formed on her lips, a smile she didn't force away.

Caleb wanted to pump a fist in victory. No walls, and a smile? Things were looking up.

"Mommy doesn't know how to cook," Kat said. "She only knows how to warm things up. Right, Mommy?"

"I never was taught to cook. I have not had much time to learn, but I have figured out a few things."

"Like?" Caleb asked.

"We eat spaghetti, yes?" She slid onto a barstool beside her daughter. "And I can fry a hamburger on the stove."

"Mommy makes good chili dogs."

Vanessa chuckled. An honest to goodness chuckle. Caleb had to turn to the stovetop to hide his wide grin. He checked the heat on the skillet, then added a dollop of butter to the pan.

"It is hot dogs, buns, and canned chili."

"And cheese on top," Kat said. "I like cheese on mine. They're really good, but you have to eat them with a fork because they're messy."

Caleb looked at Vanessa behind him. "You ever make chili from scratch?"

"From scratch? This means with only ingredients and no cans, yes?"

"Well... Not *no* cans. I use canned tomatoes and canned beans. But basically, yeah."

"This, I never do. I would like to learn someday to make chili, but between work and school and homework, there is little time for learning to cook. And little energy in the evenings."

Caleb gestured Vanessa around the island. "Come on. I'll teach you to make French toast right now, and tonight, I'll teach you to make chili." He'd have to order the ingredients, or maybe they could go to the grocery store together and pick them up. He was already looking forward to it.

Vanessa stood beside him, looking from the egg-and-milk mixture to the skillet. "I will ruin it."

"Nah, you got this. You've got a master chef teaching you."

"You are master?"

He laughed. "Not exactly, but I do like to eat." He dropped the first slice of challah bread into the egg mixture, turned it with a fork, and then added it to the skillet, where it sizzled and popped. He turned the heat down just a tad. "I use challah because it's denser and holds up better to the mixture. And it doesn't get soggy. I can't stand soggy French toast."

Vanessa nodded along, expression serious. "Challah bread doesn't get soggy. Okay. Go on."

He resisted the grin trying to spread across his cheeks. This woman, without her walls, was adorable. He handed her the fork. "Your turn."

She looked up at him. "I will ruin."

"It's only bread. How much damage could you do?"

"We will see." She dipped the bread in the mixture, turned

it over. Tried to grab it with the fork, but it kept slipping off the tines.

"You gotta angle the—"

"I have it." She finally managed to get the bread to dangle from the fork, but by then, too much liquid had been absorbed. The bread fell apart and hit the counter with a plop. "Ugh. See, I said I would ruin it." She sounded so frustrated, he resisted a laugh.

He wiped up the mess with a paper towel. "Let's try it again."

She started to back away. "Never mind. I will—"

"Uh-uh. No you don't. You never give up after a fail. Never." He looked down to face her. "You know this. You've overcome enough to know it's only a failure if you let it stop you."

Expression serious, she nodded. "Da. You are right." She dropped another slice of bread in the mixture. This time, she used her fingers to turn it over and then lay it on the skillet beside the first. She yanked her hand away as the butter splattered.

He declared it perfect.

She rinsed her hands in the sink. "Next time, I will try with the fork."

"Your method worked." He sprinkled the toast with cinnamon and directed her to do the same with her slice. She added more than he had.

"I like cinnamon," she said.

After a minute, he nudged the first slice up with the spatula. The bottom had browned. He flipped it, then handed Vanessa the utensil. "Your turn."

After a minute, she nudged up the edge, saw the bottom, and flipped it perfectly beside his piece. She beamed up at him.

"It's not hard," he said.

"I wish to learn chili."

"Tonight, Frito-chili pie."

Her nose crinkled. "Pie? This does not sound good."

He winked. "You'll have to trust me."

"See, Kat," Nadia said. "I told you he liked her."

Kat giggled. "I knew it already."

A blush crept into Vanessa's cheeks.

He'd forgotten they had an audience. An audience of two, he now realized. He turned. "Morning, Nadia. How'd you sleep?"

She shrugged. "Today is a pretty day."

Outside the wall of windows, the sun shone, the lake reflecting the deep blue sky. More leaves had turned to red, yellow, and orange overnight. Another few days and the world would be awash in color. Probably already was farther north.

"These are done, no?" Vanessa asked.

"Right. Breakfast." He slid his piece onto a plate, then Vanessa's piece went onto a second plate. "Shall we let Kat and Nadia tell us who did better?"

Kat squealed. "I bet Mommy's will be better. It's a contest!"

Caleb cut each piece in two, traded two of the halves, turned his own upside down, and buttered each. He slid the New Hampshire maple syrup—the only real syrup—across the bar with the plates. "Add plenty."

Kat took his words to heart, basically drowning her breakfast.

Nadia took a slightly more reasonable amount.

"Which one is which?" Kat asked.

Before he could answer, Vanessa said, "The better one is mine."

He chuckled and started on the next batch while the ladies ate.

"This one!" Kat pointed to the upside-down piece.

"No, this one." Nadia pointed to the other.

"A tie," he said.

Her pressed-together lips said she was displeased.

He handed her the egg-and-milk mixture. "Care to go for round two?"

~

CALEB COULDN'T REMEMBER HAVING that much fun making breakfast since... ever, maybe. When they'd used up the first batch of egg-and-milk mixture, he'd shown Vanessa how to make it, then watched as she'd whisked the ingredients together and made another few slices. There was no way the four of them would finish it. But that didn't matter. All that mattered was the smile on Vanessa's face when she finally decided to sit down to eat, the way her eyes had closed, the way she'd savored the simple breakfast, more because she'd made it herself.

Watching her brought him so much joy, he almost forgot to eat.

When he'd refused to let anybody help him clean the kitchen, the ladies went upstairs to clean up for the day.

Vanessa was the first to return. "Kat is enjoying the oversize bathtub. She may stay in there all day."

Caleb lifted the coffee carafe. "Want some?"

"I had my cup already."

He poured himself a second mugful. "Where's Nadia?"

"Blow-drying her hair."

That explained the high-pitched whine carrying down the back staircase.

Vanessa gestured to the living room. "Can we talk for a minute?"

"Sure." He followed her into the living room. She sat on one end of the couch, and he settled beside her. "What's up?"

She pulled something from her pocket but kept it closed in her fist. She kept her voice low when she spoke. "Every time Abbas let me off the yacht, I took something with me that I could sell in case I found a way of escape. Always, when we returned to the yacht, I put it back. He never knew I did it." She opened her fist, and on her palm lay a platinum ring with a jewel he didn't recognize. It was opaque, not clear, dark with bright points of color. Almost like an opal, only not cream-colored but black.

Whatever the stone was, the jeweler hadn't formed it into a perfect shape. It was oblong and a little bloated on one side. The unique color, the odd shape—something told him this was no costume trinket or mass-produced gem.

He took the ring, lifted it to the light. It was nearly an inch long. How many carats must it be—twenty, thirty, maybe? Surrounded by diamonds that looked at least a quarter carat each, the setting was... magnificent.

"I never could sell," Vanessa said. "Many times before Kat was born and right after, before I came home to Nutfield, I needed the money desperately. But I feared that maybe it would be recognized. I don't know how these things work—stolen merchandise, valuable merchandise. Is there a worldwide database or something? When I took it, it seemed like nothing, a plaything. But over time, I worried it was special. I worried I would be arrested for a thief. I worried Abbas would use it to track me. So I survived. And then, my friends in Nutfield helped me. I got a job and a home, and I didn't need to sell it. For me it has become a symbol of my freedom, my escape."

Caleb placed the ring back in her hand, and she closed her fist around it again. He wasn't sure what she was asking him or why she was telling him.

"Now... I do not know what to do. Yesterday, Abbas said he wants it back. That if he doesn't get it back, I will pay."

Caleb absorbed that news, which didn't mix well with the French toast.

"I cannot decide if I should return it to him or sell it and disappear."

"Disappearing isn't an option." He considered all she'd said. The ring, the threat. It was good news. It was the way out of this mess that Vanessa needed. "This is your home. If all he wants is the ring back—"

"This is the problem, though. I know Abbas. He will not be content to get his ring back. He will seek to punish me."

"He doesn't control you anymore."

"He will not care that I return it to him. He is very prideful, and I made him look bad. I took from him, and if he ever realized I worked against him in the poker game…"

"How could he have figured that out?"

"I fear Carlos made it clear to him later. Carlos was also very prideful, very smug. I think Carlos maybe would have found a way to tell him, to rub his mouth in it."

"Nose. Rub his nose in it. You think that, even if you return the ring—"

"He will come after me. But if I sell the ring, then I will have enough money to move, to start over elsewhere. We will need to change our names, of course."

His heart leapt. He felt like a little boy watching a home run drop toward him. His hand was up, his glove ready.

But the ball went foul.

"When you say *we*, you mean—"

"Kat and me, and Nadia, if she'll come."

Caleb wasn't a part of Vanessa's plans.

"But if I sell it," she continued, "then he'll have all the more reason to hunt me down. I think I should return him the ring, sell what I have, and run. It will be harder without that money, but maybe he'll quit looking for me if he has his ring back."

"Either way, you think you have to run."

Her head dipped, rose again. A halfhearted nod, but her eyes filled with tears. "I do not wish to go. This is my home. The people here are my family. And now, with you..." Her words trailed.

He tugged her close, wanting to speak, to say something that would reassure her but knowing his voice would sound all wrong.

She pushed against him, and he backed away. "What do you think I should do?"

That she would ask him, trust his judgment, moved him almost as much as anything else she'd said that morning. He cleared his throat. "I don't... I don't want you to leave."

"This I know. But there is no other way. To return the ring, or to sell. This is what I must decide."

To return the ring and to stay. That was the right answer. But he didn't say that. "I have a friend who's a jeweler. Let's go to him, see what it's worth and see if it's been reported stolen."

"This man, he won't call the police?"

"We can trust him."

"You think I should sell?"

"I think you should know the value of what you hold. If that ring is valuable enough that Abbas hunted you for all these years, then maybe we can use it as leverage against him. Maybe we can find a way to secure your safety."

"This is not possible."

"With God, nothing is impossible."

"Da. You are right. As usual." She reached out and laid her hand on his.

That she felt comfortable enough to initiate touch made him want to shout with victory. Instead, he flipped his hand and took hers. "You're finally learning."

Her lips turned up at the corners. "It is your most annoying quality."

CHAPTER TWENTY-FIVE

V anessa couldn't help the nervous stomach as she stared at the little store in front of them. *Designs by Tsetsilas.*

She attempted the name. "Ts...it...silas?"

"Tsetsilas," he said. "Like, tess-less."

"That does not make sense."

He shrugged. "It's Greek." He peered at the storefront. "It doesn't look like much, I know, but Artie has an eye for jewels."

In the backseat, Nadia said, "This is not like the other malls I've been to." She sounded disappointed. "Abbas took me to one in Boston. Cope-a-ley, I think he said."

"Copley," Caleb corrected.

"It was fancy. This is"—she waved at the rundown shops—"not pretty. We are here why?"

Vanessa hadn't told her sister about the ring. Though Nadia hadn't demanded her phone back—which both surprised and pleased Vanessa—based on the way her sister said Abbas's name, she still wasn't convinced of Vanessa's story.

"I have an errand to run." Caleb pointed to a party goods supply store on the far end of the strip. "Nadia, why don't you take Kat there, see what you can find?" He leaned forward, pulled his wallet from his back pocket, and extracted a bill, which he held out to Nadia. "In case you see something you can't live without."

Nadia's eyes lit up. She turned to Kat. "You like to shop?"

Kat pointed at the store window. "They have balloons!"

"Kat," Vanessa said, "you stay with your aunt. And both of you stay in the store until Caleb and I come to find you. Da?"

Nadia rolled her eyes. "Your mother doesn't trust us."

"She's always like that," Kat said. "Nervous Nellie."

Vanessa failed to keep the smile from her face. "I am no Nellie."

"Nervous Nessy. I like it." Nadia nudged Kat's shoulder. "We should call her that from now on."

Caleb said, "You two better go before Nervous Nessy changes her mind."

They scrambled out of the car and ran across the parking lot, hand in hand.

"They're two peas in a pod," Caleb said.

Vanessa considered the expression. Peas she knew—the squishy little green vegetables. A pod... This was how they grew, no? Two peas would be alike, so perhaps... "You mean they are the same?"

His smile was broad. "Well done."

"Da. They are peas. I hadn't realized how much Kat reminded me of her aunt until I saw Nadia again. My daughter is without care."

"Carefree, yes. Not exactly without care, considering how she loves you. Really, she's without worry. You did that." He lifted Vanessa's hand to his lips and kissed her knuckles. "Despite all you've been through, you managed to raise a very confident little girl."

"Too confident. She has no fear of men, no matter how

much I tell her men are not..." At the frown on Caleb's face, Vanessa redirected her remark. "Many men are not to be trusted."

"Maybe Kat is wise enough to discern the difference."

"I do not think so. I think she is naive like her auntie. Which is why I must be diligent." She nodded to the jewelry store in front of them. "You know him how?"

"He's a friend of my father's. They've known each other such a long time, I don't even know how they met. I've known Artie all my life."

"And he can be trusted?" She failed to keep the fear from her voice.

"You trust me, right?" At her nod, he smiled. "I won't lead you into trouble. I promise."

"Okay, then we go." She reached for her car door, but he tugged her back toward him. "What?"

He leaned forward, pressed a kiss to her lips. A quick peck that had her skin getting all tingly again.

"Don't open your door," he said.

"Why not? Am I not to come?"

"Be patient." He climbed out of the car and walked around it. After he opened her door, he held out his hand. "May I?"

"This is a thing, this opening of the door?" She allowed him to help her from the car.

"It's how a gentleman should treat a lady."

A lady. A little surge of pleasure rose from her middle.

Inside the small jewelry store, Vanessa stopped and looked around. Nadia was right—it wasn't fancy. Other jewelry stores were glittery and bright. Here, the scent of dust filled her nose. The glass over the cases needed to be cleaned, and the cases themselves were only half-filled with merchandise.

This jeweler could be trusted? She didn't know that she would trust him to replace the battery in her watch.

"Be right with you," a voice called from beyond a gray velvet curtain that separated the back of the store from the showroom.

Caleb took her hand and walked her to the far end of the store near the curtain, where they sat on stools and looked down. Below them, wedding sets—glittery diamond engagement rings and diamond-studded bands.

"See anything you like?" he asked.

She looked up at him, batting her eyelashes. "Oh, Caleb. I thought you'd never ask. Yes, yes. A thousand times, yes."

His jaw dropped. "Uh..."

She giggled, then slapped her hand over her mouth. What was wrong with her? She forced, "I am kidding," through her fingers.

A wide grin filled his face, crinkled his eyes. "You delight me, Vanessa. Truly."

Oh. Those words, those sweet words.

"Sorry to keep you." A man in his sixties with gray curly hair sticking out in every direction froze in the doorway. "Caleb Peterson!" He crossed the space and held out his hand, which Caleb shook. "Great to see you, son." The man turned his attention to Vanessa, and his eyebrows rose. "And your lovely friend." He shifted his hand to her. "Artie Tsetsilas."

She stood as well. "Vanessa Baker."

"Lovely name, lovely face, lovely accent."

"Stop flirting with my girl," Caleb said.

His girl. Was Vanessa his girl?

She considered the words. Possessive, yet... not. She would like to think of herself as Caleb's girl.

Artie's eyes sparkled as they took in the merchandise in the case that separated them. "Are we making it off—?"

"No." Caleb cleared his throat, adorably uncomfortable with a flush to his cheeks. "We wanted to ask you about a piece of jewelry, see if you could appraise it for us."

"Happy to. Let's see it."

Vanessa pulled the ring from her purse and held it out to the man.

Artie's amusement faded as he stared at it. "Where did you get it?"

"It is a long story," she said.

When she offered nothing else, he returned his gaze to the ring. "Do you mind if I take it?"

She feared handing it over, this last bit of hope. But she trusted Caleb. "Da. Go ahead."

Gently, reverently, the man took the ring. From below the counter, he grabbed a piece of cloth, which he laid on the glass case. He set the ring on it, then went to the back room and returned with a lamp.

Vanessa's heart pounded while Artie studied the jewel. What if it was worthless? What if she'd damaged it in her handling of it for all these years? What if it was a priceless work of art, and he'd already pressed a button and the police were on the way. That could happen, no?

Caleb pressed his hand to the small of her back, a quick reassuring gesture, as if he knew what she was thinking.

Artie turned the piece over, studied the other side.

Then, he disappeared into the back, returning a moment later with a laptop. The tapping of the keyboard was the only sound in the otherwise silent room.

"Hm." Artie tapped, muttered, "I thought..." and tapped some more. Finally, he turned the screen so they could see it.

The ring, her ring, was on the internet. "That's it." Artie watched her and Caleb as they peered at the screen. "You two agree?"

Caleb snatched the ring off the counter and slid it on his pinky finger. Even he seemed spooked now. "Yeah, that's it."

Artie regarded her again, looked her up and down. "You have an accent, but it's not Middle Eastern."

"I am Serbian."

"How'd you end up with one of the Sahim family's royal jewels?"

Royal jewels? Only she would be stupid enough to steal something that valuable, to think it was but a trinket. It was so big. Surely no stone that big could be real. "It is a long story."

Artie turned his attention to Caleb. "A story I'd like to hear."

"Maybe another time," Caleb said.

Artie spun the laptop again, clicked a few buttons, and turned it back. There was the ring again, only now on a different website. "It was reported stolen more than a decade back."

She swallowed hard.

Caleb gently squeezed her arm as if to say, *I've got you.* "We suspected as much," he said, calm as could be. "Can you tell us what it's worth?"

"It's... priceless." The color in Artie's cheeks paled. He shook his head. "I mean, not priceless. Not really. But for jewelry..." Again, he spun the laptop and clicked the keyboard. "Says here the stone—"

"What kind of stone is it?"

"A black opal."

"I didn't even know that was a thing," Caleb said.

"They're very rare, especially that size. They come from South Wales, Australia. When I say rare, I mean stones this size have names. They have legacies. You know what I mean?"

"This one is called..." Vanessa asked.

"Australian Nights," Artie said. "I guess because it sort of looks like stars in the sky."

"I can see that," Caleb said. "Its value is...?"

The man glanced at the website. "I'd guess, if one were dumb enough to sell it instead of return it"—he peered at Caleb, then Vanessa, beneath bushy gray eyebrows—"one might expect to get fifty thousand for it."

"Dollars?" Vanessa asked.

"This isn't Serbia. Of course dollars."

She pressed her hand into her churning stomach. "This explains—"

"Out of curiosity," Caleb said, "why would it be foolish to sell it?"

"You'd have to sell it on the black market," Artie said. "You'd only get fifty for it because you couldn't ask market value. Despite what the general public thinks, things are cheaper on the black market. I mean, selling this would be like trying to sell a… a stolen Degas or a Monet. Law enforcement is always searching for stolen goods. You'd be hard-pressed to sell this without getting caught. And getting caught with it would mean" —he leveled his gaze at Vanessa—"prison. That's assuming the Sahim family doesn't get to you first. They're not exactly the most forgiving people."

Caleb slid the ring into his pocket. "You've been really helpful."

Artie's lips pressed together so hard, they turned white. "You've put me in a spot here, son."

Caleb reached across the counter and laid his hand on Artie's shoulder. "There's a really good reason why she has this, and we're going to do the right thing with it. When this is all said and done, I'll tell you the story. Meanwhile, please trust me."

"I know *you're* not a thief." Artie's gaze flicked to Vanessa. That same confidence didn't extend to her.

And why should it? She had stolen the ring, after all. Considering all that happened with Abbas, she wasn't sure how she'd ended up as the criminal.

Caleb slid his hand down Vanessa's arm and linked their

fingers. "I'll call you in seven days, Artie. In seven days, I'll tell you everything. Just give us that long to straighten this out."

"I'll give you till Friday. Long as I don't find out that thing has turned up on the black market. If I do—"

"I get it. And you won't." Caleb ushered Vanessa out of the store before Artie could change his mind. Three days. How far away could she get in three days?

CHAPTER TWENTY-SIX

Caleb held Vanessa's hand as they walked the length of the strip mall toward the party supply store. He could feel the tension in her fingers.

"It's going to be okay."

"I stole something priceless. I didn't know. If I had known—"

"It's all right. This is good."

She yanked her hand away. "How can this be good? It is not. It is... It is terrible. I only thought to take something I could sell, not something worth so much it would be on"—she waved back toward the jewelry store—"on some website. A stone with a name. I am such a fool."

"Don't do that to yourself. It's not—"

"Priceless. This word keeps repeating in my brain. The jewel is priceless."

Priceless. It was reverberating in his mind as well, but for a different reason. He stopped and turned to face Vanessa. Her eyes were wide, her mouth slightly open, showing pretty, straight teeth. Her cheeks flushed in the cool breeze. "You stole something of great value from Abbas. But it has a worth, a value.

You can put a number on it. Without that ring, nobody's life has been damaged. Maybe Abbas was embarrassed. If his family found out it was lost, I bet they were angry. Good. It's the least he deserves."

"But your friend said it was—"

"My friend said it was worth fifty thousand dollars on the black market."

"It might as well be fifty trillion. I could never repay—"

"And you won't have to," Caleb said.

"Da, but still, I should not have—"

"Vanessa."

At the sound of her name, she closed her mouth.

"You need to stop this line of thinking. You did what you did because you were trying to survive. What you stole from Abbas is very valuable. Exceedingly valuable. But what he stole from you—that was priceless."

Tears filled her eyes.

Caleb pulled her close. "What he took from you was infinitely more valuable. You can return the ring to him. He can never return what he stole."

She sniffed, backed away from his embrace, and wiped her tears. "You are right. I stole because I wanted to survive. He should not have... have done all that he did to me."

Caleb was amazed at her resilience. Somehow, she'd learned to trust Caleb, despite all the ways men had hurt her in the past.

Lord, make me worthy of her faith in me. Help her to see Your hand on us in this.

He tucked her hand in the crook of his elbow, and they continued toward the store.

"What do we do now?" Vanessa asked.

"Let's just... think on it for a little while."

Her hand squeezed his upper arm. "We must act."

"I think we need to let the information simmer for a little while, see what it cooks."

"This I do not understand. We must—"

"What?"

"I do not know, but... something."

"But you don't know what. And neither do I. Don't you ever find that if you just let your mind process something while you focus elsewhere, a solution presents itself? When I have a problem, the more I try to work out a solution, the more convoluted the problem seems."

She repeated the word slowly. "Convoluted. I don't know this word."

"It means complex and hard to follow. It's like... Have you ever had to un-knot a string?"

"Like necklaces? Kat has a bunch of cheap necklaces, and she threw them once in a plastic bag. It took me days to get them apart."

"Exactly." He loved that she followed his line of thinking. Loved how hard she tried to understand him. "If you just start yanking the strands, the knots get tighter, right?"

"Da. This is how Kat tried to fix. It did not help."

"That's what I'm saying. Let's not yank on the strands of this mess." He turned to face her, placing his free hand on her shoulder. "Let's give the problem some time to simmer. More than that, let's trust God to guide us."

And then, he prayed for just that.

Vanessa bowed her head, and they stood in front of a display window, perhaps in the sight of gawking shoppers, and asked the Lord to show them the way.

When he finished the prayer, she looked up at him, eyes sparkling. "I do not think you are real, Caleb Peterson."

He pinched his arm, said, "Ouch. I think I am."

She shook her head in mock disgust, and they continued to walk.

Caleb opened the door to the party supply store, and Kat barreled out, a Mylar balloon tethered to her wrist with a blue ribbon. The balloon was pink and covered with teddy bears. She hugged Caleb's waist. "Thank you, Mr. Caleb! Thank you for the balloon."

"Katarina." Vanessa's voice was stern. "You know better. We do not hug men."

Kat backed away and looked up at her mother, expression pained. "But I thought since he saved my life—"

"Only that one time. Not again."

Behind Kat, Nadia said, "You are too fearful, Nervous Nessy. Caleb is harmless."

Vanessa's voice was harsh when she said, "No man is harmless." She caught Caleb's eyes, blinked. "You understand, no?"

Yeah. He understood. No matter what he did, no matter how hard he worked to keep them safe, Vanessa only trusted him to a point. She didn't trust him with her daughter. Would she ever get over that fear? If she didn't, how could they make a life together?

He didn't understand, and he wasn't going to lie about it. He ignored the question and focused on Kat. "I like your balloon. It's pretty."

"Thank you. I told Aunt Nadia to get one, but she said one would be enough in the car. Will it be annoying when you're driving?"

"I think I can handle it."

Nadia held her fist out. When Caleb opened his palm, she dropped his change into it. He'd given her a twenty, and she was giving him back... about seventeen.

He liked that about her, that she was responsible with money. As many negative thoughts as he'd had about Nadia, she had things to recommend her. She was trustworthy, kind to her niece, and generally happy. He'd try to remember those the next time she irritated him.

He gestured toward the car on the far end of the lot, and they started in that direction.

"Where are we going now?" Kat asked.

"Do we see leaves?" Nadia looked around at the ugly city view around them. They were in Manchester, but not a very nice area of the city. "I would like to see leaves."

"We'll go into the mountains," he said. "The leaves should be prettier at the higher elevation." He looked down at Kat. "Do you like to hike?"

She shrugged. "I like boats better."

He loved her honesty. Were all children that open? He'd never spent much time with kids. He'd always wanted children of his own, but he'd never considered what it would take to be a father. Being with Kat, thinking that maybe she could someday be his daughter...

Except that would never happen, because for that to happen, her mother would have to trust him. And she didn't, not completely. And probably never would.

No. God was bigger than Vanessa's fears.

"Could we go on a boat instead of on a hike?" Kat asked.

"Don't be rude, Kat." Vanessa's voice held more irritation than the moment called for. Was she, like Caleb, thinking of the words she'd said a few minutes earlier? Was she, dare he hope, regretting them? "We will go where Mr. Caleb wants to take us."

Nadia said something in Serbian, something that sounded angry.

Vanessa snapped back in the same language.

"She is..." Nadia shook her head. "She tells Kat not to be rude after she is unkind to you."

"I do not mean to be..." Vanessa's voice seemed pained. "I just—"

Caleb said, "It's fine," even though it was far from it. They reached the car, and Caleb held the passenger door open for Vanessa. Just before she slid into the seat, she looked at him, her pretty green eyes filled with sadness.

He tried a smile but feared she knew it was forced as she sat in the car.

He slid into the front seat, started the car, and then opened the browser on his phone. He skimmed through suggestions on things to do in the New Hampshire mountains. And then...

"Got it."

"Got what?" Vanessa asked.

"A way to make everyone happy."

AN HOUR LATER, he parked on the street in front of a little gray building on the edge of Lake Winnipesaukee. Just beyond the little building floated the Mount Washington cruise ship.

"Look at the boat, Mommy!" Kat's sweet voice pulled Caleb from the prayers he'd been lifting on the hour-long drive from Manchester. Prayers for wisdom and guidance regarding Abbas. Prayers for Vanessa's trust.

"I see it." Vanessa turned to him. In her expression, the sadness he'd seen earlier remained. Now, her lips seemed to be battling. He couldn't tell if she was trying to smile or trying not to. Either way, the expression seemed pained.

"If it's okay with you," he said. "We get to see leaves, and Kat gets her boat."

Vanessa turned back toward the lake. "It is good solution. But expensive, I think."

"Don't worry about that." He opened his car door, helped

the ladies out, and sent them to look at the boat while he bought the tickets. They'd barely made it in time for the twelve-thirty cruise, and just a few minutes after they boarded, the ship pushed away from the dock.

All the years he'd lived in New Hampshire and he'd never been on this cruise. It was a tourist trap, but as they motored across the cool water, he realized, trap or not, this was a good choice today.

As he'd hoped when they were in Manchester, the leaves on the mountains surrounding them were closer to their peak of color. Reds, oranges, and yellows were bright against the blue sky. The sun was warm but the wind chilly where they stood at the rail. Beyond the closer range, Mount Washington rose to the north, its gentle peak taller and dotted with green. He pointed it out to the ladies.

"In another couple of weeks," he said, "it'll be covered with snow, and it'll stay that way until May, maybe June."

"It is very..." Nadia said something in Serbian to Vanessa.

"Da," Vanessa said. "Gorgeous."

"Breathtaking," Caleb added.

Vanessa whispered, "Breathtaking. I like this word."

"I see fishes!" Between himself and Vanessa, Kat was looking not at the surrounding mountains but at the water through the links of the fence below the railing. At least she'd left the balloon in the car. In this wind, it would be bouncing off the adults' faces about now. "Look, Mr. Caleb. Fishes!"

He peered down. "A whole school of them."

She giggled. "They're in school?"

"That's what you call a bunch of fish that stay together. A school."

"Do they have books and teachers, too?" She giggled some more. "Look over there! That one's really big!" She was angling, trying to see through the narrow holes.

He looked over Kat's head. "Do you mind if I pick her up so she can see better?"

Vanessa covered her lips with her fingertips, staring at him.

"You're standing right there." He'd meant to keep the scorn from his voice but failed. "What could possibly happen?"

"You are right. It is fine."

To Kat, he held out his hands. "Want a better vantage point?"

She lifted her arms, and he pulled her onto his hip and leaned forward against the railing, allowing her to look down.

"The water is so clear," she said. "I can see all the way to the bottom."

"You know why?"

"Huh-uh. Why?"

"Because of all the rocks. This is the Granite State, right? Have you heard that?"

"Uh-huh." She was barely paying attention to him. He could feel Vanessa's gaze and refused to meet it.

"Big rocks and little rocks. They're everywhere in New Hampshire. They make sand, and sand is a natural filter. In fact, pool filters are filled with sand."

"Really?" Now Kat faced him, her face close enough to his that he could feel her breath. He was tempted to plant a kiss on her forehead, to pull her close. This sweet, sweet girl... Two days before, he'd barely known her. Now...

He was falling in love with her, too.

He couldn't imagine letting either one of them go.

Fear tried to creep into his heart. He couldn't let himself be ruled by it. God had made Caleb a promise, and he would believe.

He reminded himself—yet again—that his namesake had waited more than forty years for his inheritance.

Caleb prayed he wouldn't have to wait that long.

"The sand makes the water clean?" Kat asked.

He smiled at her. "Yup. If you go to other parts of the country, you'll see a lot of lakes that are muddy and ugly. But not here. Ours are crystal clear."

"Our lakes are the best," Kat said.

Caleb chanced a glance at Vanessa. And caught her watching him.

As soon as their eyes met, she turned her head forward and looked at the vista.

Through the speaker overhead, the tour guide babbled about where they were going and what they were seeing. Caleb tuned him out. He didn't know what tomorrow would bring. He would trust God to figure this out.

Only God could untangle what so many men had knotted up in Vanessa's heart.

CHAPTER TWENTY-SEVEN

Vanessa eyed the ingredients that had just been delivered from Caleb's grocery store. Perhaps one of the perks of owning the company was prompt service. Caleb returned from walking the delivery boy to the door, where, if she wasn't mistaken, he'd given the kid a great tip. Now, he spoke to her. "You still want to learn to make chili?"

There was no life in his voice, no amusement in his eyes. He was angry with her, still, after her remark at the strip mall that morning. They'd managed to have fun, but tension had hummed in the background like a running furnace.

When, an hour into the boat ride, Kat had complained that she was hungry, Caleb had politely asked Vanessa if he could buy them all lunch. She and Nadia had split a lobster roll, a first for both of them. Vanessa had loved the flavor of the tender lobster meat, dripping with butter, on the hot dog bun. Such a strange combination, but delicious. Kat and Caleb had eaten hamburgers. When Kat had eaten as much as she could—about three bites—Caleb had happily finished her meal, never once complaining about the overpriced menu.

Now, they were back at the house. Vanessa stared at Nadia

and Kat on the back patio, looking out at the lake. They seemed as happy as could be, but between Caleb and herself, tension remained.

She said, "I am sorry if I offended you."

"Do you want to help with the chili or not?"

She turned to face him. "It is one thing to trust a man with myself. This is difficult enough."

"I understand."

"I do not think you do."

He folded his arms. "You're right. I don't. I don't understand how, after everything, you can still doubt me. Do you think I'd do all I've done, spent all the—" He clamped his mouth shut.

"I know you have spent much money on us. I would promise to pay it back, but I have so little, and we will need it. And even what I have is because of you."

"Not me. The board, the job—"

"I know it was you who fought for my last pay raise. I was not in the room, but people told me. I don't understand why you care, but I know you do. All I have is due to you."

"I fought for your pay raise because you deserved it. If we don't pay you what you deserve, somebody else will offer you a better job. If I didn't care about the food bank, *I'd* offer you a better job. You're still not paid what you're worth." Though his words were kind, his voice was filled with frustration. "And I wasn't going to mention the *money* I've spent. That's irrelevant. I was going to mention the time I've spent with you."

"That, I cannot pay back."

"I know." His voice was loud and bounced off the hard countertop between them.

She stepped back, heart racing.

He started again, quieter. "Time is the only resource we can never renew. Time is the most priceless commodity in this world. And I've spent a lot of mine with you. And if it were up to me, I'd spend..." He shook his head, glanced at the windows toward Nadia and Kat. "Do you really think I'd do all I've done just to get close to your daughter? That I'd... That I'm some kind of... pedophile? I can hardly say it. It's unthinkable. And that you would think that of me is—"

"I don't think that." She desperately needed him to understand. Her voice sounded pleading. "I don't think that is your plan."

"Well, that's a relief." His tone was drenched in sarcasm.

How to explain? "It's just that men are capable of such depravity."

"As are women. But I trust you."

"You do not have a child." How could he be so stubborn? She was trying to explain, but he didn't even try to see it from her perspective. "It is not the same. I have seen men with families, with children at home, do deplorable things to others. I think maybe every man is capable of that. If given the right circumstances—"

"You think all men are closet pedophiles?"

She shrugged. "Perhaps."

"We're all sinners, men and women. But the idea that all men would..." He ran his hands over his head. "You're wrong about that."

"I cannot know this. I cannot know if you are the exception."

"It's not... I'm not the *exception*. The men you've known, they're the exception. I mean, yes, we're all sinners. We all have issues. But most men aren't looking at children like... like you think. How can you even...?" He shook his head. "I would never harm your daughter, and I'd stop anyone who tried to. If you don't know that about me, then you don't know me at all."

She'd met many depraved men in her lifetime, but perhaps Caleb was right. Perhaps there were many good men.

She wanted for it to be true. When it was just her and Caleb, she trusted him. She cared for him. But when Katarina came into the room, she couldn't help but see him as a threat. To herself, to her child. Was she wrong to feel this way?

He watched her through narrowed eyes, then lowered his head and massaged the back of his neck.

She wanted to trust him. But she was afraid.

When he raised his head, his eyes were cold. "Do you want to make chili or not?"

She did. Desperately, she wanted to spend time beside him, to learn from him, to laugh with him. But until she knew how she felt, until they could get back to the friendship they'd had before she insulted him... "I think not."

"Fine." He waved to the back deck. "Go spend time with them."

"We must talk about the ring."

"Later. I need a few minutes alone. Please."

With no other choice, she stepped onto the back patio, where Nadia and Kat were jabbering about something. They glanced her way, but she waved them off. She didn't bother to join their conversation, and, thankfully, the deck was large enough that she didn't have to. She fell onto the loveseat where she and Caleb had talked the night before and dropped her head into her hands.

Could Caleb be trusted with Kat? Did it even matter? She and Kat and Nadia were going to have to leave Nutfield forever. Unless they came up with some kind of plan to protect them from Abbas, they didn't have a choice. And Caleb's life was here. But if there were a way for her to be with Caleb...

Would she?

Would she risk her daughter's safety with this man? Because Caleb wasn't one who would settle for a casual relationship. Everything about him was intense and committed, and if they were together, he'd be intensely committed to her.

What would that be like, to have someone committed to her? She didn't have to imagine how it would feel, though. Caleb had been showing her for days.

But that would mean, if he could ever love her, he wouldn't be content with dating until Kat turned eighteen and went to college. He'd want more. He'd want them to live together. He'd want marriage.

Could she trust him to stay under the same roof with Kat for years and years? Could she trust him to be a father to her daughter?

A better father than her own had been?

You trusted him last night, the voice whispered.

She had. It hadn't occurred to her to worry over Kat's safety the night before. Did that make her a fool? Had she put Kat in danger by allowing Caleb to stay?

But God had told her to trust Caleb, and He'd confirmed that over and over. Maybe trusting Caleb was foolish, but trusting God was not.

Lord, what do I do?

His answer was the same answer He'd given her many times. *Trust Me.*

But what did that look like? She wished He'd give her an outline of His grand plan. All she knew right now was to take one step at a time. Where those steps were leading, she had no idea.

THE CHILI WAS hot and spicy, the Fritos crunchy, and the cheese creamy.

It was so good, even Nadia stopped talking long enough to eat.

Kat was shoveling chili into her mouth as if she were in a race. Vanessa was tempted to tell her to slow down.

Opposite her at the table, Caleb's gaze was on Kat too. His eyes held amusement, affection.

"It is good," Vanessa offered.

Kat looked up. "Mommy, you should have learned how to make it. Can you ask Mr. Caleb for the recipe? I wanna have this every single night forever!"

Vanessa smiled at her daughter, glanced at Caleb.

"I'll be happy to share my recipe." He looked at Kat. "Maybe you and your mom can learn to make it together."

"Can we, Mommy? And Aunt Nadia can learn, too!"

"Maybe." Vanessa twirled the food in her bowl. She and Caleb needed to talk. The food, tasty as it was, didn't appeal to her.

She couldn't think about anything but the apology she owed him—a real one this time. And the ring he still held in his pocket.

"Can I have some more?" Kat asked.

"Finish your salad first," Vanessa said. "And then you may have a little more."

Her daughter dove into the green salad with such fervor that Vanessa almost laughed.

Nadia was solemn on her side of the table.

"Are you all right?" Vanessa asked.

"I would like my phone back now."

Before she could answer, Caleb said, "You can call Abbas, if you must, but you'll have to do it where I can listen in."

"I am not to call him." Nadia glared at Caleb, then Vanessa. "I wish to check Instagram."

Caleb had brought Nadia's phone with them that day and had given it to her in the car after securing her promise that she wouldn't tell Abbas where they were staying. She'd sworn then, too, that she wouldn't call Abbas. And, as far as Vanessa could tell, she hadn't, though that didn't mean she hadn't messaged him.

"You had your phone all day," Vanessa said. "You can check it tomorrow."

Nadia stood. "I want my phone back, or I am leaving."

"Fine. Get your things." Caleb pushed back from the table and stood.

"We're not doing this again," Vanessa said. "If you wish to leave, then leave. I will not beg you to stay."

Kat looked up at Nadia and Caleb, who were glaring at each other, and then at Vanessa. "Why can't she have her phone?"

"It is... convoluted, *ceri*."

She caught Caleb's grin at her use of his word. She'd made him smile, a good sign.

"You want more chili?" Vanessa asked.

At Kat's "uh-huh," Vanessa swiped her bowl off the table and headed for the kitchen. Caleb would manage Nadia. She had no doubt he could.

"It's about your sister's safety," Caleb said, "and your niece's. I understand it's hard, but it seems like a small sacrifice, considering everything."

Everything. Da. That Vanessa had risked her life, her livelihood, her home, to save Nadia, but Nadia wasn't willing to forego Instagram for two whole days.

Finally, Nadia slumped back in the chair. "Tomorrow, I want it back."

"We'll talk about that," Caleb said. "Meanwhile, I got cake for dessert."

Nadia's expression brightened, and Vanessa hardly kept from smiling. Her silly sister was easily distracted, at least.

Vanessa gave Kat her second bowl of chili—this one barely more than a spoonful—but Kat had lost interest. "What kind of cake?"

Caleb's eyes twinkled. "What's your favorite?"

"Chocolate."

Vanessa slid back into her chair, watching Caleb's reaction.

His eyes dimmed. "Oh, no. I thought you were going to say vanilla."

"That's okay. Vanilla is good, too."

"But it's not your very favorite," he said.

She shrugged.

"It has to be your very favorite cake." He tapped his nose. "Let me do some magic, see if I can turn my vanilla cake into chocolate." He walked around the island into the kitchen. "Abracadabra, Kalamazoo." He stepped into the pantry and backed out. "Katarina likes chocolate, and I do, too!" He turned and presented the cake with a loud, "Ta-da!"

Kat clapped wildly. "Look, Mommy! It's chocolate!"

When Vanessa laughed, Caleb shot her a look of pure... affection.

How could she doubt this man? This man who'd done so much for her.

She stood and took the cake from his hands. "Since you did all the magic to get it here, at least let me cut it."

"Be my guest. There's ice cream in the freezer."

"Yay!" Kat's enthusiasm was contagious, and they enjoyed the cake and ice cream, which was a nice addition to the balloon Kat had brought home.

After Nadia had done the dishes and Caleb and Vanessa had lingered at the table not talking about anything important, Kat crashed from the sugar high. She yawned, then started whining about missing school again. "But I wanna go. I miss my friends."

Vanessa didn't have the heart to tell her she'd probably never go back. Instead, she said, "Time for bed." Which elicited more whining until Nadia offered to take her up and read her a story.

"She'll need to brush her teeth and change her clothes," Vanessa said, fully expecting Nadia to back out.

"We can do together." Nadia took Kat's hand. "Yes?"

"Yay! 'Night, Mommy. 'Night, Mr. Caleb."

They went up the stairs, leaving Vanessa and Caleb alone.

"They've made fast friends." Caleb gestured to the sofa in the living room.

She perched on the edge, and he took the chair catty-corner.

"They are peas, like you said."

He grinned, but the expression didn't hold. Their earlier conversation filled the space between them and made it feel foggy and dense.

He said, "We need to talk—"

At the same time, she said, "I must apologize."

He leaned forward and rested his forearms on his thighs. "By all means, ladies first."

"I am sorry for my words, and I am sorry I am... untrustworthy."

"Untrusting. Untrustworthy means you're not worthy of trust, which you definitely are. You're untrusting."

"Oh. Then, I apologize that I am untrusting. I try, but it is scary with my daughter."

"I'm trying to imagine how difficult this is for you."

"You cannot, though," she said. "I'm learning to trust God, and I think He wants me to trust you. I'm trying."

His fingers laced together. His gaze was intense as it held hers. "I would never hurt your daughter. She's precious. And I have to believe that, eventually, you'll trust me even with her.

Meanwhile..." He leaned back and pulled the ring from his pocket. "What do we do about this?"

"We were letting it simmer."

"We don't want it to burn." He winked. "Have you come up with any ideas?"

"I cannot sell it. This is clear from your friend. I must return it and then run away and hope he is happy to get his ring back."

"Do you think he will be?"

"If I run away, if I make it harder for him to find me, I think he will eventually give up trying. He lives on the water. Maybe if I go someplace far from the ocean... Remember we modeled our food bank after that one in Oklahoma? During our conversations, I met with one of the women there, and the others seemed very nice when I spoke to them. The real estate prices are affordable. Maybe we will go there."

"It is landlocked."

She considered the word, committed it to memory.

He stood and pulled the curtains to hide the wall of glass now that the sun had gone down. When he sat again, he said, "I don't want you to leave."

"I don't see another way. Unless you cooked up a better idea."

"It's not much of an idea, but..." His phone rang, and he answered and said, "Send them through." He tossed the phone on the coffee table. "I should have mentioned this sooner. Eric and Garrison are here."

"Now?"

"I hope it's okay. I didn't want them coming while Kat was awake."

"What can they do?" Her heart raced. It took her mind a moment to catch up with her anxiety.

Caleb seemed to sense her distress. "What's wrong?"

"I stole that ring. I will be in trouble."

"They're your friends. Nobody's going to haul you off to jail."

This she knew. Still, she crossed her arms to hold herself together.

Caleb stood and held his hand out to her.

When she took it, he pulled her to her feet and looked down at her. Inches separated them. In his arms, she felt warm and safe. It did not make sense, this feeling.

He rested his hands on her hips. "It's going to be okay."

"You act as if you are sure of this."

"And I'm always right. Don't forget that."

"Your most annoying quality."

His gaze left her eyes, flicked downward. He lowered his head, brushed his lips against hers.

Again, her body responded in a way it never had to a man's nearness. There was no fear, no urge to fight or to run. Neither was there the numbness she'd perfected over the years. This... this tingling, this yearning, this desire... This must be how normal women felt in the arms of good men.

Somehow, her hands found his shoulders, then slid up to the back of his neck. Somehow, her body arched up to meet his.

The knock on the door told her to pull away, but he held her closer. "They're here," he whispered.

She couldn't seem to make her voice work.

"I should probably answer the door," he added.

"I think yes."

His eyes twinkled. "They could wait another minute."

She pressed her hands against his chest. "Perhaps we should focus."

"Always practical," he said. "Your most annoying quality." He kissed her forehead and let her go.

As he walked to the door to let in their friends, she touched her lips. She had never understood how powerful a simple kiss could be—when it was a kiss from the right man.

CHAPTER TWENTY-EIGHT

Every nerve in Caleb's body vibrated as he walked to the front door. Vanessa was right—they needed to focus. Right now, he wanted to focus on the feel of her in his arms. But if he didn't figure out what to do about Abbas...

That was the thought that had his mind redirecting as he opened the door. Eric and Garrison stood on the other side. Garrison, at least three inches taller than Caleb's six feet, was a good ten, maybe fifteen, years older than Caleb. Though he'd been out of the FBI for years, with the authority in his stance, nobody would doubt he'd been a federal agent most of his career. Usually, Garrison was cracking stupid dad jokes, so the serious look he wore now had Caleb's heart pumping.

Eric's expression was similar.

"I take it you don't have good news." Caleb moved out of the way, and Garrison stepped in and toward the living area.

Behind him, Caleb heard Garrison say, "Good to see you, Vanessa."

She answered, but Caleb was watching Eric, who'd stayed on the stoop.

"How you holding up?" Eric asked.

Caleb shrugged. "It's been an interesting couple of days."

Eric only nodded.

"You knew about Vanessa's past? All of this stuff?"

"Not the particulars," Eric said, "and nothing about this Abbas guy. But about..." His voice trailed.

It was awkward, this dance of *Do you know what I know?*

"About Carlos?" Caleb asked.

Eric blew out a long breath. "She told you."

"Some of it."

"Did she tell you my part in it?" Eric asked.

His part? "I just assumed... You were on the force at that point, right?"

Eric's smile was sad. "Of course Vanessa wouldn't tell you without asking us first."

"What am I missing?"

"Did she say why she was in Nutfield?"

He recalled the story Vanessa had related the night before. "She said Carlos was looking for a woman and her child—his child."

"Except the kid wasn't his. He was mine."

Caleb stepped back. "Wait. What?"

"The woman Carlos was searching for? It was Kelsey. It's a very long story, but..." He shook his head. "I'm glad you know. It's been hard keeping that from you. I didn't know how to tell you without giving away Vanessa's story."

Caleb let all those pieces click into place. Since he and Eric had been accountability partners, he'd prayed for Kelsey and Eric's marriage. He'd known Kelsey had experienced trauma, and that trauma had made things difficult over the years. Their marriage was strong, probably stronger because of it. But still, there'd been rough patches.

Caleb had never known the details. Now that he did...

"I'm pretty sure this is why the Lord put us together," Eric said. "When you told me you thought Vanessa would be your..." He leaned to the side and peered behind Caleb. "You know... Anyway, I've known how to pray. I've prayed in ways you never could have, because I have an idea of the demons she's battling."

It irked Caleb that Eric knew more about Vanessa than he did. At the same time, he could see God's hand in their friendship. He could see God's hand in all of this.

This was further confirmation of what God had told him two years prior. Vanessa would someday be his bride. He would believe. Despite all the trials, all the obstacles, he would believe.

"We'd better get started."

Caleb stepped out of the way, and Eric walked into the living room. "How you holdin' up, friend?"

Caleb figured Eric was keeping himself from offering Vanessa a hug. He'd known Vanessa long enough to know she wasn't a hugger, even if he was.

"I am glad you're here. Come in, sit."

Garrison had already taken the chair Caleb had vacated, and Eric fell into the other chair.

"You would drink something?" Vanessa asked.

When they declined, Vanessa perched on the couch.

Caleb sat perhaps a little too close to her, but not as close as he wanted to. He watched her reaction when he said, "I was thinking maybe Abbas could be held accountable for everything he did to you."

"I do not think so," Vanessa said.

"Unfortunately, she's right," Garrison said. "Unless you were on American soil..."

"We were not," she said.

"There are international treaties, but..." Garrison sighed. "These things are hard to enforce, and you'd have to prove it. Do you have any evidence?"

"Only my word," she said.

"What about yesterday, though?" Caleb faced her. "He attacked you."

Vanessa touched her neck. "Da. But—"

"What happened?" Eric's voice was too loud in the quiet room, and he shot Caleb an angry look. "I thought you were going to protect her."

The urge to defend himself rose, then collapsed with the truth. "I screwed up."

"It wasn't his fault." Vanessa took Caleb's hand but spoke to Eric. "He warned me. I was to leave the room before Abbas got there, but I wouldn't leave without Nadia. It was my fault."

"It was Abbas's fault." Anger throbbed in Garrison's voice. "You didn't call the police?"

"It didn't occur to me." Vanessa glanced Caleb's direction.

"Me, either. I just wanted to get her out of there. I blew it six ways to Sunday." Vanessa squeezed Caleb's hand, and though the feeling was nice, the gesture was meaningless. He'd accompanied her to Boston in order to protect her, and he'd messed up all around.

Garrison leaned back in the chair. "It probably wouldn't have mattered. Even if you had, local cops would consider it a domestic disturbance. He'd be taken into custody and then, my guess... Released. Especially considering the guy's a foreign prince."

Vanessa startled at the words. "A... what? A prince?"

Garrison's gaze flicked to Caleb and back to Vanessa. "You didn't know?"

She turned to Caleb. "Abbas is a prince?"

"Yeah." Caleb rubbed the back of his neck. "I probably should have mentioned that. Abbas bin Fahd *al Sahim*. That last part means—"

"He is royalty." She fell against the sofa and hid her face behind her hands. "I cannot fight him. I can never get away."

"Let's not get ahead of ourselves," Garrison said.

Eric added, "You might not have to fight him."

Caleb liked the sound of that. He tugged Vanessa's hands down and threaded his fingers with hers.

"This family has come under fire before for alleged sex crimes." Eric's Texas accent grew thicker when he was angry. "One of these so-called princes was accused of some ugly behavior in LA a few years back, and there've been other cases abroad."

Garrison looked as angry as Eric. "The problem is that the family uses its influence to whisk these guys out of the country before they can face any penalties."

"Da. I am not able to fight. I am... destroyed."

Caleb glared at his friends. "I'm really hoping there's a *but* to go along with all your good news."

"But," Garrison said, "the royal family cares about its reputation. They might not let one of their members rot in an American jail, but neither are they happy when these accusations fly."

"We're thinking," Eric said, "maybe we can contact someone who'll have influence over Abbas and offer a trade. Y'all give them the ring, and they get Abbas off American soil— and keep him off."

"They would do this why?" Vanessa asked. "The ring is theirs. I must return it or face charges, no?"

"Well," Eric drawled, "if you face charges, then you'll go into court and tell why you stole it in the first place. I'm guessing that's not a story Abbas—or the Sahim family—wants in the public record."

Caleb saw what they were getting at. "And we could make it very public. Nate's still with the *Wall Street Journal*, right?"

"He is, and Rae isn't without resources." Eric nodded to Vanessa. "We could destroy him."

She tapped her lips with her fingertip. "And this royal family, you think they will care about his reputation?"

Garrison fielded that. "We don't know how they'll react, and, even if they agree to our terms, we don't know if Abbas will do what they say. But, unless you have a better idea…"

She glanced at Caleb, and some of the tension softened from her eyes. "I was going to return the ring anyway. Maybe I can return it and not run? Maybe… it is worth to try?"

He didn't correct her use of the English expression. He was too focused on those beautiful words. *Not run.* That was what he wanted. Vanessa, here in Nutfield. With him. Forever.

"I'm trying to track down someone who can get us in touch with a Sahim royal," Garrison said. "Do you think you can lie low another day or two?"

She looked at Caleb. "We will have to deal with Nadia tomorrow."

"That's your sister?" Eric asked.

"Da. I don't know if she believes me about Abbas. She has been patient but soon she will want to call him." She turned to Caleb. "What do you think?"

"We'll take her somewhere tomorrow and let her use her phone, like we did today. I don't want her on her phone here."

"Smart," Garrison said.

"Da. We can wait another day or two. But then, I fear Nadia will want to return to him."

"If she does, she does," Caleb said. "It's harsh, but you can't force her to believe you."

"This I know. But I also can't let her go back."

He didn't know how Vanessa planned to prevent Nadia from doing what she wanted.

He cared about Nadia because Vanessa did. And he wouldn't do anything to harm the girl. But if Nadia wanted to return to Abbas, he wouldn't prevent it. Because to prevent it meant putting Vanessa and Kat in danger, and Caleb wouldn't allow that, not under any circumstance.

Her head tilted to the side as if she were trying to read his mind. He was glad she couldn't. She wouldn't appreciate what was going on in there. His thoughts about Nadia. His thoughts about Vanessa and Kat, their safety. And Vanessa's lips, full and red and...

The sound of a throat clearing had Caleb snapping out of his daze.

Vanessa's cheeks pinked.

"Anyway," Eric said. "I was thinking that y'all should come to the prayer meeting tomorrow night. We don't have to share any of the details with the group, but I know the folks there would pray for you. I've learned over the years that all our plans are nothing when God isn't in them."

Caleb turned back to Vanessa. How many times had he invited her to the monthly prayer and worship night their church sponsored? How many times had she turned him down?

Was she considering it, or was she about to refuse?

"Do you believe in the power of prayer, or don't you?" Eric asked.

"I do, yes," Vanessa said. "But I am not comfortable asking for help. Especially not after everything you have all done for me already."

"Prayer is a privilege," Garrison said. "Don't rob your friends of the opportunity to pray for you."

"It might be good for Nadia," Caleb added. "I tried to talk to her a little about my faith today while we were on the boat. She seemed ambivalent."

"Ambivalent," she repeated. "This means what?"

"Like she had mixed feelings. Like she wasn't sure what to think. But in the company of believers, maybe she'd open herself to the idea of Christ."

"Da. Maybe." She squeezed Caleb's hand. "You are such a good man. I thank you for that."

He tried not to show the impact that her words had on him.

Eric said, "Garrison, you'll work on reaching out to the royal family. I'll distribute Abbas's photo to the force, make sure we're keeping our eyes out for him. Caleb, you stick to Vanessa and Kat like Velcro."

"Tough job"—he winked at Vanessa—"but I'll take one for the team."

She bumped her shoulder against his. "You are martyr for the cause."

She'd made a joke. A silly one, but he loved that she could find humor despite the fear that must be plaguing her. "Just call me Joan of Arc."

"Who is this?" she asked.

He wrapped his arm around her shoulders and squeezed. Funny that she could be so smart and so poorly educated at the same time. "Never mind."

She settled against him. "You will explain later."

Later. Tomorrow. Next month. Next year. If their plan worked, they'd have all the time in the world.

CHAPTER TWENTY-NINE

Fortunately, Caleb's company had a good management team that he trusted. Still, he'd not planned to be away this week, and work beckoned. As long as they were waiting to hear back from Garrison about reaching out to the royal family, he might as well dive into his laptop.

By the time the girls had come down the next morning, he'd caught up on his emails, though there were still issues that needed to be managed. He'd deal with them later. He put work out of his mind and focused on Vanessa, Nadia, and Kat.

From the moment Nadia sat at the breakfast table, he picked up on her discontentment. It was evident in the way she snapped at her sister, in the way she picked at her meal. Later, it was evident in the way she criticized the mall in Manchester for not having the stores she preferred. In fact, she finally gave up on shopping and spent a solid two hours sitting in the food court, sipping a soda and staring at her phone while Vanessa, Kat, and Caleb browsed. Those two hours were the most enjoyable of the day, despite the fact that Vanessa adamantly refused to let Caleb buy them anything.

One of these days, she'd learn to take gifts from him. One of these days, he would shower them both with treasures.

They went to McNeal's for a late lunch, and Vanessa introduced Nadia to some friends who happened to be there. Nadia was polite enough, but it was clear she was growing impatient to leave. While they filled their bellies with comfort food, she regaled them with stories of night clubs and casinos and fancy shopping districts she and Abbas had visited all over the world.

It wasn't until Nadia told Katarina not to settle for living in a "tiny town filled with old people and children," that Vanessa had had enough.

Their spat—in Serbian—had diners at nearby tables turning to look.

And then, when Caleb asked Nadia for her phone before they headed back to the house, she'd put up a fight. He didn't want Nadia to leave, but her presence was far from enjoyable. Part of him was eager to return her to Boston.

But the stories Vanessa had told him about her time with Abbas wouldn't let that thought linger. *Open Nadia's eyes to the truth. Until You do, give me patience.*

God had promised to teach Caleb patience, and He'd served up plenty of lessons the last few days.

What amazed Caleb most, though, was the change in Vanessa. Or maybe he was only seeing her differently than he had before. Because of the Lord's promise that Vanessa would eventually be his bride, Caleb had been trying to care for her for two years. Trying— and often failing. Her prickly personality made her difficult to love. But now, he saw beyond the veneer she displayed to the world. She wore thorns like a cactus in order to prove she was able to care for herself with very little nourishment. The truth was, she was more like an orchid. Tender, vulnerable, and desperate for love.

She'd opened herself up to the love of God.

And, just a little, she opened up to him. She'd smiled that day. She'd laughed. She'd teased her daughter and made silly jokes.

Caleb couldn't wait to see how she would thrive when she opened herself up to his love completely. When she let him shower her with affectionate words, acts, and touches, she would be the most beautiful orchid in any garden.

He shook himself out of his musings. Orchids and cactuses indeed. He needed to focus.

It was late afternoon, and he was seated at the bar with his laptop, catching up on the day's emails. Vanessa and Nadia had walked down to the lake. He'd worried at first, but the neighborhood was secure, and there was no reason to believe Abbas knew where they were. Plus, the neighborhood's security had been told about the threat, so those at the gate and those at the water would be watching closely. The ladies should be safe.

Behind him, Kat was bouncing on the sofa and watching TV. Vanessa had trusted him to keep an eye on her. That fact, more than Vanessa's casual touches that day, more than their stolen kisses, made his hope take flight.

God's plan was perfect, and nothing would thwart it.

Caleb returned his focus to his email. As soon as he finished it, he'd take Kat to the driving range at the golf club in the neighborhood. Obviously, she had too much energy to watch TV, and the coloring books and crayons her mother had given her were sitting unused on the coffee table.

But there was a problem with one of the store managers that needed to be dealt with. Usually, these issues were taken care of by Caleb's leadership team, but this one had been kicked up to him.

He was agonizing over the email when a crash, then a cry, had him spinning.

Kat lay on the floor beside the sofa holding her head.

He hurried to her. "What happened?"

She held her hands up, and he lifted her into his arms.

"Are you hurt?"

"I bumped my head." Tears streamed down her cheeks. Her hand was pressed against her forehead.

He sat on the sofa. "Can I see it?"

She moved her hand, and he studied the spot. A red mark, a bump... Bumps on the head were good, right? He thought he remembered that from when his own siblings were little. A bump meant the swelling was happening outside the brain and not inside. Not that this was that serious.

He kissed the spot. Kat's eyes were wide and focused on him. Tears still dripped, but fewer now. "I bet that really hurts."

When she nodded, he was sure she'd climb off his lap and return to the cartoon playing in the background. But, if anything, her expression darkened. "Why were Mommy and Aunt Nadia fighting today? Is Aunt Nadia going to leave?"

He patted Kat's back. "I hope not. Do you want her to stay?"

Kat nodded. "Except she makes Mommy mad. And you said she isn't safe. Why isn't she safe?"

Uh-oh. Had he said that? Maybe not in so many words, but Kat was savvy. She could read between the lines. "Aunt Nadia's safe. It's just that... You should talk to your mommy about that."

"Mommy won't tell me anything. Aunt Nadia won't tell me anything. But I'm scared."

When he pulled the little girl close, she wrapped her thin arms around his neck. He inhaled the scent of her. She smelled like strawberry shampoo and the crackers she'd been munching on. She fit perfectly tucked beneath his chin. This sweet, sweet girl, this girl who would be his daughter. The very thought of it had tears filling his own eyes. *Thank you, Lord. I had no idea what a gift she would be to me. As if Vanessa weren't enough.*

"Should I be scared of Aunt Nadia?"

"Oh, sweetie. Your Aunt Nadia won't hurt you." *Give me wisdom, please.* "Nadia has a friend, and we don't think he's safe."

"Is her friend going to hurt me? Or Mommy?"

"Of course not. Nobody's going to hurt you. I promise, I'll keep you both safe."

She stared up at him with those wide brown eyes. Those beautiful eyes. Someday, a young man was going to fall for this precious girl. Caleb would be fending off suitors for years. It might be wise to invest in a shotgun, just in case.

"Mr. Caleb?" She backed away and looked at him with such eagerness in her face. "Are you going to be my daddy?"

Oh. He hoped so. He prayed so. "Would you like that?"

She nodded. "I don't have a daddy, and you don't have a little girl. I think it would be good."

He pulled her close to keep her from seeing the emotion in his expression. "I hope so. We'll just have to wait and see."

He was still fighting the rise of emotion when the glass door slid open.

Vanessa stood in the threshold.

The look on her face—loathing, disgust, and fear all mixed together—had Caleb setting Kat on her feet.

But it was too late.

CHAPTER THIRTY

Vanessa almost cried out as images flooded her mind, all the things she'd been forced to do by evil men, things that made her a very, very good girl. And here was Caleb, his hands all over Kat. His filthy hands.

"Get away from my daughter!"

"She fell. I was just—"

"You get out. You get out now."

"English, Vanessa." He had the nerve to look confused. "I can't—"

"Get out!"

Behind her, Nadia said, "What is wrong with you? He wasn't doing anything."

Vanessa rounded on her. "This is none of your business." And then to Caleb. "I should never have trusted you."

Beside him, Kat bawled. "But Mommy—"

"Go upstairs!" Vanessa turned and snapped at Nadia. "You, too. You give her a bath. Now."

Nadia shot Caleb an apologetic look and took Kat's hand. "Let's go upstairs. No reason for you to watch your mommy go crazy."

"You have no idea what you're talking about!" Vanessa forced herself to take a breath, to think.

Nadia paused and looked at Caleb. "I know you can't understand a word she says, but trust me. You're not missing anything."

Serbian, English. It mattered not what language she spoke. Nobody understood. Nobody would ever understand.

When Nadia and Kat disappeared up the stairs, Caleb said, "She was bouncing on the sofa, and she fell off and bumped her head. She was crying, so—"

"So you took advantage."

That vein pulsed in his jaw. "I don't know what you think you saw."

"I know what I saw. The first minute I turn my back, and you were touching my daughter."

"I was hugging her! I was comforting—"

"I have seen all the moves. I have heard all the excuses. You will leave now."

"Vanessa, I would never—"

"I will not allow it!" Her scream echoed off the walls. She clenched her fists and, once again, forced herself to calm down. She spoke slowly so he wouldn't miss a word. "I will not allow you to hurt my daughter."

He crossed to where she stood, stopped a foot away.

The urge to step back was strong, but she didn't do it. Caleb wouldn't hurt her. Would he?

His words hummed with anger. "I will not defend myself for caring for your daughter."

"Good, because I will not listen to your defense. I will not believe you."

His rage seemed to fade. "Please, Vanessa. Don't do this. Don't let your past ruin what we have."

"We have nothing." Emotion flooded her veins, but she kept

her shoulders back, kept her voice even. She wouldn't crack, not while he still stood in front of her.

"I love you." He sounded so sincere, but she knew what she'd seen.

What a smooth liar he was. "For those words, I hate you all the more. Get out."

VANESSA STOOD IN THE FOYER, guarding the staircase to keep Caleb from having further access to Kat, and waited for him to emerge from his room.

When he was gone, she would break down. When he was gone, she'd let the flood of emotions come. She'd analyze every moment from when she'd first peered through the glass and seen her daughter in his arms to the moment when he'd told her he loved her. But not yet.

He walked down the marble-tiled floor toward her, carrying his small suitcase. He stopped a foot from her. "Don't do this, Vanessa. You can trust me."

"It is done. And I don't."

He seemed to be waiting for something else. She had nothing for him but contempt. Finally, he reached into his pocket and pulled out Abbas's ring. "Give it to Garrison at the prayer meeting tonight. He'll have a plan—"

"I am not going to pray with your friends."

"My friends? They're your friends too. They're our friends."

"There is no *our* anything."

The last bit of affection slid from his expression. "Take the" —he pressed his lips together as if holding in a bad word—"ring. It's yours."

She didn't want it. For many years, she'd held onto it as a symbol to remind her of all she'd overcome. Now, it was only a symbol of her foolishness. For taking it in the first place. For not returning it years ago. For believing she could ever be free. For believing she could ever trust anyone.

For believing she could trust Caleb.

"You give it to Garrison, have him do whatever he wishes with it. We are leaving Nutfield."

His jaw dropped. "No. Stay here. Stay where it's safe."

She took in the cold marble foyer, the wealth and privilege all around her. "This is not my home. This is not my life. We leave today."

"But Nadia—"

"Nadia will come with me. After our talk, she understands what Abbas is. She doesn't wish to return to him."

"She says that now, but... You have to be careful."

"I don't need your help. I have managed by myself for many years. I can survive without you."

"What if I can't survive without you?"

She straightened. "You are a man of pretty words, Caleb Peterson. This does not make you a good man."

He stepped back as if she'd punched him. He fisted the ring. "You're running away from the people who love you most in the world. Hate me if you want, but don't leave this town. The people here are your family. They want to protect you."

"I don't need them, either." She crossed her arms. She would not stay here. Abbas could find her here. Maybe, if Garrison could find a way to have him sent out of the country, she would be able to return. But with Caleb here, with the reminder of all she'd lost?

She'd started over once before. She could do it again.

He turned for the door. A moment before he opened it, he stuck his hand in his pocket, pulled something out, and left it on the entry table beside the fake flowers. Nadia's phone. After he'd opened the door, he turned back to face her. "I won't apologize to you, because I've done nothing wrong. Despite your accusations, my feelings for you haven't changed. Someday, you'll realize all you lost when you refused to believe in love."

The door slammed in his wake.

She stared at the wood that separated her from the man she'd trusted just long enough to feel the sting of his betrayal.

And that's what it had been. Betrayal.

She could still see his arms around Kat's tiny body. See how he'd enveloped her little girl.

For days, she'd accused her sister of being a fool. But she was the fool. She who'd known better, who'd believed Carlos's pretty words all those years ago, who'd had enough experience with the worst of mankind to know better. She had almost been sucked in again.

The footfalls on the steps behind her had her swiping at the tears she'd forbidden from falling.

Nadia stalked across the marble tile. "Your daughter has a bump on her head." The Serbian words were too loud in the cold room. "She told me she fell, and Caleb picked her up and kissed her injury. And for this, you sent him away?"

"He is not to touch my daughter. He knows this."

"You're insane! You don't trust him. You don't trust Abbas—"

"Do not put them in the same category! They're not the same!"

Nadia folded her arms and lifted one eyebrow. "Then why did you send him away?"

"It is not..." She didn't know how to explain. And anyway, Nadia would never understand. Nobody could understand what she'd been through, what she feared. "Pack your things. We're leaving today."

Nadia glared at her, but Vanessa turned her back on her sister. She needed to think.

She marched through the house and out the back door, where she collapsed on the loveseat.

Their loveseat.

No. No. She couldn't let herself think that way. She'd promised herself she would never let what happened to her happen to Katarina. She was only protecting her daughter. If that meant she sacrificed every other relationship in her life, so be it.

She didn't know how long she sat there, replaying what she'd seen, reliving every moment of the horrible scene, when the back door opened.

Kat stepped out, hair still wet from her bath. Eyes red from crying.

An ugly bump on her forehead.

"Does your head ache?"

"Why did you send Mr. Caleb away?"

She patted the seat beside her, and Kat scrambled up. "He said he wanted to be my daddy."

The words filled Vanessa's stomach with acid. Why would he say such a thing? Was he so evil that he could think of Kat as his daughter while planning to harm her?

Or perhaps he'd said the words to gain Kat's trust.

Man's depravity never ceased to surprise her.

"You don't need a daddy," Vanessa finally said. "You have me."

"He said he'd protect us from Nadia's scary friend. Who's going to take care of us now?"

"I will take care of you, *ceri.*"

Kat launched herself off the loveseat and faced Vanessa. "I want Mr. Caleb."

"He is gone. But I am—"

"I want Mr. Caleb!" She stomped her tiny feet.

"Do not yell at me. He is not coming—"

"I hate you!" She screamed the words, then ran back into the house, sliding the door closed with such force that it bounced against the frame.

Vanessa shouldn't let Kat get away with insolence. But right now she couldn't force herself off the loveseat. She dropped her head into her hands and wept.

CHAPTER THIRTY-ONE

Dinner needed to be fixed. Bags needed to be packed. Arrangements needed to be made.

She'd wallowed enough. It was time to move on—from her home, from Nutfield, from Caleb. These were small sacrifices to save her sister.

And her daughter.

She would not mourn Caleb any longer. She'd brought this heartbreak on herself by trusting him, but no longer. Caleb was a man, just like all the rest. She only thanked God that He'd revealed Caleb's true colors before Vanessa had made the biggest mistake of her life.

When she stood from the outdoor loveseat, she realized how cold she was. And no wonder. The sun had dipped below the trees, and tonight nobody had brought out a blanket to drape over her. Nobody had snuggled up beside her to share his body heat.

Stop it.

Inside, Kat was watching TV. She glared when Vanessa walked in. Tear tracks marked her cheeks. Vanessa's heart broke for her daughter, but Kat would recover from this. They all would.

Nadia was probably staring at the TV in her own room. And sulking. Everybody was sulking.

Vanessa opened the refrigerator. There were no meals, only ingredients to make meals, which she didn't know how to do.

She checked the container of leftover chili, but there wasn't enough for the three of them.

Sandwiches, then. She fixed three turkey and cheese sandwiches, set them on plates, and added a handful of potato chips to each.

When dinner was prepared, she ran upstairs to pack their things quickly. They'd eat after they loaded the car.

Except... her car wasn't there. It was at her house. She froze inside her bedroom door. What to do about that? She could call someone, but... She checked her watch. Everybody she could think to call would be at the church for the prayer and worship meeting.

Uber, then. She started packing her things and Kat's. After they ate, she'd call for a ride. And she'd call the police and ask them to meet her at her house, just in case Abbas was there watching for her. As long as she was going home anyway, she could grab more things. Not everything, but more than a few days' worth of clothes. Maybe whatever household goods she could fit in her minivan. The rest she'd have to consider a loss.

As much as Caleb liked to think he and this town could protect Vanessa's family, she knew better than that. Abbas would get his revenge for the ring she'd stolen, and he'd do his best to find Nadia if for no other reason than to soothe his damaged ego. But she wasn't going to make it easy for him. She wouldn't wait around like a... what was that English expression? A sitting goose?

She could almost hear Caleb's voice when the proper word came to her. *Sitting duck.*

Tears stung her eyes and made their toiletries swim in her vision. *Caleb. Why couldn't you have been the exception?*

She swiped the tears and grabbed the toothbrushes. She was doing what she had to do. To save Nadia from Abbas, to save Kat from Caleb, to save herself from all of it. They had to run.

When the bags were packed, she stripped her bed and Kat's, dumped the sheets in the hallway. The least she could do was get them started, even if she didn't have time to wait until all the beds were made. She knocked on Nadia's door.

Nadia yanked it open. "What do you want?"

"I need to wash your sheets. Also, I made sandwiches." Despite all the craziness in her life, it was nice to speak her native language. Comfortable. "We should eat before we go. And..." A thought occurred to her. "Caleb bought all those groceries. We should take what we can. We won't have a lot of money while we travel, and—"

"I'm not going anywhere with you."

"You said..." Panic rose. "You promised you'd come. You promised you'd stay with us."

"If you don't trust Caleb, then..." Nadia shook her head. "Caleb is the nicest man I've ever known. Even nicer than Tata. If you don't understand that, then you don't understand anything."

Vanessa grabbed her sister's wrist. "Nadia, you have to come. I've given up everything to protect you. I've sacrificed—"

"I didn't ask you to do that!" She yanked her arm away. "You're crazy, and I'm not going anywhere with you."

Vanessa backed up and leaned against the wall. She could fix this. She could still keep them all safe. "I understand you're angry with me. There are other options." She thought fast. What could she do? "I'll buy you a ticket home." The cost would eat up a good portion of her savings, but at least Nadia would be safe. "You have your passport, no?"

Nadia's laugh was anything but kind. "I'm not going back to Serbia."

"Then what? What do you want to do? Just tell me, and—"

The doorbell rang. A moment later, someone pounded on the door.

Nadia headed toward the stairs, suitcase in hand. "He's here."

"Wait!" Vanessa followed, but Nadia didn't slow. "Who's here?"

"Who do you think?"

With the suitcase banging behind Nadia, Vanessa couldn't reach her to stop her as they went down the stairs.

They were in the foyer by the time Vanessa grabbed her sister's arm to stop her from opening the door. It didn't make sense. Nadia had no way to contact...

She glanced at the table inside the front door. The table where Caleb had dropped Nadia's phone.

The phone was gone.

"Please tell me you called Caleb to take you back?" *Please, please let it be Caleb.*

"After what you did to him today, do you really think I'd ask him for help? Don't you think he's done enough?" She reached for the door, but Vanessa smacked her hand away.

"Please, please, Nadia. Please don't answer it."

A bang on the door vibrated through her entire being. "Open up."

Acid filled her stomach.

Nadia's eyes were cold. "Get out of my way."

"You don't understand. He'll kill me."

"Right. He can't be trusted. Like Caleb can't be trusted. I almost believed you, sister. But now I understand. Why did you make up all those stories about Abbas? Are you jealous he wants me and not you?"

Despite the familiar language, Vanessa couldn't process the words her sister was hurling at her. She could only think about the fact that Abbas was on the other side of the door. How had he gotten past the guard at the gate? Maybe he'd hurt him or killed him. Or maybe he'd just slipped him a bribe.

It didn't matter. None of it mattered now.

Kat stood in the doorway and watched the scene.

"If you want to go with him, then go." Vanessa glanced at the door as if he were standing right there. She had to focus on Nadia. "I won't stop you. But please don't let him in yet. Let me get Katarina away first. Just... I'm sure the police could be here in seconds."

"You don't have to fear me, Nadia." Abbas's voice carried too easily through the door. "You know this. Your sister has no reason to fear me, either."

"Just give me ten minutes," Vanessa said. "Please, ten minutes—"

"I'd like to clear things up with you, Vanessa." Abbas's refined English accent, always charming, always dripping with deception.

Nadia shoved her out of the way and reached for the door.

Vanessa was out of options. She ran across the foyer, pulled Katarina into her arms, and hurried to the back. Behind her, the front door swung open. She heard Nadia's cheerful greeting.

She and Kat were almost to the slider when she saw movement through the glass and froze.

The guards Abbas had used for years were on the deck. His servants and friends. Men who would do whatever he told them to do, no matter how horrid.

Behind her, footsteps.

With trembling fingers, she yanked her phone from her

pocket, but before she could dial, Abbas snatched it out of her hand. He spun her around, and she backed against the wall of glass.

He kept in step with her. So close she could see the gray in his beard. So close she could feel the heat coming off his skin. But he didn't touch her.

"Hello, again, Vanessa." His attention turned to Kat, who hid her face against Vanessa's neck and wrapped her arms and legs around her as if she'd never let go. "And who have we here?" He reached toward Kat's hair.

"Do not touch her."

His arm lowered, and a slow smile spread across his face. His hand came toward her, and she flinched, but he didn't make contact. He angled close, reaching for something behind her. She heard the click of the lock on the door.

It slid open, and the guards filed in.

Abbas focused on Kat again. "She's as pretty as you were. Of course, you were a bit older when we met."

Guards on one side. Abbas in front. She was cornered. She had to think, *think*. She had to get Nadia to understand the danger. Only if they worked together did they have a chance at escape. And they had to escape before Abbas got them back to his yacht. Once that happened, all would be lost.

Vanessa straightened her shoulders. "My daughter is seven. Not much younger than I was. Though I lost track of the years. How old do you think I was when you purchased me, Abbas? About twelve?"

Behind her, Nadia said, "See, I told you. She's gone crazy."

Abbas smile never wavered. "They told me you were thirteen. If so, barely. You became a woman aboard my ship." His gaze flicked to the guards, but she dared not take her eyes off Abbas. "Do you remember? We had to make an unscheduled stop to buy her feminine products."

One of them chuckled. She'd heard their names, but she'd always thought of them as Beast One and Beast Two. That chuckle came from Beast One, the meaner and more sadistic of them. Beast Two had a shred of humanity. Sometimes he would sneak her extra food. He was the one who cared for her when she became ill. He was the one who insisted they make that unscheduled stop when she'd first gotten her period. No mother to ask questions. No women at all. Only herself and the three men who used her like an amusement park ride.

She would die before she let them touch her daughter.

The problem was, her death was likely Abbas's goal. And then who would protect Katarina?

"Wait." Nadia stood beside Abbas. "You met when she was twelve?"

Abbas swiveled and took Nadia's hand. His shoulders lifted and fell. "I saved her from a terrible life. I sheltered her on my ship. I fed her and cared for her."

But Abbas's words didn't settle the fear in Nadia's face. "You said you lived with her. You said she was your girlfriend. You acted as if..."

He ran his knuckles down Nadia's cheek. "Semantics, my love."

"I don't understand."

Vanessa said, "That's because he's lying to you."

The pinch came from beside her, a sharp pain in her upper arm. If not for Kat blocking the way, he'd have pinched her shoulder. She'd been punished by Beast Two that way more than once. He was the kinder one, but only by a degree. He leaned close and whispered just loudly enough for her—and Kat —to hear. "Watch your mouth, whore."

Whore.

The name she'd gone by for years and years. The name

she'd gone by for so long that her own name might have been forgotten if she hadn't repeated it to herself every night.

I am Vojislava Bakočević. I have a mother who loves me. I have brothers and sisters who love me. I am loved. I matter.

She had mattered then, and she mattered now.

Nadia still looked confused, though... was the look forced? "You're saying you rescued her, and then you fell in love with her?"

"Precisely." Abbas shifted to look at both of them. "And after all I did for Vanessa, she left me." He squeezed Nadia's hand. "But I never cared for her as I care for you."

Nadia's normally easy smile didn't reach her eyes. "Let's just leave. Vanessa obviously doesn't want to come with us. Let's leave her and Kat here."

Oh, Nadia. She was trying to undo what she'd done. As much as Vanessa had wanted to spare her sister, she would allow Nadia to sacrifice herself to save Kat. Anything to save Kat.

"Ah, but you see," Abbas said, "she took something from me, something I need to get back."

Nadia glanced at Vanessa. "If she gives it to you, then you'll leave her and Kat here?"

Abbas turned to Vanessa. "Do you have it?"

She didn't, not with her, and it was just as well. Even if she did, she wouldn't admit it. Apart from the ring, Abbas had no reason to leave her alive.

"It's in town."

His brows lifted toward his curly brown hair. "In this town? In this dinky little town, you left my priceless jewel?"

She scrambled to think... Was the downtown bank open this late? Would Abbas notice if it wasn't?

She didn't know the answer to any of those questions. All she knew was that her only hope to save her daughter would be to get into town. "It's in a safe deposit box at a bank on Crystal Ave."

He glared at her for a long moment, then walked closer until his face was less than an inch from hers. "Jalil, take Nadia and get her settled into my car, please. And stay with her to make sure she's safe."

To make sure she doesn't escape. And to threaten Vanessa. Did Nadia understand that?

Beast Two grabbed Nadia's arm.

"Wait!" Vanessa sidestepped Abbas. "Nadia, take Kat with you." Whatever Abbas was about to say to Vanessa, to do to her, she didn't want Kat to witness it.

Kat squeezed Vanessa tighter, but she said nothing.

Beast Two looked at Abbas for permission. He nodded, and the guard stepped back.

Nadia's eyes were wide. She looked as if she wanted to do something, to say something, to fix all of this. But there was nothing to do now but let it play out.

Please, God. Please let it play out differently this time. Please protect us.

She crossed to her sister. "*Ceri*, go with your Aunt Nadia."

"I want to stay with you." Her little voice was low and scared.

"Trust me, daughter. Go with Nadia."

Nadia took Kat's waist, and Vanessa gently pried Katarina's hands from her neck.

When Kat was in Nadia's arms, Beast Two ushered her toward the front, snatching her suitcase on the way.

The door slammed behind them, and a wide smile spread across Abbas's face. "Noble of you to try to protect your daughter. As if it will help."

"I will give you your ring back if you let my daughter go."

His head tilted to the side. "You think you can negotiate

with me?" He glanced at Beast One, amusement in his expression. "Our little whore has grown up."

The guard chuckled.

Abbas reached behind his back. When he showed his hand again, it held a pistol. He didn't point it at her, just rested the barrel against the side of her head. "If the ring isn't in my hand by the end of this day, I'll sell your daughter to the highest bidder. And your sister. You"—he eyed her, head to toe—"you've lost the youth that made you attractive. You belong in the trash heap."

She didn't allow his insult to permeate her skin. She knew who she was. Besides, what happened to her was irrelevant.

"Hear me on this." Abbas pinched her chin in his fingers.

He was dying to get a reaction from her, dying to see her cower as she used to. She kept her face impassive. She'd learned much since she'd left Abbas's yacht. She'd learned to hide her feelings deep inside. To pretend she was tough. To pretend she was unafraid.

Abbas watched, waited. After a moment, he dropped his hand. "That ring is worth more than the three of you combined."

"If I give it to you, you will let us go?"

His smile, charming, fraudulent, spread across his face. "Of course."

He lied, of course. She wouldn't trust a word from his mouth. The ring was the only thing keeping her alive right now. If it could get her downtown, maybe, maybe she could save Katarina.

CHAPTER THIRTY-TWO

The last place Caleb wanted to be was at church. Every month, Christians from multiple churches in Nutfield gathered to pray for the town, the state, the nation, and the world. Tonight, Caleb didn't care about any of that. He didn't think he could stomach an hour of thinking about local and world leaders. But his friends would also pray for individual needs, and he needed that desperately.

The real reason he'd come was much less spiritual and much more practical. Garrison had texted and said he had information. For that, Caleb had forced himself to drive to the downtown church. When he stepped into the vestibule, he caught sight of Eric and Garrison in conversation in the corner. Between himself and them, a gathering of couples chatted and laughed as if all were right with the world.

Attempting to smile at familiar faces, he made his way past the crowd to his friends.

Eric took one look at him and said, "What's wrong?"

He hadn't planned to tell Eric or anyone what had happened that day. What if they thought, like Vanessa did, that Caleb had overstepped with Kat? What if Caleb was in the wrong? He knew his own heart, knew he'd had nothing but kindness and love for Vanessa's daughter on his mind, but maybe Garrison and Eric, both parents themselves, would take Vanessa's side. Maybe they'd never look at him the same way again.

His friends studied him while he debated. Eric was his closest friend and prayer partner, and Garrison knew as much as Eric did about Vanessa's past. Caleb couldn't fix this on his own. He needed God's help. Which meant he needed his friends' prayers.

"I was watching Kat, and she fell and bumped her head. I was only trying to console her, but—"

"Vanessa didn't see it that way," Garrison guessed.

"She ordered me out. She's planning to leave Nutfield for good."

Eric clasped his shoulder. "I'm sorry, man."

"We can't let her leave with that ring," Garrison said. "If she does, not only will Abbas be looking for her, but so will law enforcement."

"I have the ring." Caleb pulled it from his pocket and handed it to Garrison. "She wouldn't take it back."

"Well, that's good news." He pocketed it. "Still, she shouldn't go. We're close to getting this taken care of. I've got a friend in the State Department working on contacting the Sahim royals right now. He's very confident they'll agree to keeping Abbas off American soil in return for the ring."

"Did you tell her that?"

"I thought she'd be here tonight."

"She won't," Caleb said.

Garrison pulled his phone from his pocket. "I'll call her right now." He stepped outside.

Most of the crowd had moved into the sanctuary, but Eric stayed with Caleb. "I don't know what to say, man."

"Nothing to say. I blew it."

"No," Eric said. "Vanessa's just afraid. She's come a long way in the last seven years, but, from what I can tell, fear is always her first reaction. And for her, fear means building walls, keeping people out. More than once, Kelsey's had to break through her walls anew after something's frightened her. She's like... like a turtle, retreating into her shell at any sign of trouble."

Caleb leaned against the wall, arms crossed. His friend's analogy was as good as his own. Turtle, cactus. Either way, how was he supposed to get past the protective covering?

How did one cuddle a cactus?

How did one remove the flesh-and-blood turtle from its protective shell?

Inside the sanctuary, praise music started, and the worshipers sang along.

Garrison came back in. "No answer. I left a message and sent a text. I'll try again after the meeting."

"I don't think I can stay," Caleb said. "I need—"

"You need to be here," Eric said. "We're breaking into groups tonight. Women here, men in the annex."

They broke into groups every week, occasionally by gender. It would be easier to ask for prayer from the men alone, and it would be more comfortable in the smaller building next door than in the large sanctuary.

What were his options? Stay here surrounded by the presence of God and His people, or go home and brood.

A very big part of him wanted to go home and brood.

Instead, he walked with his friends into the sanctuary. He'd try to worship. Later, when they moved into the annex, he'd ask for prayer. Because he was at the end of himself. He had no idea how to fix this. Only God could change Vanessa's heart. Only God could protect her now.

CHAPTER THIRTY-THREE

Vanessa had no plan.

When they reached the entrance to the neighborhood, Vanessa looked for the guard in the little shack who opened and closed the entrance gate, but she saw nobody inside. Nobody to signal they needed help.

"What did you do to him?" she asked.

Abbas said, "Don't worry, my dear. A little bump on the head. He'll recover."

The guard would be no help. Now, her only hope would be found in downtown Nutfield. Maybe somebody would see them. Maybe somebody would contact the police. Even if she drove right by one of her friends, though, she wouldn't be seen in the backseat of Abbas's car.

Beside her, Kat gripped her so hard that Vanessa's fingers ached. She lifted her little hand and kissed it, then met her frightened eyes and tried to reassure her with a smile.

The look didn't fool her daughter.

In the seat beside Abbas, Nadia faced forward and chattered, telling Abbas about everything they'd done since she'd been in New Hampshire. About the boat, about the pretty

279

foliage, about the mall. Though she'd complained about the mall earlier that day, now she made it sound charming.

Abbas murmured responses occasionally, but Vanessa didn't think he was buying Nadia's forced cheerfulness. It was obvious Nadia was overcompensating. Abbas had to have known she no longer trusted him.

And Nadia knew he knew.

Yet, Nadia continued to chatter.

Vanessa tried to drown out the words. *Lord, help me.*

But how dare she ask God for help now after all the stupid choices she'd made? They were clear now, clear as if someone had put a magnifying glass over them. If Vanessa hadn't ordered Caleb out of the house, then Nadia wouldn't have gotten angry with her. Caleb wouldn't have left her phone unguarded, and even if he had, Nadia wouldn't have called Abbas because she'd have continued to believe Vanessa's account of the kind of man Abbas was. Vanessa could blame this all on Caleb, but...

As they rode the dark meandering back roads of Nutfield, she forced herself to relive the scene she'd witnessed at the house. Caleb had hugged Kat. He'd kissed her forehead. He'd held her close. Not like a lover. Not like an abuser. Like a father. Even Kat knew that—and longed for it.

Like Tata used to hold Vanessa.

Caleb wasn't Abbas. Caleb was nothing like Abbas. Even at Kat's young age, she knew this. She embraced the goodness in Caleb, trembled at the evil in Abbas. And the fact that Vannesa'd ever thought Caleb was anything like Abbas made her the biggest fool of all. This was all her fault.

Her sister, her daughter, herself—all lost because Vanessa had refused to believe in Caleb.

No. It was more than that. What had Caleb said before he'd walked out of the house?

He was right. She'd lost everything because she'd refused to believe in love.

Father, forgive me. The words felt hollow now. If only she could go back and do everything differently. *I know this is all my fault. Help me fix it. Help me save my baby. Help me save Nadia. I can't do this alone. I need help. Please, send help.*

The glow of town was visible ahead. They were nearly there. Abbas would have to let her out of the car to go into the bank. Of course, he'd accompany her, so she wouldn't be able to signal for help. But maybe somebody would see. The bank was just a few doors down from the police station, and Eric had alerted all the cops in town to be on the lookout for him. Maybe a police officer would spot them.

The problem was that Abbas wouldn't leave Nadia and Kat alone. No, he'd make sure the Beasts were guarding them.

She glanced out the rear window. They were following in a second car, watching. Always watching.

Abbas turned onto Crystal Ave, and the sight at the far end had her heart pounding. The church. The parking lot was on the far side, hidden from their view. From here, the church looked as if it could be deserted, but she knew all the people within. Her friends. And they *were* her friends. It was too late, but she realized that these people had become friends and more. They were family to her.

And Caleb would be there.

If she could get Kat to the church...

Nadia continued chatting in the front seat.

Vanessa turned to her daughter, put her finger over her own lips, and unlatched Kat's seatbelt. She leaned down and whispered, "When I say, I want you to run to the church. Run as fast as you can. Don't turn around, no matter what. Don't stop, no matter what. You understand me?"

She backed up to see her daughter's expression. Eyes wide, lip trembling. But she nodded.

Vanessa leaned in again. "Find Mr. Caleb. Tell him what happened. He'll take care of you."

As soon as she heard the words from her own mouth, she knew they were true. Of course Caleb would take care of Kat. He loved Vanessa, and he loved Kat.

It was as simple and as beautiful as that.

She hugged her daughter, inhaling her scent, perhaps for the last time. Would she ever again feel these precious arms around her? Would she ever again look into those big brown eyes? "I love you, my sweet girl."

Kat trembled against her. *Please, please, God, save us.*

Abbas ran through a yellow light. Behind him, a car horn blared.

Abbas swore under his breath.

She turned to look. The guards' car was stopped at the intersection.

"Where are we going?" Abbas said.

"Just beyond the church." A lie. They were passing the only bank on the street now. And then the police station. She watched the front, but nobody stepped out. Nobody saw.

Another block until the last stop sign before the church. From there, Kat would have to cut across the common, then cross the street, to make it to safety. If Vanessa could keep Abbas from getting out of the car for about a minute, Kat would get away. Then...

She had no idea what would happen then. Maybe Abbas would kill her. Maybe he'd kill Nadia. But Vanessa didn't think so. He needed that ring. He didn't need Kat to get it. And killing her or Nadia wouldn't help him.

She thought, she hoped, that he'd let her daughter go.

She glanced behind. Two cars separated them from the guards.

Abbas neared the stop sign. She squeezed Kat's hand, then reached across her and grabbed the door handle.

When Abbas stopped, she yanked the handle, pushed the door, and yelled, "Run!"

Kat bolted from the car.

Vanessa wrapped her arm around Abbas's neck and squeezed.

His hands came up, grabbed her forearm, dug in.

Nadia pummeled him from the side, a string of curses in Serbian flying from her lips.

"Nadia, run!"

But she didn't. She hurled herself at Abbas. Then, she backed up, his gun in her hand. She whacked him on the head.

"Go!" Nadia screamed as the gun slipped from her grip and fell.

Abbas quit fighting. His head slumped.

Nadia opened her car door.

Vanessa went out Kat's door and grabbed her sister's hand. They bolted across the corner of the common.

Shouts chased after them. The guards had seen and were following.

Vanessa and Nadia were almost there. They made it up the steps, pushed through the door, and burst into the back of the church.

CHAPTER THIRTY-FOUR

Vanessa froze with Nadia beside her, their breathing heavy in the room's silence. Twenty-five, maybe thirty women, all faced them.

Kat was standing in their midst.

Marisa was on her cell. Probably dialing 911.

Rae was on her cell, probably calling her husband, the chief of police.

Kelsey was crouched down, Kat in her arms. Sam was on her other side.

Harper came forward. "What happened? Are you all right?"

Then Ginny, Angel, and even Chelsea were there. They surrounded her, touching her, drawing her and her sister into the sanctuary. Protecting them.

She was overcome. She couldn't think.

Until the door behind her slammed open.

In an instant, the women turned to face whoever had come in.

Abbas, followed by Beast One and Beast Two, stepped into the worship center.

The fury in his eyes was instantly masked by that charming smile. "Good evening, ladies."

Her friends moved to shield her, Nadia, and Kat. A wall of kindness and love.

Rae stepped forward. "Can we help you with something?"

"Actually, I think I can help you." His refined accent bounced off the walls as he looked around. "I've never been inside a Christian church before. It's lovely."

Kelsey slipped her hand in Vanessa's. Vanessa realized all the women were holding hands now.

She felt her daughter behind her and reached back to include her in the chain.

Nadia gripped Vanessa's arm. They were connected. They wouldn't be separated again.

"We're having a prayer meeting," Rae said. "Would you like to join us? The men are meeting next door."

Abbas chuckled, and the sound was lighthearted, as if he hadn't a care in the world. "I think not. But you need to know that a few of those in your midst don't belong."

"How so?" Rae asked.

"Christians are supposed to be good and pure and moral, isn't that right? But the woman you're sheltering now is far from it. You see, I am a Sahimi prince, and she stole something from me. She is a thief and a whore."

The women bristled, muttering and shifting.

But Rae only laughed. "You obviously don't know anything about Christianity."

Abbas's confidence slipped, though probably Vanessa was the only one who knew it. She'd spent too long studying his face, his moods.

"You see," Rae said, casual as could be, "we believe everyone is a sinner, and all sinners are equal. When we believe in Jesus, He makes us clean. And when we're saved, all Christians are equal. God shows no favoritism. We're all sinners saved by the grace of God and the blood of Christ. Whatever you think you know about our friend Vanessa, you're wrong. She's pure and sweet and free."

Rae's words rang in Vanessa's ears like the clearest church bells.

Abbas's scoff was cut off by the doors opening.

He and his guards turned as Eric and Brady entered, other police officers at their sides.

More streamed in from the side doors at the front of the sanctuary. Many had their guns drawn, aimed at Abbas and his guards.

And, just like that, Abbas and the beasts were disarmed and taken into custody.

A moment later, more men poured in. They found their wives and girlfriends and daughters and sisters and friends. She heard choruses of concern.

Are you okay?

What happened?

Did they hurt you?

These men... these good, godly men had swarmed in to protect the women they loved, they cherished. These were nothing like the men in her past. These were men the way God intended.

In the words of the people surrounding her, she felt the praises to God, the gratitude that He'd protected them. She felt the embraces all around. But she couldn't take her eyes off the man standing in the entry now.

Caleb had stayed there. He'd watched Abbas and the guards handcuffed and marched out of the church. He'd spoken with Eric. And now, he turned to face her.

Before she could think what to do, Kat yanked her hand away and ran to him.

He opened his arms, and she threw herself at him. She was crying and babbling as he lifted her, held her against himself, and walked Vanessa's direction.

Over the din of the crowd, she heard her daughter's words. "Mommy told me to come find you. She said you'd take care of me."

Caleb met her gaze. "Of course I will, sweetheart. Always."

Vanessa couldn't make her voice work. It had all happened so fast. One minute, she was sure she would die.

The next moment...

Caleb held his free arm open, and she stepped into his embrace. "I'm sorry. I should have trusted you. I should have—"

"English, please."

Oh. She looked up, held his eye contact, and switched to English. "I'm a fool. I should never have doubted you."

"You don't now?" His gaze flicked to Kat. "It's okay?"

Vanessa said, "Da. It's perfect."

His mouth closed, his eyes filled, and he looked toward the church's high ceiling.

Praising God. As she would do, all the days of her life. But right now...

She looked around at the people who surrounded her. Her friends. True friends. These women who'd placed themselves between her and Abbas. Who'd put themselves in danger to protect her.

As difficult and closed off and suspicious as she'd been since she'd lived in Nutfield, these people had loved her and supported her. They'd taken her in and helped her.

She still longed for her mother and her siblings. As for her father... Whether he'd known or not what he was selling her into when he took that handful of bills, she had to forgive him. Because she'd been forgiven much. And she'd been given much.

Because, somehow, she'd found a new family, right here in Nutfield.

Poor Nadia seemed overwhelmed as she took in the scene. All these people, this church. This peace.

Vanessa grabbed her sister's hand and pulled her into their group hug. Herself, her daughter, her sister, and Caleb, and the amazing people around her. Her true family.

CHAPTER THIRTY-FIVE

Caleb still couldn't believe it was over.

He kept himself from asking Vanessa what had happened, knowing he'd get the whole story eventually. He stood quietly and listened to Eric's first round of questions at the church, then drove Vanessa, Nadia, and Kat to the police station. He stayed with Kat in the waiting area while Vanessa and Nadia went deeper into the station, where Eric surely asked more questions and filled out his reports. Caleb was dying to know the details, but, God willing, he'd have the rest of his life to learn them. Now that Abbas was in custody, there was no rush.

Finally, Vanessa and Nadia came out, and Kat clambered off his lap and ran to her mother, who lifted her and held her tight.

This strong woman and her precious child, these two he loved and had almost lost.

Two years he'd questioned God's will. In four days, God had turned his world upside down.

The same God who had created an entire universe in just six days.

When Caleb had rushed into the church, had seen Abbas and his two goons, he'd been overcome with rage. Rage and fear and... he'd never be able to name all the emotions that had filled him in that moment.

He forced himself to concentrate on Kat. She hadn't said much since the ordeal. He hadn't pushed her. Over time, she, too, would open up about what she'd been through. She'd recover from this and be stronger for it. That ability to take hardship and turn it into strength—that was another one of God's specialties and something Vanessa had learned well. He had no doubt her daughter had inherited that trait.

He reached out, and Vanessa slid her hand into his.

"You're all set?" he asked.

"Eric said we could go." Vanessa sounded tired. "Abbas and his guards will remain in custody. We're safe."

He pulled her close and kissed her forehead.

Behind Vanessa, Nadia stood with her arms crossed, staring at the floor.

He turned her way. "You all right?"

"I'm sorry. I did not believe—"

"A thousand times," Vanessa said, "I have told you this was not your fault. I'm the one who made you doubt me by kicking Caleb out."

"Wait," Caleb said. "What?"

But Vanessa just waved off his question and spoke to Nadia. "If not for that, you'd have continued to believe. This was my fault."

"You're both wrong," Caleb said. "This was Abbas's fault. And now it's over. All is forgiven, all is past, and all is well." He opened the door to the crisp evening air. "Come on. Let's get you ladies home."

They slid into his car, and he drove toward Vanessa's house.

"Our things are still at Ginny and Kade's," Vanessa said.

"They went over there and grabbed them for you," Caleb said. "While you two were being questioned, Kade loaded your bags into my car." He met Nadia's eyes in the rearview mirror. "The police recovered your suitcase from Abbas's rental. I have it, too."

"Thank you." Her voice was small in the backseat. She still blamed herself. What a mess Abbas had left in his wake.

"I left their house before cleaning." Vanessa said. "I left sandwiches on the table and chips out. I stripped the beds and left the sheets in a pile in the hallway. I feel terrible."

He squeezed her hand. "They understand, and they don't mind one bit. They were happy to help."

"They are good people," Vanessa said. "All of our friends are good people."

Our friends. He loved that phrase.

Vanessa's house looked just as it had the other day. The bike was still outside. On the front porch, the golf club was still leaning against the wall. Funny how so many things had changed and others were exactly the same.

Inside, Nadia and Kat went to the kitchen to fix something to eat. Apparently, they hadn't eaten since lunch, which felt about a million years ago.

He held the ladies' bags. "Want me to leave them here, or—?"

"If you don't mind taking them back," Vanessa said. "I'll show you the way." She led him down a narrow hallway and pushed open the last door on the left. "Leave Nadia's suitcase in here."

He stepped into what had to be Kat's room—painted white furniture, baby blue walls, and butterfly decals. More butterflies decorated the bedspread, along with decorative pillows and a mountain of stuffed animals. The room was tidy, despite the dolls and doll furniture in one corner, the easel and drawing materials in another.

He left Nadia's suitcase on the end of the twin bed and stepped to the room across the hall.

"My suitcase and Kat's duffel will go in here," Vanessa said.

Unlike her daughter's, Vanessa's room was sparse. No pretty comforter, no headboard, no fresh coat of paint. One drawer hung off-kilter on the bureau. She'd gone all out for Kat and had done nothing to beautify her own private space.

It was a picture of Vanessa's life. She'd sacrificed her own luxury for Kat's, and she'd risked everything to save her sister.

Two more reasons he loved this woman.

She stood in the doorway, arms crossed, eyes downcast. If he didn't know her better, he'd say she looked self-conscious. He left her suitcase and Kat's duffel bag on the end of the bed and slipped past her and down the hall.

"Thank you for... you know."

When he reached the living room, he turned to face her. The last thing he wanted was to leave, but he said, "I guess I'll call you tomorrow."

"I would like you to stay for a little while, if you don't mind. We need to eat, and then I must get Kat settled, but—"

"I'd love to."

He joined them at Vanessa's little kitchen table and munched cheese and crackers. It was after eleven when Nadia bid him good-night and Vanessa shooed Kat down the hallway to brush her teeth. Before she followed, Vanessa waved to the TV. "I don't have cable, but we have that Disney streaming service. There was a special, so..."

He kissed her forehead. "Take your time."

He settled on the couch and found the local news on TV but couldn't concentrate. Instead, he listened to the voices coming down the hall. Vanessa getting Nadia settled in Kat's room, tucking Kat into her own bed. The normal sounds of family life, sounds he couldn't wait to be a part of.

Vanessa poked her head into the living room. "Kat would like a kiss good-night."

"Oh." His heart swelled just a little as he followed Vanessa down the hallway and into her bedroom.

Kat was curled up under the covers on Vanessa's queen-sized bed. He crouched down beside her. "How you holding up?"

She shrugged her tiny shoulders.

"Did your mommy say your prayers with you?"

"Uh-huh. And she read me a story, too. But I'm still scared."

"Do you mind if I say a prayer?" He held out his hand, and she slipped one of hers from beneath the blanket and took it. He turned to Vanessa, who stood in the doorway, and held out his other hand. When she joined him, he closed his eyes.

He thanked God that they were safe and prayed for His peace and protection over them. The words were forgotten the moment they left his lips, but the peace of God filled their space, connected their family, as only He could.

When he finished the short prayer, he kissed Kat's forehead. "Sleep tight."

She slid her little arms around his neck and hugged him fiercely. Then she snuggled under the covers.

Five minutes later, Vanessa curled up at his side on the sofa. She didn't say anything, and he didn't expect her to. He found a movie, and they sat in silence, eyes on the screen, while he reveled in the feel of her against him. They'd been sitting like that for thirty minutes when Kat stepped into the room, her blanket in her hand. "I can't sleep."

Vanessa patted the space beside her, and Kat lay on the sofa, rested her head on her mother's lap, and, within a few minutes, drifted off.

Vanessa must have, too, because he could feel her even breaths against his chest. That she would feel comfortable enough to sleep in his presence, to let her daughter sleep in his presence... What a difference a few hours had made.

When the credits rolled, Vanessa sat up and yawned. She turned to him with a sheepish smile and whispered, "I'm sorry."

He planted a kiss on her forehead. "I'm happy just to be with you. But"—he removed his feet from her coffee table where he'd perched them and started to stand—"I should go."

"I wanted to talk to you, but I got comfortable... Wait just a moment, please." She scooped Kat into her arms and walked down the hall. A moment later, she returned. "She's still asleep."

"Poor kid's had a rough day."

Vanessa sat, her knees touching his. "I tried to apologize earlier, but you wouldn't let me."

He stifled the urge to tell her it wasn't necessary. Brushing off an offense wasn't the same as dealing with and forgiving one. So, he let her talk.

"I should never have accused you of being unappropriate with my daughter."

"*In*appropriate."

"That is what I said." She barely smiled with the words. "Either way, I jumped to wrong conclusions. Will you forgive me?"

He took her hands and squeezed. "I already have."

"I cannot promise I will never do it again. This is my reaction whenever any man gets near her."

He nodded slowly. "Fair enough. I promise to try to be patient with you and not do anything that makes you uncomfortable."

Her intelligent green eyes studied him, and in them, he saw not relief at their conversation but... fear?

"What's wrong?" he asked.

"You said something to me earlier, something I still struggle to believe. But you are an honest man. My inability to believe it does not make it untrue, yes?"

He thought of the words he'd said, the last-ditch effort to get her to believe him back at Kade and Ginny's house. They had been true. If he could take them back and say them for the first time at a more appropriate occasion, he would. "I shouldn't have—"

"It was not true?"

"I wouldn't have said it if it weren't true."

"This I believe. But at the time, I did not receive it well. My response was cruel."

"Also honest, I think."

"It was stupid and misguided, and I am sorry."

"Forgiven and forgotten. Let's just move on and not worry—"

"I am not finished." She lifted one of his hands in both of hers and gazed down at it. His wide palm looked rough and powerful over her smaller one. She was so delicate, so very breakable. That she sat beside him, vulnerable...

For a moment, he had the tiniest inkling of her anxieties. Every moment she spent alone in his presence, she was pushing away the past, pushing away her fears and worries. Every moment, she was working to trust him.

This was true, he supposed, for almost all women, who were physically weaker than almost all men. But not all women understood the gravity of it. Not all women had had the education Vanessa had in the utter depravity and evil of man.

Caleb would never truly comprehend what Vanessa's trust in him meant, but he would do everything in his power to earn it nonetheless.

He looked away from their joined hands to see her eyes shining with emotions he couldn't decipher.

"I wanted to say..." Her voice trailed, and she trailed her finger over the back of his hand, sending tantalizing, agonizing responses throughout his body. He dared not move, afraid she would stop. Afraid to scare her away.

"I don't know how it happened," she said. "I didn't plan it, and I don't know what to do with it. And it scares me more than I can express." She met his eyes. "But if I am being truly honest, then I need to tell you that, somehow, you broke down all my walls. Or maybe you figured out how to wiggle your way through the holes."

"Like a cockroach?"

The grin she gave him broke through the tension that had been building since she'd returned to the living room. "Maybe a mouse. One of those cute little white ones."

"How about like a warm breeze on a cold day?"

"Better. Like that, then." Her smile faded, and she swallowed. "Anyway, now you are inside the walls. Now, somehow, I need to tell you that... I love you too."

"Oh." *Oh. Oh, man.* She loved him? And she'd trusted him enough to confess it? He pulled her against him, fought emotions as strong as he'd had in the church earlier. He fumbled for what to say.

He held her shoulders and leaned away to look at her. Her expression still held fear. In fact, she seemed downright terrified.

"I love you too." He kissed her forehead. "We're going to take this very slowly. We're going to give it time to grow naturally. We're not going to rush. Okay?"

The fear faded, and a smile touched her lips. "Yes. This is good."

"You're going to let me shower you with gifts."

"You do not need—"

"And you're not going to argue with me about those gifts." He winked to bring levity, though he wasn't kidding. "We're going to go on dates and hold hands and kiss at the movies. We're going to make sure Kat is on board with the idea of you and me. And then, someday..." Someday, she would wear a white wedding gown and walk down an aisle toward him. He could picture the gown already. He'd seen it in his dreams. "And then, we'll see what God has for us next. How does that sound?"

She snuggled against him. "Perfect. It is perfect."

CHAPTER THIRTY-SIX

Reluctantly, Vanessa kissed Caleb good-bye and locked up behind him, engaging the alarm out of sheer habit. She would happily have slept on the sofa resting against him all night long, but if Kat woke, she'd be frightened. Vanessa needed to be at her side.

And Caleb needed to sleep, too.

Vanessa was desperate to climb into bed, but, irrational as it was, she was certain she could detect the lingering effects of Abbas's touch on her skin. Before she changed into pajamas, she would shower.

And then she would be free of all of it.

In the bathroom, as the water heated up, she slid off her clothes. She'd shoved her phone into her pocket at the police station when it was returned to her. Now, its ding bounced off the tile in the small room, and she cringed at the volume. She'd be sharing a room with Kat tonight, and she couldn't risk the phone waking her daughter. She silenced it and glanced at the screen. *Good night, my love.*

How could a man like Caleb call her *his love*?

She caught her silly grin in the mirror and almost forced it away. But why? As hard as the events of the last few hours had been, she'd found plenty to smile about. The memory of her friends gathered around her at the church, Caleb's arms. Her daughter was safe. Her sister was safe. She was safe.

She quickly typed *Sleep tight* and added a little heart. She wasn't accustomed to using the L-word with anyone but Kat. She would get used to it, and Caleb would be patient with her as she did. He was such a patient man. And good. And honest.

Still listing his attributes, she stepped into the hot shower and scrubbed away the events of the day.

In the years since she'd killed Carlos, she'd worked to truly feel and internalize the freedom that was hers. Not just the physical freedom from Carlos and Abbas and every other man who'd treated her like property. Not just the freedom from prison after she'd shot and killed Carlos nearly eight years past. But the spiritual freedom she was still struggling to understand —that Christ died to set the captives free.

Vanessa had been a captive, first to men and then to her own anger and bitterness. Though she'd learned the truth, it had been a process to believe it.

Now, as the lingering effects of Abbas's touch swirled down the drain with the cleansing shower water, she let all that left-over bitterness and anger and shame go with it. She could never go back to the girl she'd been at ten years old. Though she'd never willingly go through what she had, nor would she ask anyone else to go through it, she could see that her struggles had shaped her. They'd made her tough, and they'd made her compassionate. They'd taught her to appreciate things others took for granted, like the freedom of owning her own vehicle, old as it was, which allowed her to come and go as she pleased. The freedom of renting her own little home. The freedom of working hard and earning her own money.

And now, Abbas's ring, the last lingering thread that had

held her to her past, was gone. Abbas was gone. She could really and truly put it all behind her. Now, she could step into her future.

Through the glass shower door, she saw her phone light up on the bathroom counter. Probably Caleb sending another text. The thought of him made her giggle as she rinsed the shampoo from her hair.

But Nadia invaded her thoughts. There would be no more pretending Vanessa had no family back in Serbia. Now that her sister had found her, Vanessa would have to face her past. For the first time since she'd left them, she felt strong enough to do it.

She heard a faint hum and glanced through the shower doors. Her phone was vibrating again. Probably the second reminder for the text that had come in a moment before.

She ran the razor over her legs. She'd forgotten to take it with her when she'd packed on Saturday night—and again when she'd come back here on Monday—and the hair had gotten stubbly. She might have learned to live with unshaved legs had she stayed in Serbia. She was no longer the girl Tata had sold. She was grown. She was free. And, now that Nadia was back in her life, she would call home. Maybe, someday, she would even go to visit. She'd hug her mother and her siblings. She'd meet the sister who'd been an infant when Vanessa had left. She'd introduce Katarina to her grandmother and her aunts and uncles.

It occurred to her how much such a trip would cost, but the familiar worry slipped away. Caleb wanted to lavish her with gifts. This was a gift she would allow herself to accept.

A sharp pain jabbed just above her ankle, and then a drip of blood mixed with the water. She'd sliced a good chunk out of her skin with that pass of the razor.

She finished and dried off, wincing when she ran the towel over the raw and bleeding cut. After quickly wrapping her hair, she snatched her dirty clothes off the floor. She'd forgotten to bring her robe into the bathroom with her, so, with her towel wrapped around her, she dabbed at the blood to keep it from dripping onto the carpet and opened the door. Chilly air snaked around her feet in the hallway as she hurried into her bedroom. Kat didn't stir when Vanessa entered and slipped off the towel and into her bathrobe. She dumped her clothes and hurried down the hallway toward the kitchen, where she kept a box of Band-Aids—a handier spot for all of Kat's little wounds.

She heard the vibration of her cell phone again. Who would be calling that late? As soon as she got the bleeding under control, she'd check that.

An itch on the side of her foot had her wiping the dripping blood. The last thing she wanted was to scrub the carpets. But... too late. She saw at least one red droplet on the beige rug. At this rate, she'd never crawl into bed.

An unexpected scent gripped her attention as she neared the kitchen. It was... the scent of leaves, of forest? Had she left a window open?

In the kitchen, she grabbed the bandages—princess-themed, thanks to Kat's help at the grocery store. She pulled one out and lifted her foot onto a kitchen chair. Blood slithered from the cut to the bottom of her foot. She reached for a paper towel, losing her balance in the process. When she gripped the kitchen counter to keep from falling, blood from her fingertips smeared on the laminate. She got the paper towel and pressed it to the wound. After about ten seconds, she added the bandage and hoped it would contain the bleeding.

She'd survived Abbas and Beast One and Beast Two only to be done in by a silly shower razor.

The towel unwound from her head, and she yanked it off and tossed it over a kitchen chair, finger-combing the wet locks.

Where was that chill coming from? Maybe Nadia had

opened a window. But... no. The alarm would have gone off. She knew she'd set it after Caleb left. Any door or window opening would set it off. Besides, it was chillier here than nearer the bedrooms. The kitchen windows were all closed. She was about to step into the living room when she heard a creak.

The old hardwood floors made that noise when someone walked across them.

The flood of adrenaline made no sense. Abbas and his guards were in custody. She was safe.

But... the chill in the air, the scent of the outdoors, the late-night phone calls.

She yanked open a kitchen drawer, reached for a knife.

A hand slid over her mouth, a forearm pressed against her neck.

"You will be silent." Abbas's voice was low and cold.

No, no! How could he be here? She was dreaming. A nightmare. Except there was nothing dreamlike about the pressure against her windpipe.

"You will be silent, or I will kill you and your daughter and your sister. Do you understand?"

Against the pressure on her neck and her mouth, she nodded.

"There's no point in screaming. Nobody will hear you but those you want most to protect. You understand?"

Again, she nodded.

He spun her around and pushed her through the kitchen into the living room and toward the front door. If she opened it, the alarm would sound.

Except, how did Abbas get past the alarm?

It didn't matter. He was in her house. He was no longer in custody. None of it made sense.

They reached the door.

His voice was low in her ear. "Disable the alarm and open the door."

There was a code to silently trip it and, miraculously, she remembered the numbers. She punched it in, and the alarm appeared to be disabled.

"Open the door and step outside."

"You're going to get your ring back. I have someone working to return it to your family. What do you want from me?"

He flipped her around, pressed her against the wall near the front door. "You thought you could get away with it, didn't you? You thought you were so clever, but I figured it out."

"What are you...?"

His hand pressed against her mouth again. He leaned in close, and she felt his breath across her cheeks. "You helped him. Somehow, you told that Latino pig when to bet and when to fold. You cheated me."

She should deny it, pretend ignorance. But he knew. When he moved his hand to let her answer, she told him the truth. "It was easy, and you were a fool to believe you had my allegiance. I would have done anything to get away from you."

In the darkness, she could hardly make out the expression on his face, but she didn't need to see it. She could feel his rage.

"And now, you will be punished." He yanked her away from the wall and turned her toward the door. "And when you are dead, I will sell your daughter and recoup my losses."

Abbas's words should have sent fear through her body, but she felt an odd sense of peace. She couldn't decide if it was fueled by utter hopelessness or by the great hope of the Living God, Who saw, Who knew, and Who would not forsake her.

She reached for the door, eager to put distance between Abbas and her family. If only she'd had time to grab the knife.

She needed a weapon.

A weapon.

She thought of what was on the porch, what had been on the porch for days. If she could grab it...

She pulled open the heavy door, pushed open the screen. As she stepped onto the porch, Abbas close behind, she snatched the golf club. With all the force she could muster in such close proximity, she jabbed the end into Abbas's side.

"Ooph." His grip on her lessened, and she spun away.

She stepped back and lifted the club.

And swung hard at his head.

The metal connected with his skull with a resounding *thwack*. He stumbled.

She swung again. *Thwack!*

He fell onto the porch.

Abbas, who'd planned to punish her for escaping him.

Abbas, who'd planned to kidnap her daughter and destroy her.

Abbas, who deserved no mercy.

There was no way she'd let him hurt her again. No way she'd let him hurt her sister. No way she'd let him hurt her daughter.

She lifted the club.

CHAPTER THIRTY-SEVEN

Why wasn't she answering the phone? Caleb careened around a corner and hit redial.

He'd been trying to reach her for twenty minutes, ever since Eric called to tell him Abbas had been released.

Released? It made no sense, no sense at all.

When Eric called, he'd assured Caleb that Abbas had been taken to Boston and was probably nowhere nearby. Just to be on the safe side, though, he'd had a radio car drive by her house. So far, there was no indication that anything was amiss.

As if a cop could tell from the comfort of his cruiser.

As if Abbas would leave a car in the driveway for all the world to see.

The federal official who'd taken Abbas into custody had assured the Nutfield Chief of Police that Abbas had been ordered to leave the country immediately. But would he?

Caleb didn't know. What he did know was that Vanessa wasn't answering her phone, and until he put eyes on her, until he assured himself she was safe, he wouldn't rest. And he wouldn't leave her side until they were certain Abbas was gone for good.

Why in the world had the authorities let him go?

Fury coursed through his veins. Who cared that Abbas was related to royalty? He'd kidnapped three people at gunpoint. He would have killed them, or stolen them away. What would he have done to little Kat? Remembering Vanessa's story, Caleb had a pretty good idea of what Kat's fate would have been.

The State Department was worried about an international incident. Somehow, that was more important to them than the three beautiful souls whose lives were, once again, in danger.

As he turned onto Vanessa's street, he caught sight of red and blue lights reflecting off his rearview mirror, coming up fast. Something was wrong, very wrong.

Caleb whipped his car onto Vanessa's long, winding driveway.

On the front porch, the glint of metal caught his eye.

A gun? Where would Abbas have gotten a gun? Surely his hadn't been returned to him. At this point, Caleb would believe anything.

He slammed the gearshift into park and bolted from the car.

The sight on the porch had him slowing. It wasn't a gun, and it wasn't in Abbas's hand.

Vanessa stood on the porch wearing nothing but a bathrobe, her hair dripping. She held the golf club like a baseball bat.

Abbas was on the concrete, pushing himself up.

"Watch out!" he shouted.

But Vanessa seemed wholly unaware that Caleb was there. She shouted something at Abbas in Serbian.

Abbas made it to his hands and knees. Then, his hands and feet.

He would lunge at her, take her down.

Caleb was running their direction when Vanessa swung the club. It connected with Abbas's skull.

The thud of metal on bone was loud in the silent night.

The man collapsed at Vanessa's feet.

She stepped away, wielded the club again, and prepared to swing.

Abbas didn't move.

Cops were right behind him. What would this look like from their point of view? Like her defending herself? Or like her bludgeoning a defenseless man?

She'd killed a man once, and the authorities had called it justified—a shooting in defense of another, thanks to the eyewitness accounts of the people at the scene.

The authorities wouldn't be as understanding a second time.

"Vanessa, don't."

But she didn't react, didn't seem to hear him. She was too deep in the moment, the opportunity to protect herself and her family from this monster.

Again, she shouted in Serbian. The club started its swing.

Caleb reached her, wrapped her in his arms. The club whacked him on the shoulder, but he barely felt its force. "It's okay. It's okay."

She was screaming, hitting him, trying to get away.

"It's me. It's Caleb. You're safe."

"He will kill me! He will take my daughter."

"The police are here. You're safe."

The words seemed to penetrate. The tension released from her muscles. "You should have let me kill him." Her words were muffled against Caleb's chest. "He will never stop."

A man's voice split the silence. "Drop the weapon and step away."

He spun to look over Vanessa's head and saw a cop holding a gun aimed in their direction.

Caleb lifted his hands from around Vanessa. Grabbed her shoulders. She didn't move, didn't seem to hear.

"Drop the club, Vanessa," he said. "You need to drop it and lift your hands. Now."

Her eyes widened. The golf club fell to the ground with a clang.

"Lift your hands up and turn to face the police," Caleb said. "They need to know you're not dangerous."

She did as he said, and the police moved in. He was quickly frisked. The cop gave Vanessa a quick once-over.

"You don't need to frisk her to see she's not carrying a weapon," Caleb said.

The officer patted the pockets of the bathrobe and then gestured to the yard. "Step aside and don't move."

Caleb glanced down at the man sprawled on the concrete as they passed him. Blood dripped from Abbas's head. His eyes were closed. His chest rose and fell.

Caleb helped Vanessa off the small porch into the yard, and they watched as paramedics examined Abbas and then loaded him into an ambulance. Based on the bit of information Caleb overheard, the man was in bad shape.

He knew it was wrong to pray for Abbas's death, but Vanessa was right. If he survived, he would continue to be a threat. *Lord, You know what to do. I will trust You. Please, protect my family.*

Nadia stepped outside wearing a too-thin nightgown.

Which was more than Vanessa's bathrobe. Only now did he notice the blood on her hands, on her foot.

He lifted her arm, then the other. Searched her face for cuts, the bathrobe for blood. Had she been stabbed? "Medic!" he shouted, then to Vanessa said, "Where are you hurt?"

She rattled something in Serbian.

"English, Vanessa."

"Da." She blinked, seemed to work to focus. "He did not injure me."

"You're bleeding."

She looked at the smeared blood and switched back to Serbian.

Nadia translated. "She cut herself in the shower."

Shaving. Thank God. He'd nearly had a heart attack over a razor wound.

A paramedic jogged their way. "What is it?"

"I panicked," Caleb said. "Let me get her inside before she freezes to death."

Vanessa seemed to feel the chill only when he mentioned it. Her teeth started to chatter. She took a step toward the door. Her bare feet had to be aching on the cold ground. And shock was probably setting in.

He swung her into his arms. "Nadia, hold the door."

She did, asking, "What happened?" as he passed.

"Abbas."

Nadia gasped as he stepped around the sofa and set Vanessa on the couch.

"Grab that blanket," he said.

Nadia pulled a fleece throw from the back of a chair and tucked it over her sister, whispering in Serbian.

Vanessa didn't answer. She didn't seem able to speak through the chattering teeth.

Caleb held her until a paramedic made him step away, then watched as they dressed the wound on her ankle, examined her for other wounds, and treated her for shock. Throughout the appraisal, she insisted Abbas hadn't hurt her.

When Eric stepped into the house, Caleb rounded on him. "What the—?"

"I know, I know." Eric lifted his hands. We shouldn't have trusted—"

"You shouldn't have let him go!"

"Wasn't my call, and the chief had no choice."

"Brady should've—"

"Protected her. I know." Behind Eric, Brady Thomas filled the doorway. "The agents promised me he would be taken straight to his yacht. They assured me they'd watch until he'd launched. They didn't."

"Why?"

Eric glanced at Vanessa, who'd turned to watch the conversation. "Let's try to calm down."

"Easy for you to say. It wasn't Kelsey who was nearly murdered tonight."

Except Vanessa had held her own. Beautiful, strong Vanessa had done what none of them could.

"Not easy," Eric said. "None of this is easy."

Little Kat stood in the entry to the hallway, blanket in hand, eyes wide.

Caleb glared at his friends, then scooped her up. "Hey, sweetie. Sorry if we woke you."

"Where's Mommy?"

He turned so Kat could see her mother, who was still huddled beside her sister on the couch and speaking to the paramedic.

"Your mommy is fine," Caleb said. "Everyone is safe." He let his own words fill his mind. For the second time that night, he assured himself they were safe. At least Abbas wouldn't be running loose anytime soon. What had happened that night, and what would happen next, he had no idea, but at least for now, they were safe.

CHAPTER THIRTY-EIGHT

Abbas was dead, and Vanessa wasn't sorry.

She was at the police station when Brady—Chief Thomas in this place—entered the conference room and gave her the news.

Abbas hadn't survived the multiple blows to the head. He'd been pronounced dead on arrival at the hospital.

She didn't speak, didn't say anything. She knew from the last time she'd killed a man that the best thing was to keep quiet. And, before she'd been taken away from him, Caleb had made her promise to do just that.

He would send an attorney, and until then, the police weren't to ask her any questions.

A man she considered a friend sat at the end of the long table, catty-corner to her. He'd already gotten her coffee, which she couldn't make herself drink, and offered her food, which she'd declined. He squeezed her shoulder. "I'm not here to question you."

"I am not afraid of you, Chief. And I'm not afraid of the truth."

"I'm still Brady, Vanessa. I'm still your friend."

She wanted very much for that to be true.

"We're all on your side," Brady said. "Nobody in this department wants to see you behind bars. But we have to do this by the book."

"There is a book?"

"We have to follow the rules," he clarified. "But understand me. Nobody thinks you need to be punished. If anybody deserves to be punished, it's those idiots who let the man go."

Da. This was true, and it was good that her friend believed in her.

He ran his hand over his head. "I'm one of those idiots, but..." He shook his head. "Their authority trumps mine. When the State Department tells you to do something, you do it. You trust that they know what they're doing."

"And if they tell you now to prosecute me?"

"It's not my decision. I don't know why they'd push for it."

She knew from last time that the decision to prosecute would not be made by Brady or Eric or anybody else on the police force. The county prosecutor would make the call. A man was dead—a wealthy and well-connected man.

This wasn't like when she'd killed Carlos, the ringleader of a human trafficking operation. Nobody had cried for Carlos. Nobody who had influence, anyway.

This was different. This was worse.

But she wasn't sorry. Abbas was dead, which meant her family was safe.

Except...

"Will they seek retribution?" Vanessa asked. "His family. If I am released, will they want to see me punished?"

Brady lifted his broad shoulders and let them fall. "Let's not borrow trouble."

"Borrow trouble." She repeated the phrase, tried to work out its meaning. "Why would someone borrow trouble? Or loan it?"

His smile was slight. "It means to worry about all the things that might go wrong but haven't yet. Let's deal with one obstacle at a time."

"Da. This is good, but hard. I will try."

The door opened, and a woman stepped in. Despite the late hour—just after two in the morning—the woman looked fresh and polished in a tailored gray suit over a teal blouse. She was nearly six feet tall, only a couple of inches shorter than Brady, who stood to greet her.

"Glad to see you, Cass."

"You haven't been questioning her, right?"

"Just keeping her company. We're friends." Brady stepped back. "Vanessa, Cassandra Laurent."

Vanessa stood and shook the woman's hand.

"I'll be representing you." Ms. Laurent gave Brady a pointed look, and he slipped out of the room.

For the next thirty minutes, Vanessa recounted the events of the evening while the lawyer scribbled notes furiously. When Vanessa was finished, Ms. Laurent set down her pen and gave Vanessa an intense look. "One question. Did you want to kill him?"

"Yes."

Ms. Lauren sat back, seemed to tense. Maybe that had been the wrong answer. But she'd told Vanessa to be honest.

"Otherwise, he would never have given up." Vanessa stood and backed away from the woman. "I escaped him nearly a decade ago. All those years he looked for me, eventually dragging my sister into this nightmare." Her voice shook, but she didn't stop. "He told me tonight his plan was to kill me and then take my daughter, my sweet, innocent child. He said he would sell her. I know what he does to innocent girls. I would not have it. You ask me if I wanted him dead? After what he did to me? After what he promised to do to my child? The answer is yes. I wanted him dead. I am not sorry he's dead. And if I go to prison for that, then so be it."

Ms. Laurent nodded wordlessly. After a moment, she said, "Tonight, were you trying to kill him?"

"Trying to? No. I was only trying to make him stop. I hit him, and he kept coming at me. I hit him again, and he fell, but he was getting up. I shouted at him to stay down, but he was pushing to his feet. And... I realize now I was speaking Serbian, which he doesn't speak. But my meaning was clear. He would have attacked me. He told me he was going to kill me. I couldn't..." The memory of it was too fresh. She squeezed her eyes closed, but the images came anyway. "I hit him again. And then..." And then she would have hit him again, and maybe again and again. She'd been out of her mind with fear, with fury.

But Caleb had stopped her. Caleb had wrapped her in his strong arms and promised her she'd be safe.

Ms. Laurent said, "Even though you wanted him dead, you weren't trying to kill him."

"Da. Yes. This is true."

"Okay." The lawyer read her notes, said again, "Okay." A long, slow breath released from her mouth. "What a mess. Why'd they let the guy go, anyway?"

Vanessa flipped her hand toward the door. "They had no choice. The American government came. He is royalty."

"That doesn't make him more valuable than you are."

Vanessa held the woman's gaze. "This is true. I am valuable. My sister is valuable. My daughter is precious. Maybe we don't matter to the government."

"That's not it. Don't let the actions of one person, or even one group of people, taint you to the whole country." Ms. Laurent pushed back her chair. "Someone screwed up royally,

Vanessa, but you matter. Sit tight and I'll see about getting you out of here."

It wasn't Brady or Eric who questioned Vanessa but a man and a woman she'd never met before. Perhaps having strangers question her was in the book they were going by. With the attorney at her side, she answered their questions honestly and then, finally, she was released.

Eric led her to the waiting area. When she entered, Caleb stood, and she stepped into his arms. "I am free to go."

"Thank God." He kissed the top of her head and held her close, speaking over her head to Eric. "She's not being charged?"

"We're not sure yet." Eric's voice was level, a soothing tone he probably used often enough in these kinds of situation. "We're on her side."

The tone seemed to irritate Caleb, or maybe it was the words. She felt his tension in his chest and stepped away, turning to face Eric.

"What did you find out about the people who let him go?" Caleb asked.

"We're still working on that."

"Basically, you don't know anything."

She expected Eric to bristle at the words, but he kept that even expression as he glanced at the wall over the door. The clock read four-fifteen. "Give us a little time, man. Maybe a few daylight hours. I promise we'll find out what happened."

A quick glance at Caleb's face showed he was not satisfied with that answer.

Eric crossed the space and gripped Caleb's shoulder, but he directed the words to Vanessa. "You're safe, and you're free." He turned to Caleb. "Be thankful for that."

Caleb's Adam's apple bobbed. "Yeah." He kissed her forehead. "Yeah, I'm trying."

"Get some rest." Eric patted Vanessa's upper arm. "We'll talk tomorrow."

Caleb drove her back to her house in silence. At home, she left him in the living room and found Kat curled up on Nadia's twin bed in her aunt's arms. Poor, sweet girl must have had a terrible night. Thank God she'd slept through the worst of it.

She pressed a kiss to Nadia's forehead and then carried her daughter to her own bed and tucked her in.

When she returned to the living room, she found Caleb lying on her sofa.

"Hope you don't mind," he said, "but I won't be able to sleep at home."

"I'm safe now."

"I know. But..." He swung his legs to the floor. The poor man looked exhausted. "I can go if you want me to."

From her place behind the sofa, she ran her fingers over his brown hair. "You're welcome here."

He caught her hand, looking up at her with sleepy eyes. "Thank God you're safe."

She leaned over and kissed him. "Sleep tight... my love."

The smile that split his face she carried to bed with her. She would let go of all the horror of this night and hold onto that pleased smile.

CHAPTER THIRTY-NINE

As Eric had promised, they discovered the truth the next day.

It seemed Abbas had convinced the federal agent who'd collected him from jail in Nutfield that he couldn't launch the yacht until he hired more crew, as his men were being held in a jail cell. The excuse made sense to the agent, who dropped Abbas at the hotel in Boston, accepting the man's assurances that he'd prepare to leave as soon as possible.

The agent had taken Abbas's passport and wallet, promising to return them when Abbas called. He hadn't worried about Abbas's ability to get back to New Hampshire. Abbas's rental car had been towed, and, without ID, renting another would be impossible. What he hadn't considered was Abbas's sizable bank account.

It seemed that, the moment the agent walked out of the hotel, Abbas told the concierge he was in desperate need of a car that night. He'd offered the man five thousand dollars cash for the use of his own. The concierge took the cash and handed over his keys.

An hour later, Abbas was back in Nutfield.

Caleb paced across Vanessa's living room as he listened to Eric's explanation. So far, he wasn't pleased with any of it.

He glanced at Vanessa, who was seated in the corner of the couch, her knees pulled up to her chest. She'd sent Nadia and Kat for a walk to give herself, Caleb, and Eric some space for this conversation.

Vanessa had been quiet since she'd woken up that morning. She'd fixed breakfast—scrambled eggs and toast—and had kept up a steady stream of conversation for Kat's sake, but Caleb could tell the effort wasn't easy. The stress, the worry that she might be arrested, had eaten at both of them all morning.

Now, she dropped her feet to the floor and leaned toward Eric. "What I don't understand is how he got all the way down to Boston and back before we learned he'd been released."

An excellent question. Caleb spun and glared at his friend. Unfair, since Eric'd had nothing to do with any of it. Brady had released the man, and then only because he'd been ordered to.

Seated on the chair adjacent to the sofa, Eric focused on Vanessa. "The chief thought the agent would do as he promised. He wanted to spare you the worry, figuring he'd tell you after we were sure Abbas was off US soil. When Brady called to confirm that Abbas's yacht had sailed, he learned what the agent had done."

Vanessa took in the information. "What time was that?"

"I'm not sure exactly," Eric said.

"Brady should be here," Caleb said. "Why'd he send you to explain his actions?"

Eric leveled his gaze at Caleb. "A man was killed last night, a very well-connected man. Believe it or not, there're some issues to be managed by the chief at the station." To Vanessa, he said, "Brady didn't want you to have to wait until he was available to talk to you, but of course you can call him with questions

I can't answer. You might just have to wait a few hours to get a response."

"I understand," Vanessa said. "I appreciate that you're here."

Eric's explanation made sense, but it didn't cool Caleb's ire.

Eric continued. "Brady insisted the agent double-check to make sure Abbas was at the hotel. We were still waiting on confirmation when I first called you and, when you didn't answer"—his gaze flicked to Caleb—"you."

"And then I started calling," Caleb said. "And when you still didn't answer…"

Vanessa smiled at Caleb, and the look calmed him. He turned back to Eric. "Is that why you showed up, guns blazing, last night?"

"Nope." Eric turned to Vanessa. "We got an alert that your alarm went off. I figure Abbas didn't know about it, and when he opened the door—"

"I tripped it," Vanessa said. "He knew the alarm was there, and somehow he'd gotten inside, but there's a code to make it seem disabled. A panic code, I think it's called."

"Smart," Eric said.

"She is, isn't she?" Caleb stood behind her on the sofa and ran his hand over her silky hair. "Level-headed in a crisis."

"My head was not level. It was God who reminded me of that code. I had forgotten about it."

Of course his brilliant, beautiful bride wouldn't take credit. He loved that about her. He loved everything about her.

He had to stop thinking of her as his bride, though. If he let that slip, he'd scare her away.

She leaned into his touch. They both needed to concentrate on Eric right now.

"Do we know yet if I will be charged?" she asked.

"That's what I came to tell you. Based on your statement,

Caleb's statement, and our recommendation, the prosecutor has decided your actions were in self-defense."

Vanessa sat up. "I am free?"

Eric smiled. "You're free."

Caleb wanted to celebrate, but... "What about Abbas's family?" He rounded the sofa and sat beside her. "Do we need to worry they'll come after her?"

"Garrison never told his contact in Washington Vanessa's name. We're holding the details of Abbas's death close to the vest."

A look of confusion crossed her features.

"They're not sharing the details," Caleb explained. "They're keeping them secret. Close to the vest—like a hand at cards?"

"Ah." She repeated the expression, then nodded for Eric to continue.

"They'll know just enough to know that Abbas was killed in self-defense, but even the State Department agrees that it's in everyone's interest that your name be kept out of it. The royal family will get their ring back, take his body home, and that'll be the end of it."

"What of his guards?" Vanessa asked.

"Rather than risk them being released in this country after they serve a sentence, they're being shipped back to their country. They'll be blocked from ever entering the USA again."

Vanessa's gaze left Eric and rested on Caleb's. "It is over?"

"It's over."

She wrapped her arms around him and held him tight. This woman who'd recoiled at his touch just five days earlier was now spontaneously hugging him. He was feeling pretty good about himself until she released Caleb, pulled Eric up, and hugged him too.

Caleb glared at his friend one more time for good measure,

but Eric only chuckled as he took her shoulders and set her at arms' length. "You're a whole new Vanessa today."

"Today, I am a free Vanessa. I think maybe..." She reached out to Caleb, and he slid his hand into hers. "I think maybe I am not only free from prison. Today, I am free for my future. Free to be who God wants me to be."

Caleb let her words soak through him. He had no idea all of God's plans for this remarkable woman, but he knew one part of what God wanted her to be. Caleb's wife. Someday, he'd tell her how long he'd known that. Someday, he'd tell her about all the prayers he'd lifted for her in the past two years. He'd even tell her how hard he'd resisted God's plan at first, before he really knew her. Someday, but not yet.

For now, though Caleb didn't deserve her, he'd take her and cherish her for the rest of his days.

CHAPTER FORTY

Vanessa looked down at the outfit Caleb had insisted she wear today, one he'd bought her on a recent shopping excursion—a pretty pale green wraparound dress. She wore the emerald necklace, earrings, and bracelet he'd bought her, saying they matched her eyes.

In the backseat, Kat was dressed in a similar outfit, hair fixed beautifully. Vanessa had even let her wear a little lip gloss for the occasion.

As she drove, she couldn't help but think about the events that had taken place nearly a year before. Abbas's ring was returned to his family and, according to Brady and Eric, there was no indication they cared to know who'd killed him.

Caleb had bought Nadia a ticket back to Serbia, and she'd resumed her studies at university. Vanessa had spoken to her mother and her siblings on the phone numerous times since then. At first, the conversations were difficult, stilted, but over time, they got to know one another again. They were learning to be comfortable with each other.

She hadn't spoken to her father, though she would have to. She had forgiven him for what he did. But Tata wouldn't talk to her. Mama said he was too ashamed. Someday, she would need to fly there, to hug them all, and to tell her father in person that he was forgiven. She would tell them all about the hope she'd found in Christ and the family He'd given her in New Hampshire. She was eager to make that trip, but now that school had started, it was difficult to find the right time.

Summer had faded and the leaves, once again, were exploding in color. Caleb had decided they needed to have their pictures made. She would have been content to ask a friend to snap a few photos with a cell phone, but Caleb didn't do anything halfway. He'd proved that during the months they'd dated, lavishing her and Katarina with gifts, taking them places Vanessa never would have gone on her own to do things Vanessa could never have afforded to do. They'd taken ski lessons that winter. They'd gone tubing that summer. They'd seen Red Sox games and plays in Boston. They'd gone on a whale watch and visited museums. They'd eaten out at least once a week, eaten at home—either at hers or his—most other nights of the week. Caleb had taught Vanessa how to cook, taught Kat how to bake, and taught them both, slowly and patiently, how to trust him. How to receive the love he so freely gave.

He had promised to take their relationship slowly, and he'd been true to that promise. So true that often, when they kissed, she was the one longing for more. She'd never thought she could desire a man the way a woman should, but God had even healed that broken part of her. The Bible told her she was a new creation, and she believed it. She was new. She was free.

Vanessa parked her old minivan on the side of the road by the Nutfield Town Common and checked her reflection. Like Kat, she'd taken extra care with her appearance that morning. The pictures were important to Caleb. Therefore, they were important to her. She'd even put on makeup, which she almost never did, and curled her long hair.

Oddly, cars lined the street, but the common was empty this Saturday afternoon. Vendors would begin preparing in just a few days for the annual Harvest Festival, which would start the following Friday evening. On Saturday, there would be a parade and, this year, Vanessa would ride the float. She was no longer trying to hide. She was free of all of that.

She and Katarina walked across the grass toward the little stage on the far side. She glanced at the church, her church. The bright white steeple reflected the setting sun and seemed to glow against the pale blue sky. It was a beautiful evening for photos, and this was a beautiful place to shoot them.

Caleb had chosen a dark suit and a green tie that matched her dress. He was talking to Marisa Boyle, who had a camera hanging around her neck. Vanessa had forgotten Marisa had taken up photography in recent years. She was a great painter, but she'd found a new passion through the lens of a camera.

Nate stood nearby holding a step stool in one hand, a canvas bag in the other, acting as his wife's helper today.

When Caleb saw her, he smiled and walked her direction. He stopped about five feet away and whistled. "You look... Wow."

"How 'bout me?" Katarina twirled, spinning her skirt in a wide circle.

"Absolutely gorgeous." He closed the distance and kissed them both.

"It's the perfect night," Vanessa said.

Caleb rubbed his hands together. "A little chilly, but this won't take long. And I brought blankets if we need them." He took their hands and walked them toward a little grouping of trees.

Marisa made them stand in a few different poses, which felt totally unnatural but, she assured Vanessa, would look beautiful. Vanessa did what she was told, not holding back the smile that came easier all the time.

After a few minutes, Marisa said, "Just a few more," and posed Vanessa again, this time with Katarina slightly behind her. It felt odd to be facing away from her daughter—and at nothing—but she thought Marisa must know what she was doing.

"You're up." Marisa nodded to Caleb.

He joined Vanessa, and Vanessa expected Marisa to come over and tell him to stand a different way. But she didn't.

And then, Caleb fell to one knee and took a ring box from his pocket.

Vanessa gasped. Her hand flew to her mouth.

What was happening? Was this what she thought it was?

Behind her, Kat gasped.

Caleb winked at her before focusing on Vanessa again.

"There are so many things I want to say to you," Caleb said. "If I tried to say them all right now, we'd be here until midnight."

A single sob escaped her mouth.

Katarina's little hand brushed against her hip, but Vanessa couldn't take her eyes off the man kneeling at her feet.

"The more I get to know you, the more I believe God created you just for me. Or maybe me just for you. I don't know. All I know is that I love you. If you'll have me, I'll spend the rest of my days providing for you and protecting you, raising our..." His voice hitched, and he reached out to Katarina.

She slid her hand into his and looked up at Vanessa with a look of wonder on her face.

Caleb smiled at Kat and returned his gaze to Vanessa's. "Raising our daughter and, God willing, more children some-day. I will love you both to the very best of my ability." He opened the box and lifted an emerald ring on a platinum band.

"It's not traditional, but then, nothing about you is. If you'd prefer a diamond—"

"I love it," Vanessa said.

His shoulders relaxed slightly. "Will you marry me?"

"Yes. Yes. Yes."

He stood and wrapped her in his arms. Everything felt perfect there, more perfect, if that were possible, when he kissed her. Then, he lifted Kat and kissed her, too.

"Put on the ring, Mommy!"

Caleb grinned as he set Kat down. He slid the ring onto Vanessa's finger. A symbol of forever.

She stared at it as it glimmered in the evening light. It was the most beautiful ring she'd ever seen. She was overwhelmed.

And then people streamed onto the grass.

Marisa continued to snap photos, snapshots of their friends coming from every direction. Angel and Donovan, Dylan and Chelsea, and Harper and Jack came from one side of the stage. Rae and Brady, Eric and Kelsey, and Sam and Garrison came from the other.

Caleb's family came from behind a nearby bush with outstretched arms and shouts of "Finally!" and, from Essie, "I knew it!"

Before Vanessa had processed what happened, she was surrounded by friends offering hugs and kisses and shouts of congratulations. Tables were set up, food was brought out as more friends came, many volunteers at the food bank, some clients. Friends from church, friends from Kat's school.

Suddenly, the crowd hushed, and everyone turned back toward the stage. Who was missing? Everyone she knew was already there.

Nadia walked into view, but Vanessa barely glanced at her sister. She couldn't take her eyes from the couple at her side.

They were older than Vanessa remembered, smaller from

her grownup perspective. Lines etched Mama's face, but the wrinkles only added to her beauty as she smiled across the grass at Vanessa, tears streaming down her face.

Beside Mama, Tata walked, slowly, tentatively. His gaze never left hers. He looked... afraid. She had never seen such an expression on her father's face before.

Caleb squeezed her hand. "I hope it's okay."

Lines of worry creased his brow.

"Maybe it was too soon," he said. "But I thought—"

"It is..." Her voice clogged with emotion. She squeezed his hand, then walked across the grass to her parents, her siblings behind them, barely glancing at her friends as they looked on.

She wanted to hug her mother so badly, her arms ached at her sides. But she aimed at her father.

He froze, dropped Mama's hand and stepped away as if he worried Vanessa might harm him.

Everything was grayer—skin, hair, eyes. And he was shorter than she remembered, barely taller than herself. He pressed his lips together, seemed to brace for what would come.

"Tata." It was all she could manage.

"I'm sorry, my darling." His voice had hardly changed. It shook now, though from age or emotion, she didn't know. "I'm so sorry. They told me... I was afraid—"

"Stop." She didn't want to know what he'd thought would happen to her. She didn't want to hear his excuses. He'd come, he'd faced her, he'd apologized. He couldn't make up for what he'd done, and she wouldn't listen to him minimize it.

They weren't her feet that stepped closer to him. They weren't her hands that lifted to cup his wrinkled cheeks. They weren't her eyes that saw the torment in his. Only the God who filled her and wiped away her sins gave her the strength to say, "I forgive you, Tata."

Tears trailed down his cheeks. His shoulders hunched, his gaze lowered to the ground.

She wrapped her arms around him, and they wept together.

A moment later, she hugged her mother for the first time in sixteen years. And greeted Milos and met his pretty wife. She hugged Anya, who wore glasses and looked every bit the serious scholar she'd been at six years old. She met her baby sister, Tasya, an awkward teen who seemed overwhelmed.

Vanessa understood how Tasya felt. She was overwhelmed, too, as her friends and family offered congratulations and exclaimed over the pretty engagement ring and looked at the digital images on Marisa's camera. Her friends introduced themselves to Vanessa's family. Her parents' English was broken and stuttered, but her siblings spoke the language well enough to be understood.

Kids arrived and started games of tag, running and laughing. Before she knew what had happened, a party had broken out on the town common. A party to celebrate her engagement. A party for her birth family to meet her New Hampshire family.

Caleb approached her on the edge of the group. He slipped his arm around her hip and pulled her close as they watched their loved ones. "I hope it's okay. I know you don't like to be the center of attention, but"—he shrugged—"I couldn't help myself."

"It is... perfect. Before, I was afraid always, of everybody, but today..." She looked into the eyes of the man she loved. "Today, I am free."

He turned to her and rested his hands on the sides of her face. "My love, free looks beautiful on you."

∼

I HOPE you enjoyed Vanessa and Caleb's story and all of the stories from Nutfield, New Hampshire. I'm excited to begin a whole new series, this one in the fictional town of Coventry, New Hampshire. Turn the page for a sneak peek of GLIMMER IN THE DARKNESS.

ONE MORE THING. I don't want you to miss a brand-new Nutfield novella, *Sleigh Bells and Stalkers*, featuring familiar friends from Nutfield—and some new friends as well. *Sleigh Bells and Stalkers* is just one of the stories in the *Christmas in Nutfield* boxset. Little Daniel from *Innocent Lies* is all grown up, coming home from college, and you're going to love his story. It releases November 2024.

Secure your copy now.

Nothing could get her home...but this. worked hard to shake off her tragic childhood. As a foster child with a mother in prison for murder, Cassidy was an outcast in her small town until she met James. But she and James's little sister were kidnapped. She escaped, but Hallie didn't survive, and everybody assumed Cassidy killed her. Like mother, like daughter, after all. With public opinion and the authorities united against her, young Cassidy fled. A decade later, another little girl has been kidnapped, and Cassidy may be the only person who can find her.

He doesn't know who to trust. James never believed that Cassidy killed his sister. When his best friend's daughter goes missing a decade after Hallie's murder, he finds Cassidy sneaking around his property. His thoughts turn dark. If she's not behind the recent kidnapping, what is she doing back in Coventry? Her answer—that she's returned to find little Ella, and she needs his help—has him reeling. Can he trust Cassidy? If there's any chance he can save Ella, he has to try.

Pulse-pounding suspense, second-chance romance, and a precious little girl who only wants her daddy. Start reading *Vanished in the Darkness* today.

AFTERWORD

Dear Reader,

I've been looking forward to writing this book ever since I "met" Vanessa when I was writing *Innocent Lies* in 2017. She was originally intended to be a villain, but I fell in love with her and knew her character would need to be redeemed. For three years, Vanessa has been whispering in my ear—Serbian accent and all—telling me her story. When I sat down to write it, it almost felt as if I were recording actual events.

Well, it wasn't *that* easy.

A few things to note:

Frustrating as it is, high-ranking dignitaries and those related to them are too often given special privileges in the US. When writing Abbas's story, I referred to a 2015 article involving two members of the Saudi royal family in Beverly Hills, who were arrested on multiple sexual abuse charges, then released and whisked out of the country before they faced those charges. In real life, I highly doubt Abbas would be released the same night he was arrested, but sometimes, fiction requires some bending of the rules.

Human trafficking remains far too common worldwide, despite greater reporting and a greater understanding of the problem. At one point, Serbia was a hub of such activity, but the nation has worked hard in recent years to curb human trafficking.

Fortunately, many homes have cropped up around the United States that offer freed human trafficking victims a place to live, along with counseling and education and guidance.

A couple of random notes:

Because Serbian uses the Serbian Cyrillic alphabet, the Serbian words I use are Anglicized versions of the originals. I hope those who speak Serbian will forgive me if I've terribly botched the beautiful language.

The Boston hotel is modeled after the Marriott Long Wharf, but I took some liberties with the lobby and so renamed it. The Long Wharf is a beautiful hotel on the water in Boston. I highly recommend a visit.

I got the idea for the final line of this story, "Free looks beautiful on you," from a book by a friend of mine, Christy Johnson titled *Free Looks Good on You*. The book's subtitle says it all: "Healing the soul wounds of toxic love." I mention it here because there are plenty of women in the world who've never been caught up in human trafficking but who need healing from toxic and abusive relationships just the same. I highly recommend Christy's book.

Thank you for sticking with me through the eleven books of the Nutfield Saga (twelve if you read the novella, *No More Lies*, which is available here.) I fell in love with my fictional town of Nutfield way back in *Convenient Lies*, and I'm sorry to say good-bye. I hope you'll join me as we travel up I-93 into the White Mountains to the little town of Coventry, NH, where we'll settle into a charming lakeside town nestled between two mountains and meet a whole crop of new friends. It starts with *Glimmer in the Darkness*. I think you're going to love it. .

God bless you, my friends.

Robin

ALSO BY ROBIN PATCHEN

The Wright Heroes of Maine

Running to You

Rescuing You

Finding You

Sheltering You

Protecting You

Capturing You

Defending You

Fighting for You

Anchoring You

Shadowing You

The Coventry Saga

Vanished in the Darkness

Redemption for Ransom

Betrayal of Genius

Traces of Virtue

Touch of Innocence

Inheritance of Secrets

Lineage of Corruption

Wreathed in Disgrace

Courage in the Shadows

Vengeance in the Mist

A Mountain Too Steep

The Nutfield Saga

Convenient Lies

Twisted Lies

Generous Lies

Innocent Lies

Beautiful Lies

Legacy Rejected

Legacy Restored

Legacy Reclaimed

Legacy Redeemed

Sleigh Bells & Stalkers

One Christmas Night

Amanda Series

Chasing Amanda

Finding Amanda

ABOUT THE AUTHOR

Robin Patchen is a *USA Today* bestselling and award-winning author of Christian romantic suspense. She grew up in a small town in New Hampshire, the setting of her Nutfield Saga books, and then headed to Boston to earn a journalism degree. After college, working in marketing and public relations, she discovered how much she loathed the nine-to-five ball and chain. After relocating to the Southwest, she started writing her first novel while she homeschooled her three children. The novel was dreadful, but her passion for storytelling didn't wane. Thankfully, as her children grew, so did her writing ability. Now that her kids are adults, she has more time to play with the lives of fictional heroes and heroines, wreaking havoc and working magic to give her characters happy endings. When she's not writing, she's editing or reading, proving that most of her life revolves around the twenty-six letters of the alphabet. Visit robinpatchen.com/subscribe to receive a free book and stay informed about Robin's latest projects.